VS. 689

Winter of the Eagle

Winter of the Eagle

by
K. M. Campbell

London
GEORGE ALLEN & UNWIN
London   Sydney

First published in 1980

GEORGE ALLEN & UNWIN LTD
40 Museum Street, London WC1A 1LU

© K. M. Campbell, 1980

British Library Cataloguing in Publication Data

Campbell, K M
    Winter of the eagle.
    I. Title
    823'.9'1F   PR 6053.A48

    ISBN 0-04-823166-5

Typeset in 11 on 12 Baskerville by
Red Lion Setters, Holborn, London
and printed in Great Britain
by Billing & Sons Ltd, Guildford, London and Worcester

To Diana

1

Among the steady, disciplined veterans of Ney's Third Corps,
Captain Charles Hippolyte de Fezenque Larguien of the 46th
Line Regiment stood on a knoll a little ahead of the light
company which he commanded. He had been there for some
time, peering through his glass at the fir trees across the river
where young Matthieu thought he had seen Russian skirmishers.
Below him, on the rugged slope running down to the river, a
scattered handful of his men formed a slender picket line,
watching for the enemy.

It was a beautiful afternoon and the sun was golden before the
onset of winter and, casting blue across the sky, it picked out here
and there the white dusting of high cirrus cloud. The trees
seemed gentle in their dappled shade with memories of summer,
and Captain Larguien fancied their perfume carrying to him
across the clean air. Yet there was little warmth in this late
sunlight and it glittered on the frozen earth without bringing
thaw. Ice had wrapped its black shadow over the floodlands and
the marshes, broken only where heavy vehicles had ploughed into
the mud. The roads had been broken in this fashion so that where
they were not treacherously iced for the poorly shod horses they
were nothing better than clinging quagmires where wheels sank
deep and would not move.

In the east the guns rumbled as they had done since dawn, and
the drifting smoke from the batteries blotted the sunlight from
the fighting men as the shattered rearguard tried to fight its way
out of the trap which had so nearly closed. Ruined columns of
stragglers mingled with the baggage vehicles, blocking the roads
and impeding the movement of the embattled troops; they
scattered when Platov's Cossacks swept down in long deadly
charges, screaming their war cries in an orgy of plunder and
death until they were repelled at last by the gallant remnants of

1

the retreating corps. At the narrow bridge where the river ran round Viasma the frightened people crushed together in loud disorder, pressing forward to escape. They carried the tumult into the suburbs and already buildings were burning and a growing pall of smoke was rising, hiding the town from the gentle sun. The sharp smell of the fires wafted away to mingle with the stench of burnt powder and give warning to men that the refuge which they sought was being destroyed.

The Third Corps, drawn up in proud lines, waited in the cold sunlight on the long ridge below the town, commanding the road from the south. Larguien's men had been engaged several times already as the advance guard of Kutusov's slow-moving army probed forward to be driven back in indecision. Everyone was aware that the old rearguard was being destroyed behind them but they stood steady, waiting to take over its role, confident in themselves and in their commander, Ney. A brother officer had informed Larguien that the Marshal was over with the rearguard at that moment trying to sort out the mess that Davout and Prince Eugene had created between them, and by the look of things it would be some time before the corps would be in action again. Ney's old soldiers could relax a little and allow themselves the luxury of contempt for the motley remnants of inferior corps that were breaking up under a little pressure.

Larguien continued to stand there with his glass, surveying the trees. Although he was aged only twenty-one, it was a seasoned eye that he brought to bear on the offending woodland, for he had served the Emperor since Austerlitz. It was at Austerlitz that his brother had fallen before the Russian guns, and broken the hearts of his ageing parents. For it was the boys' dream of Imperial glories that had drawn the family back from exile in Britain. Now, seven years later, Captain Larguien still carried his dead brother's sword as he stood, tall and arrogant, watching for the same Russian enemy.

He tensed as he saw movement in the trees and looked again, his eye straining. He thought he could see a face and then, as he brought it into focus, forms sharpened and he could see them clearly, their green uniforms half hidden among the frond-like branches. Sharpshooters; a dozen at least, probably more. He scrutinised the adjacent ground but could see no others. With a snap he closed his telescope and turned to the two men beside him.

'Quite right, René,' he said sharply, addressing the younger man. 'Half a section of them. There may be more. Just keep your eye on them and signal if they try to cross the river. The picket line won't be able to see them.'

He handed his glass to the youngster, Lieutenant Matthieu, a boy of sixteen whose fair moustache was no more than a light down above his lip. The boy was unsure of himself; entrusted with the responsibility, his eye wavered. His child's face was ridiculous under his heavy shako, the plume ducking as he saluted and turned to begin his vigil. The third man of the group fell in at Larguien's side when he moved to stroll back to the company.

'It should be quiet enough for a bit, Sergeant-Major,' Larguien commented, looking at the well-built man beside him. His hair was greying and there was an almost clerkish anxiety which had become much more noticeable recently with the old soldier worrying about the deteriorating condition of the men in his care.

'I hope so, sir.' But Sergeant-Major Garnard's nervous eyes were elsewhere and Larguien followed his gaze. There was some sort of disturbance on the right flank of the company. A high-pitched scream came to them across the gun-torn air.

'Cannot Sergeant Bernoit keep his men under control?' Larguien snapped. Garnard shrugged expressively. Bernoit was one of the longest-serving men in the regiment and made his own rules. They could see his small wiry figure now, his long yellow plume dancing erratically as he ran back from the line in pursuit of three recalcitrant soldiers.

It was Necker, the corporal, who saw the pig first, his scavenger's instinct drawing his eyes over to the hollow where the snuffling beast had just appeared. He grinned gap-toothed at the man beside him, nudging and pointing in glee and then, with a wary look over to where Sergeant Bernoit watched the officers on the knoll, he slipped his musket to the man in front and darted off with Andrieux and fat old Boudin waddling along behind. They almost had the pig cornered when Boudin spoilt it all; he threw his gross weight round its neck, but his fat arms slipped so that the sow squealed in terror and broke free. The other two ran after it, but they were clumsy on the broken ground and the pig wriggled from their hands and, leaving them sprawling, scurried into a thicket.

3

'What the hell d'you think you're doing, Corporal?' the familiar voice barked from above, and they looked up to where the little figure stood above them, bristling with irritation. Despite his diminutive stature Sergeant Bernoit was a man of authority, standing there in his worn uniform, neatly patched, with just a few days' stubble on his craggy face, his black moustache carefully trimmed.

Necker stood up and shrugged self-consciously, his mind still teasing with the pig, wondering if he dare give chase again, without taking time to explain to the angry sergeant. The pig itself solved the problem for, breaking from the thicket, it charged straight at Bernoit and he had to jump clear to avoid being knocked over. Yet even as he did so the sergeant unslung his carbine and, dropping on one knee, aimed carefully and fired. The pig staggered on for a step or two and then rolled over, dead. Bernoit rose and looked down at the others, ironically.

'You pathetic bastards,' he said, and turned back to his post leaving them to attend to the carcass. The men had gathered excitedly, watching the scene, chattering loudly, but now as Bernoit strode down on them they fell silent, seeing his wrath.

'Face your fronts! Get fell in! What do you think this is? God, you're worse than those three. No wonder Ivan's having it so easy.'

Sheepishly the soldiers re-formed, cursing him under their breath. When he was satisfied that they were in order again Bernoit began to reload his carbine and, cocking an eye over to the little group by the pig, paused to bellow:

'Corporal Necker! Get a move on. I need you here. You're sodding indispensable.'

One of the men chuckled loudly, but winced at the invective which Bernoit, whipping round, lashed at him; and Necker, seeing, bit off the retort which he had ready. Instead he muttered to his two companions, 'Christ, you'd think he'd be pleased,' for it was a long time since any of them had eaten fresh meat.

Now Larguien was approaching with Garnard padding along beside like a worried spaniel. Bernoit came to attention.

'Cannot you keep your men in hand, Sergeant?'

Bernoit looked at him coldly, annoyed at the rebuke. When he had been fighting at Valmy this officer had been a frightened baby hiding in Britain. In those days they had known how to treat arrogant aristocrats. He decided not to mention the pig.

'High spirits, Captain. The lads were getting bored.'

Larguien, nettled by the other's indifference, spoke sharply.

'And the shot, Sergeant? Why did you fire? Who was involved? What is going on?'

Garnard's darting eyes had seen Necker and the other two men, busily hacking up the dead animal, and he intervened.

'I think Sergeant Bernoit has killed a pig, sir.'

'A pig?' and Larguien's eyes glittered with anticipation.

'A very small pig, Captain,' Bernoit affirmed.

Larguien smiled sardonically. 'Even a small pig will make a pleasant change from old bread.'

Bernoit shrugged. The granaries in Viasma had been destroyed. There would be no new bread and he wondered how long the old supplies would have to last. It had been a hungry campaign thus far and with winter there would be little to forage. He saw the thought reflected in Larguien's hazel eyes and Garnard's frown. The pig had had no business to be there, a lucky chance, no more.

'You can always rely on Necker to find anything that's going,' he assured them.

'Well do try to arrange things in a more orderly fashion in future, Sergeant. We are in the enemy's presence, after all,' and Larguien moved away to resume his former position in the centre of the company. Garnard paused to add:

'Try to get the pig divided up as quickly as possible, Paul. We may be in action again at any moment.'

'Now Jacques, I'd never have thought of that,' Bernoit retorted.

Here was Necker's little detachment running up, laden with raw meat, some crammed into their haversacks and some clutched in armfuls of bloody flesh.

'Get that shared out *rapido*,' ordered Bernoit, taking a substantial piece to squeeze into his own pack. He felt the additional weight settle discouragingly on his shoulders and adjusted his straps to make it lie more comfortably. The men had settled down again and he let his eyes drift back to the young Matthieu still standing on the knoll, watching the enemy movements to the front. The company trumpeter had joined him now, waiting motionless two paces back. There seemed to be no sign of activity and Bernoit looked further round, along the blue ranks of the battalion in deep lines of three to where the eagle, borne by his closest friend, the Regimental Sergeant-Major, sparkled in the

5

sun, and the Colonel sat on his patient horse. Beyond, the second battalion and the rest of the corps waited as Viasma burned behind them and the guns drew closer from the east. He was unperturbed and wondered how long it would be before the generals got things sorted out and brought the real soldiers of this corps into the main battle to put matters right.

A darting movement caught his eye on the other side of the ravine and he saw that a Russian horse battery was galloping up into position. It was a sight of breathless beauty, of flying manes and dashing hooves. The drivers struggled to keep their balance on the lurching limbers as the guns bounced behind them and the crouching gunners hurtled forward on their lathered mounts. Brasses and buckles flashed in the brilliant light. He could hear the jingling harness now and the hooves thundering with the grinding of the wheels on the frozen ground. Already they were within half a mile of him and, as he watched, their commander reared his horse and his bellowed orders came loud to Bernoit's ears. The hooves, long-spiked for winter, crunched into the frosted soil as the cursing drivers wheeled into line. Urgent gunners flung themselves from the saddle and scurried to unlimber and swing the guns round to face the French and instantly the beautiful vision mutated into ugly black-mouthed menace.

'I wondered when they'd think of that!' called Necker from the ranks.

The limbers were open now and the gunners were running with powder and shot. The mounted officer, gold lace aglitter, was riding up and down, his voice high-pitched as he urged his men into action.

'We'll be moving forward now, you'll see,' Necker prophesied, but the others stirred nervously as the gaping muzzles moved slowly round, pausing for a moment to rest directly upon them and then to everyone's relief going on to bear on the line companies of the regiment. They waited tensely for the bombardment to begin. Then, suddenly, the rattle of small arms fire broke out from the dead ground by the river.

'Skirmishers, by God!' exclaimed Andrieux and at that instant the battery opened fire. Bernoit felt the black grip of fear clawing at him, his stomach stabbing with pain. The familiar old symptoms but getting worse these days; he had been at war for too long. He brought himself under control and found that he was shaking. He hoped that the others had not noticed.

Larguien was running long-legged to join Matthieu, who was dancing with anxiety on the knoll. They would be going down into the ravine in a moment. Bernoit fought to control another wave of near panic and tried to make a joke.

'Now Boudin, you'll have your chance to run off some of that fat.'

'Can't do that, Sarge. It's the only thing that's keeping me warm.'

Larguien only required to take one quick look at the scene below before turning to snap a quick order to the trumpeter who nodded and brought the instrument up to his lips. The strident notes rang clear, summoning the company forward.

'Skirmish order,' Bernoit noted automatically and, as his men moved off, he ordered, 'Check your locks!' He unslung his own carbine and opened the priming pan to make sure that the powder was still in place.

With all their battle experience the company fanned out easily as they came up to their officers and then, advancing over the brow of the ridge, they began the difficult scramble down the side of the ravine. Below they could see the brown puffs of smoke and for a minute they were detached witnesses as the picket line was pushed back by the Russian skirmishers who had managed to cross the river unnoticed. Then they were engaged themselves and the air was alive with crackling bullets and whining ricochets and the sudden little spurts of dirt kicked up from the assailed ground. Here and there men fell stricken and over on the left someone began to scream. Just ahead, the picket commander, Sergeant Thomas, rose from the rocks where he had been concealed and made to sprint back to them. A bullet tore his throat open and he tumbled over with a clatter of equipment, but was otherwise silent. Bernoit remembered that he still had the bullet-mould which Thomas had lent him a fortnight before and he hoped irrationally that the dead man had not needed it.

Overhead the air was rent by the howling of roundshot from the enemy battery and, looking up, Bernoit observed that the light company from the second battalion was coming down in support. That at least was a source of comfort. The line companies remained on the summit, drawn up in their rigid ranks, enduring the cannonade, and among them men began to die. Once there had been four battalions of the regiment, but starvation and disease had taken their toll during the long

7

marches, and then there had been the appalling fighting before the redoubts at Borodino. At Moscow they had reorganised into two weak battalions, and now men were dying again.

Bernoit ducked instinctively as a bullet dug splinters from the boulder where he was sheltering. He looked up and saw Andrieux's rueful grin, lopsided with the long scar from Austerlitz fiery as it always was in action. Andrieux shook his head.

'Too close,' he said. 'That's the second time.'

'I think they've got a rifle down there. Listen.'

Again there was a crack, sharper than the familiar musketry. Andrieux nodded, but made no comment. The British in Spain had taught them about rifles with their long range and deadly accuracy. Bernoit grimaced. He could see that the rest of the company had moved into a forward position.

'Come on, it's time to move.'

He stepped out from the friendly protection of the boulder, shouting orders at the rest of his section and the ragged line began to struggle down the rough, frozen hillside. He distinctly heard the bark of a rifle and saw one of his men go down but then they were in cover again and it was possible to take aim and fire at the half-seen enemy.

A man broke into the open about fifty paces ahead and they saw the short firearm he was carrying and knew that it was a rifle. Andrieux swore for he had not finished reloading and Bernoit's hurried shot went wide. One or two of the others fired, missing the running man, and for a moment it looked as if he was going to escape, but MacDonald, over on the right, brought him down. MacDonald was the best shot in the regiment but at that range it had been a very lucky hit. Over there Necker was grinning broadly and slapping the big marksman on the back, but the tall fellow was dour and expressionless as ever. He claimed that his grandfather had been a Scottish lord and that he was related to his namesake, Marshal the Duke of Taranto. No one in the regiment ever teased him about this, however, for the dark humourless man was a lethal killer and they called him the 'Black Giant', but never to his face.

The air was heavy now with gunsmoke, acrid in the cold as it rolled into the gorge, and visibility was diminishing. The company stumbled forward again and it was satisfactory to note that the enemy were falling back without too much resistance. Bernoit's section spread out to cover the right flank and it was

8

there that they found the rifleman lying where he had fallen. He was badly injured and in pain and he appealed to them as they approached. They stopped for it was German that he spoke.

'You bloody traitor,' Andrieux cursed him in anger. Everyone knew that Germans had defected to the Russian camp, but this was the first such renegade to have fallen into their hands.

'You can't trust any of these German bastards,' growled MacDonald who had joined them, and he kicked the wounded man so that he shrieked in agony. They saw that MacDonald had picked up the German's rifle and Bernoit took it from him and examined it with admiration.

'A good weapon, this,' he commented.

'Accurate,' MacDonald agreed, taking it back. 'I'm keeping it.'

'You'll need the right bullet-mould then, Mac,' Andrieux addressed his friend. 'Our balls are the wrong calibre.'

The other grunted assent. 'I'll see what I can find,' and he roughly rolled the screaming man over and started to search his pack.

'Well, don't be long; I need you,' Bernoit asserted, 'and hold on to your musket in the meantime. Come on Andrieux.'

They had not gone more than a few paces when the screaming stopped and a wheezing cough told them that MacDonald had cut the German's throat. They paused for a second and Andrieux cocked an eyebrow.

'German pig,' he muttered.

'Deserter,' affirmed Bernoit.

The afternoon progressed. They killed a few more of the enemy and a few more of their own men were killed; they shot a few gunners and the gunners slew men in the line companies. And all the time the ruined rearguard fell back through Viasma and the guns in the east moved closer until they were in the north and at every hand men were dying.

It was not till after nightfall that the regiment was afforded respite and drawn back to rest awhile with the guns pounding all around and the sky alight, glowing red with the flames of the burning town. A new stench came to them carried on the star-blotting smoke, mingling with the bitter smell of burning timber and charred stone. It was the sweet scent of scorching flesh as the dead and crippled in Viasma were consumed in the inferno.

The soldiers eased their packs from their shoulders and stacked their weapons. Glimmering flames sparked in the dark as they lit their fires, and here and there were little groups with pots to cook and hot food to eat instead of the flint-hard stale bread. Bernoit's company was such and from their pots tonight drifted the aroma of stewing pork so that others, less fortunate, drew near and envied them and tried to curry favour. By Boudin's fire men grew impatient as he seasoned the dish with herbs collected during the summer, and drew his bayonet to defend the pot, while young Gautier sat with calf's eyes and waited with the others until Boudin pronounced himself satisfied.

'The Emperor would be honoured to eat such a dish.' But Andrieux, hungry and impatient, replied:

'The Emperor would have you shot for taking so long.'

Bernoit was not eating yet and his lump of pork stayed in his pack to be shared later with his friend, Étienne Vernier, the Regimental Sergeant-Major. First, however, there was the conference that Larguien had called. As he walked towards the officer's bivouac Bernoit breathed in the delicious smells with mouth-watering anticipation. He drew his greatcoat tighter around him and snuggled into the woollen scarf which he had bought in Moscow for Étienne's wife, his sister Émilie. It was very cold, tonight.

2

It was a tiny group that assembled around Larguien and as Bernoit looked at their faces in the firelight he felt depressed. There were so few of them left.

'We will not be marching tomorrow. The corps will maintain its present position and defend the crossings. This will allow an orderly withdrawal.'

Larguien's voice was harsh and abrupt and for the hundredth time Bernoit strove to overcome his dislike. He found it difficult to adjust to Larguien who had assumed command of the company during the reorganisation at Moscow. As an old republican Bernoit despised the ancient aristocracy and loathed the arrogance which seemed to be its marching companion. Yet, listening to him now, Bernoit had to acknowledge that the captain was an able commander and his tone was reassuring as he made light of the day's disasters.

'I understand that First Corps is in some disorder. That does not astonish me — all these Germans and Spaniards, and conscripts of course. It's going to take Marshal Davout all his famous discipline to sort that lot out and in the meantime we've got to protect him from the Russians. That doesn't bother me. It's better that we form the rearguard ourselves than have to keep coming back to rescue them as we did today. We all know that the two divisions of this corps are well able to do the work of Marshal Davout's precious five. And we won't take so long about it!'

That brought a laugh for it was the stern Davout's painstaking withdrawal which had made the day's action necessary. The captain's words were comforting and Bernoit found himself wondering if things were better than he imagined. Yet three corps had preceded them through the burning shell of Viasma and experience told him that there must be dreadful ruin in all

11

three. He realised that Larguien was trying to betwitch them by his rhetoric into a feeling of security. He wondered if the others appreciated that they were being misled, then looking up he met Larguien's eyes and saw there an appeal to him, an understanding and a respect. Suddenly in sympathy Bernoit knew that the situation was very serious and that the officer expected him to comprehend and support him. Involuntarily he shrugged and half smiled and Larguien's eyes flickered momentarily in acknowledgement that they, at least, could rely on one another.

The others in the group stirred and when Bernoit looked around at them he felt safer in the knowledge of the silent compact he had just made. Matthieu, the only other officer, was courageous enough no doubt, but he was completely without confidence and would be even worse after his performance that afternoon. Distracted by the Russian horse artillery, he had allowed those skirmishers to slip across the river unobserved. Even making allowance for the lad's age, he was a liability, no more than a frightened schoolboy who almost certainly lacked the stamina for what lay ahead. It was a harsh judgement, but they all knew that, had it not been for Matthieu's inattention, Sergeant Thomas would now be standing among them.

Garnard was an old comrade and it was tragic to watch his deterioration under the gnawing anxiety of recent months. He was a nervous old woman now, very different from the tall fusilier who had stood beside Bernoit at Marengo. His new fussiness had become a demoralising irritation and Bernoit shook his head sadly, and considered that the sergeant-major should be pensioned off. He caught the last member of the group, Sergeant Yvel, watching him and wondered if he was thinking similar thoughts about Sergeant Bernoit. But Yvel, for all his cynical wit, was youthful, and brash with his recent promotion. As Bernoit looked back to Larguien he felt he had cause for relief in the new trust which had been established between them.

Larguien was talking about stragglers, referring to the clouds of disbanded men from other corps, and his audience nodded. They remembered the unruly hordes blocking their way ahead. So be it. They would sweep the rabble on before them when they withdrew and Larguien emphasised that there would, of course, be no such disorder in Ney's corps.

'Remember, the Emperor has placed his trust in us. We have Marshal Ney, the finest corps commander in the army. We will

12

not betray their faith in us. Let others straggle if they wish. There will be no stragglers from this company. The regiment will march in close order from now on and no one will drop out without permission. Any fit man straying from his battalion area will be treated as a deserter. Foraging will be carried out only by authorised parties.'

Larguien paused to let them absorb the change in marching order. It would be very different from the amiable system which had existed before, with everyone marching more or less where he pleased. Garnard expressed anxiety about the regiment's camp followers. Would the married men be allowed to march with their wives and families, he wondered, and what arrangements were to be made for the cantinières?

'The women and children will march with the baggage in advance of the corps. An escort will, of course, be provided. No one from this company will march independently with his family.'

'But the men won't like that, sir,' Garnard protested. 'They've always been allowed to march with the women—to afford them protection.'

Larguien's reply was sharp. 'The men will have to endure it. The best protection we can offer the women is a strong rearguard and we can't have that if half the fit men are running around looking after the needs of their womenfolk. Look what happened to the First Corps today. It will be hours before all the able and willing men rally to their regiments.'

Bernoit nodded in agreement. If some such method had been operated in Spain his wife might be alive today. He felt the cold of the night bitter around him as he recalled the misery of those hours high in a Spanish pass, trying to find comfort and succour for the dying woman he had loved. It had been snowing then, he remembered, as he stumbled on alone with the lifeless form in his arms, too miserable even to weep. He pulled himself back to the present with a wrench. He must be getting old, he thought, living in memories. He was wearying of war. But Larguien had said something that needed further discussion.

'The cantinières to go forward as well, Captain? And all the sutler's people? But how will we manage for supplies?'

'Foraging will be organised at company level as I've explained but otherwise...' and Larguien went on to outline the revised arrangements in a technical discussion which was more optimistic

13

than practical. As he took part and listened to Garnard's plaintive statements and Yvel's sarcastic but useless contributions, and watched young Matthieu, round-eyed, chewing his lip and silent, Bernoit was grateful to remember the pork in his knapsack. He would have to make it last for some time, it seemed.

Larguien had one final order to transmit before the conference broke up.

'No able-bodied straggler will be permitted to approach our bivouacs. The pickets are to be instructed to chase these people away from the fires. Any straggler coming in to join the ranks must first report to the duty officer.'

Yvel whistled, but Bernoit could see the reasons behind this command. The woods must be full of fit men who had deserted their eagles and were marauding like brigands. The presence of such men could only lead to disorder if they were allowed to mingle freely among those in the ranks.

At last the conference was over and he could walk away with Garnard and Yvel to join the rest of the battalion's sergeants where they sat gathered around their fires. As they approached, a sudden ripple of flashes lit the sky, followed almost immediately by the crash of guns echoing and re-echoing in the ravines. Again and again they fired and other batteries, alarmed, took up the cannonade so that the whole world seemed tormented by the pounding discharges, dancing distorted from rock to gully, pulsating across the hillside from every direction. The three sergeants stopped awestruck, and tried to identify the source of the appalling noise which affronted them.

'Someone's catching it over there,' Yvel shouted over the din.

'There might be a general alarm,' Garnard volunteered.

'Shouldn't think so,' replied Bernoit, sounding more confident than he felt. He was badly shaken by the racket and the thumping shock waves from the explosions.

'That's a major bombardment going on. Just listen to it,' Garnard argued.

Bernoit shook his head. 'They're just wasting powder. It's the ravines that are exaggerating it. It'll die down in time, when the gunners get too hot.'

'So long as nothing happens before I eat,' Yvel declared, leading them forward to their fires.

It was a pleasure to stop by the fire and slip off their heavy

14

packs. There was always an agreeable light-footed feel at this point of the day and Bernoit paused to savour it, leaning over the fire for a moment, arms outstretched, enjoying the heat, before turning to hang his sword belt and cartridge pouch over their stacked carbines. He handed his water-bottle to Garnard and said:

'Do me a favour, Jacques, and dig out my cooking gear. I'm going to find Étienne.'

The other grunted in assent: it was a familiar routine. Garnard seemed more relaxed for already the gunfire was abating. Bernoit smiled this thanks and turned away to amble among the fires looking for his friend. He passed one sergeant who was sitting by a fire, alone with his wife, and saw that she was in tears at their imminent separation. He wondered when the women would be escorted away. The gross figure of La Sylphide, their cantinière, appeared from the shadows.

'Hey Bernoit, my chicken,' she called, 'what's this rumour I hear about you chasing me away?'

'Not me, my love—I shall be inconsolable without you. Blame the Colonel.'

'Ah well, if you want any little comfort you will have to search for me then. I shall be with the baggage since it seems my services here are dispensable. Seven years I've served this regiment and never been treated like this.'

'I am disconsolate, Sylphide—whatever shall we do without you?'

'Starve and go thirsty,' she replied succinctly. Bernoit remembered an immediate service she could perform.

'Go to Garnard and give him some of your excellent tobacco for me—he'll find money in my forage cap. Oh—and have you still got my brandy on that thieves' cart of yours? Then leave me a bottle.'

La Sylphide grinned toothlessly. 'I had hoped you'd forgotten about that, my pigeon. You're lucky there's any left.'

'I'm looking for Étienne. Do you know where he is?'

She shook her head. 'Strange—I haven't seen him around tonight.'

They went their separate ways and still Bernoit could see no sign of his friend. There was nothing strange in this; any regimental sergeant-major would be busy on such a night. Bernoit spoke to several people who had not seen Étienne

Vernier, before he stopped a quartermaster corporal.
'Have you seen Sergeant-Major Vernier?' he asked innocently.
'Haven't you heard? He copped his today.'

For a moment Bernoit could not understand. It was not possible that Étienne was dead. He could not die here, not in a pitiful, useless skirmish where the regiment had hardly been engaged. They had been together for most of their service life, had been recruits together. They had stood shoulder to shoulder at Valmy, at Marengo and Austerlitz. Bernoit shook his head in denial.

'Yeh,' the corporal confirmed, 'just as we was coming out of action. That horse battery that done it.'

The corporal was ready to amplify his bald statement with more interesting details for after all he had been in the colour party and had recovered the eagle from Vernier's dead hand. They had let him carry it in, too. Messy it was, though. Besides, it was not every day that you saw the same shot strike down the sergeant-major and the senior major. Then he saw Bernoit's face and remembered that 'Old Valmy' and the Sergeant-Major were as thick as thieves. Related, someone had told him, brother-in-law if he had got it right. The quartermaster corporal quietly withdrew and left Bernoit alone with his sorrow.

Someone had spoken. A voice had dropped into the well-depth of his misery and sent ripples of thought running out like a pebble splashing into a dark pool. He stood there and made the effort to focus his thoughts, his eyes moist so that the dancing bivouac fires were painful pinpricks of blurred light piercing his sorrow. The voice spoke again.

'I see you have heard.'

It was said kindly, with compassion, and Bernoit knew the voice well and was moved. He forced himself to reply.

'Yes, Colonel, I've just heard.'

'I'm sorry—I too regarded him as a friend. We have all lost friends today.'

'Is he still out there, Colonel?'

'Yes.' The commanding officer was quiet for a moment, before adding, 'They are all lying out there. Major Marlot was killed by the same shot, you know.'

'Then, Colonel, I grieve for you. We have both lost our closest today.'

16

'Yes,' said the Colonel wearily, thinking of the silent ranks lying out on the freezing hillside.

'I'd like to . . . ' Bernoit began, gesturing in that direction.

'Yes, of course. On you go.' He hesitated again before adding, 'It's not pretty—it was his head—you . . . er, that is . . . you may have difficulty . . . finding him.'

Bernoit nodded, understanding, but without appreciating. He knew now that his cheery, one-eyed friend had lost his head, smashed by a round shot, but it was too grotesque to comprehend. He saluted and turned from his commanding officer, leaving him alone with his own grief.

Bernoit stumbled unseeing through the camp, past the soldiers settling down for their cold night's sleep, past the women gathering together in tearful readiness to leave their menfolk behind, past the little tent where the surgeon still laboured in the gloomy lamplight, removing limbs, repairing torn flesh. He passed the picket line and walked back along the broken road where already the frost was setting on the muddied pot-holes and bands of stragglers lurked, seeking comfort in the night. Down to the bridge he walked, where the river swirled softly, and past the sentries there and the demolition party waiting for the outlying pickets to come in. Slowly, he climbed back to the hill where they had stood all day until, at last, he found himself among his fallen comrades.

The stench of death was here already and with it the pungent smell of wolves, shadows seen flitting among the ample carrion, occasionally raising a head in mournful howling, a fit celebration of the dead. Further over, a battery opened fire again and the cacophony of bounding echoes began once more as other guns took up the song, while Bernoit stood alone surrounded by the mangled, silent wreckage of his friends.

Not all were dead for there were wounded lying all around, crying for succour. Some wanted aid, others water and some few sought most of all a merciful bullet to end their suffering. One man, wearing a grenadier's epaulettes, seized Bernoit's coat and clung to him, crying piteously:

'Oh Sergeant, dear Sergeant—oh Jesus, don't leave me. Take me in, oh Christ Jesus, Sergeant, take me in.'

Bernoit was looking for his fallen friend and heeded no other, so he pushed the clinging hands away and continued regardless on his search. Behind him the man screamed for water and swore at Bernoit for his harshness. Bernoit ignored the noise and held up the lantern in his hand. For a moment he looked at the flame curiously for he had no recollection of bringing it with him. He supposed it must have come from the engineers at the bridge though he could not be sure.

In the lamplight he moved across the trampled ground and approached the place where the colour party would have stood. There was a hollow where many cannon-balls had come to rest and he paused to look at the torn forms lying there among the frost-covered shot. The man he sought was not there and he moved on, careless of the wounded groaning around him. He slipped on some half-frozen matter near one corpse and slithered down a slight slope. As he rose he saw a familiar face in the beam of his lamp. Almost on a level with his own face it seemed to look at him, but he saw the dead eyes and the mortal pallor, the lips drawn back in a snarl. It was Marlot, the senior major, and as Bernoit stood up he saw that Marlot had been cut in two, and already the thick blood was freezing on the flint-hard ground. He knew that Étienne Vernier was near at hand.

He examined the huddled corpses around him and at first he did not see Vernier lying there. He had been looking for some time at one body before he realised that his quest was over. He saw the silver epaulettes and knew by these badges of rank alone that he had found his friend, for Étienne Vernier was headless and there was no other way of identifying him. Bernoit stood transfixed, too horrified to approach. This ruined carcass was not his friend, but an empty spoilt shell and it was then that he knew that Étienne was dead, and he knew the meaning of it.

Death was no stranger to Bernoit and it seemed that all his life he had heard its wings rustling ominously at his shoulder, but always selecting others. Most of the old crowd had gone now, one way or another, the old band of brothers who had stood together at Valmy, but somehow he and Étienne had always managed to come through. It was inconceivable that life could go on without Étienne Vernier at his side. Yet there it was, and this stiffening corpse had been a brother to him.

He forced himself to kneel down beside the body and ignore the horrid mess which had been the head. He pulled at the straps on the pack to ease it off, determined to collect the few small things which now meant so much. As he drew the pack away the body half turned and he saw

18

the medal of the Legion of Honour still pinned to the breast.

'I'll have that,' he thought and fumbled with the clasp until the pin came free and it slipped into his hand. He held it there in the lamplight, a thing of beauty with its worn red ribbon and the white enamel cross. His mind drifted back to the dreadful hours at Austerlitz when the air was humming with flying shot and all the officers were down and Étienne, blinded in one eye, blood streaming from the empty socket, led them on against the Russian grenadiers. They called him 'Cyclops' after that, those who knew him well.

His mind filled with memories of Étienne's face, the black eyepatch and the neatly trimmed whiskers, the mouth curling humorously; taut and firm in the gunfire at Jena; laughing with him in German taverns; grim in the long marches in Spain; and smiling and gentle, as they sat round the warm embers of the fire which Émilie kept burning in Paris, and told their soldiers' yarns to young Paul sitting at his uncle's knee and gazing at his wonderful, one-eyed father.

Yet it was back to the early days that Bernoit's thoughts strayed, days of innocence which had been destroyed before the mill at Valmy. There they had stood together and first heard the .pulping smash of broken bodies. There they had suffered the Prussian cannonade, and had endured, and had wagered on the beetles scurrying in the earthworks. Later, Dalours had been hit in the face and had taken a long, noisy time to die.

In time that baptism of fire had ended and he was thick in the advancing columns, and realising that it was over, that somehow the ragtag and bobtail of the Republican army had thrown back the military might of Prussia. And in the cheering, unruly mob he had found Étienne Vernier, smoke-blackened and grinning, and that young man, his clear blue eyes twinkling, had shouted across to him:

'Hey, Bernoit! Don't forget the beetles—you owe me twenty sous!'

Bernoit neither saw nor heard the approaching horsemen, even though they halted, attracted by the lantern.

'What's this,' a voice demanded, 'a fellow robbing his fallen comrades?'

He was superbly mounted and the gold fringe on his embroidered shabrack stirred in the cold wind. He sat there, wrapped in a splendid blue cloak, the gold lace glittering in the lamplight, his cocked hat seemingly alive with fluttering white feathers. But his face was greater than these, solid and fiery, framed by his ginger whiskers and, above all, commanding. Now it was angry and contemptuous.

'Well? Answer, soldier,' the man commanded and behind him the others, his staff, stirred in their saddles.

Bernoit hesitated, choosing his words with care, for this man was Marshal Ney and Bernoit was disturbed to have so innocently incurred his wrath.

'The man was my friend,' he said simply. Then he saw Ney's eyes taking in his sergeant's stripes and the long service chevrons and he added, 'We have been together since Valmy.'

The Marshal looked down and his frown softened.

'Valmy,' he murmured as if his mind was back in those giddy days, at the head of his troop of hussars again. Ney's gaze fell on the medal in Bernoit's hand.

'The Emperor himself bestowed this after Austerlitz.'

Ney nodded. 'We have all lost friends today. Ours is a sad life ... I know you! You were in my old Sixth Corps weren't you. What's your name again?'

'Bernoit, sir,' he replied, proud to be remembered. 'I was with you in Spain.'

'Ah yes, I remember now. You were a sergeant-major then.'

Embarrassed, Bernoit wondered how Ney could recall such details, and ruefully replied, 'I trod on forbidden ground.'

'An officer's mistress or the mess funds, eh? Ah well, I don't want to know. We old fellows are thinning out, are we not?'

The bond of comradeship was between them now. They had been fighting in the same struggle for over twenty years. It did not occur to Bernoit that he was poor while the other was wealthy and privileged. They were mutually proud. That was enough.

'Aye Marshal, there are few of the old ones left.'

'And a soldier's death at the end of it all. It is enough,' and the Marshal cast his arm around to embrace the fallen. Then he was the corps commander again, anxious to be on his way. He gestured to his staff to move off and nudged his horse forward, pausing for a last word.

'Don't delay too long, Bernoit. Get back to your battalion. The bridges will be down shortly.'

Then they were gone, the horses carefully picking their way

over the dead, a glittering group of riders fading into the shadows as they resumed their survey of the position. Their clipping hooves slipped into silence and somewhere near at hand a wolf howled, calling its message to the heavens.

Bernoit knelt down again and placed the lantern beside him on the ground. It was an honour that the Marshal had spoken to him thus, and he felt strengthened by it. A man like that understood what this business was all about. It was good to know that he had things in hand. Everything would be all right. He was right too, about death, and Étienne's death seemed less pointless now. What had he said? 'A soldier's death.' But oh, it was hard to bear the loss. He looked at the medal in his hand and sadly shook his head.

'He spoke to us both, Étienne. He's a real old-timer, that one.'

He decided not to search Vernier's pack immediately, but to carry it back to the bivouac and, with a final heave at the straps, he drew it free and put it to one side. Carefully he went through his friend's pockets. There was little enough there, a few coins, a tinderbox, the silver whistle on its white lanyard which had been a present from Émilie. He slipped them into his own pocket together with the medal, and was about to stand up when he saw something lying near the corpse's shoulder. Like a little medallion it was, with a rat's tail of soiled cord. He picked it up curiously and saw with distaste that it was covered with brain and blood. Gingerly he wiped it clear and pulled off the broken cord which he now saw was a little chain clogged in the sorry mess. Disgusted, he threw the chain away.

It was a locket which he held and he pressed the delicate catch to open it. Inside was a lock of auburn hair and he knew that it belonged to his sister, and on the faces were matching portraits of them both, Étienne and Émilie. The little paintings were crude but simple, and they both looked very young. They must have been painted when the couple had just married. Bernoit had never seen the locket before and now, with the faces of his friend and his sister smiling at him from their youth, he broke down and wept.

How long he had been lying there he could not be sure. The lantern was guttering and he knew that it was late. He remembered Ney's warning and hoped that the bridge was still standing. It would be very awkward to be stuck on this side of the river and

21

anxiously he looked around him. The night was still and there
had been no gunfire for some time. From where he stood the
bivouac fires of the Russian army seemed very close, and in the
deathly stillness he felt fear beginning to grow within him.
Suddenly he was in a fever to be away from this horrible place.

He rose and bent to pick up Vernier's pack. The locket was still
in his hand and he stopped, noticing it again. A thought came to
him and he took out the lock of Émilie's hair and leaned down to
tuck it carefully into his dead friend's coat, just over his heart,
where the medal had been. Then he slung the pack on his
shoulders and picked up the spluttering lantern and, pausing for
a moment, he stood to attention and saluted.

'Adieu, old friend,' he said and then turned his back on the
lifeless form.

He had not gone far when he heard movement ahead and he
thought of dousing the tell-tale lantern. Before he could do this a
figure loomed on the skyline and he saw that it was a woman. He
held up the lantern and recognised her as Sergeant Thomas's
wife. Widow now, he amended and knew that she had been on a
similar mission to his own.

'Who's there?' she called anxiously.

'It's all right, Jeannette. It's me, Bernoit.'

'Oh thank God. I'm lost, Bernoit, lost.'

In the lantern light he could see that her face was pale and
tear-stained but as she drew close she smiled wanly.

'You too have been weeping,' she whispered.

'Yes.'

'We have lost our dearest today. . . . Oh God! He was so—so
cold.'

Bernoit sighed. She was encumbered with belongings which
she had taken from her husband's body—indeed it seemed that
she had collected all his accoutrements—and Bernoit took the
dead man's knapsack to ease her load. He remembered the bullet
mould which he had borrowed and wondered if he should
mention it, and then decided not. She would have no use for it.

'We must hurry. They're going to blow up the bridge,'
he urged, and he led her towards the road. Wolves moved
sulkily from their path and on seeing the flitting images
Bernoit shuddered and thought of them tearing at Vernier's
body, and the lock of Émilie's hair falling unnoticed from
the sundered clothes, to be blown away by the chill uncaring

22

Russian winds. The silent shapes reminded him of rats.

'Like the rats at Saragossa,' he murmured, 'eh Étienne, my friend.'

'Pardon?' the widow asked, and he wondered if she too had seen the grim shadows and imagined them gnawing at the body she had loved. He tried to shrug it off, but she had looked where he was looking and said quietly:

'Ah yes. The wolves.'

'If only we could have buried them...' he began apologetically but she shook her head and tried to sound matter of fact.

'It's not important. The ground is too hard. His sufferings are over, at least.' And then she broke again and began to sob. Her body shook in her grief and, helpless and tragic, she turned to him. Pity welled in him and he put the lantern down and freed his arm to wrap round her and tried to bring her comfort.

'There,' he said gently, 'I saw him fall. He felt nothing.'

She nodded at this new knowledge, but her sorrow was not eased. Bernoit reflected that Étienne Vernier had likewise known nothing, unaware of the flying shot even as it smashed his head away.

'Come,' he said, and his voice was gruff. 'The bridge will be down if we do not hurry.'

Yet even as they moved away there was another delay. A wheezing broken figure was wriggling across the ground in their direction and it began to whine at them.

'Oh my treasures — for the love of God — don't leave me. Take me in. Jesus help me.'

Bernoit recognised the grenadier who had caught at his coat-tails earlier, hours ago it seemed. He was anxious to be away from this hillside and made to move around the wailing man. Jeannette Thomas stopped him.

'Oh! We must help him,' she protested.

'There's no time — the bridge...'

The man had reached them now and was clinging to the woman's skirts. Bernoit tried to push him away but the woman stopped him.

'We must help him,' she affirmed.

'Yes, yes,' the man whined, 'help me — take me in.'

'For God's sake,' argued Bernoit, 'we'll never get across the river. The Russians will be around here soon.'

'Yes yes,' the grenadier waited, 'the Russians — soon — don't leave me to them.' And he turned to Bernoit, his eyes wide in terror and pain, and he lowered his voice to add in horror, 'There are the wolves too.'

The woman settled the matter by kneeling down to support the wounded man.

'It's all right, we're going to carry you back,' she said quietly, and before Bernoit could protest she turned to him defiantly and added, 'We are going to, aren't we, Bernoit?'

Bernoit shrugged. He knew when he had been defeated, so he now turned his attention to the problem of moving the crippled man. Bernoit saw that the man's legs had been smashed and he was clearly incapable of helping himself. He must have endured atrocious agony to crawl across to them. It seemed so pointless to waste precious time in assisting the man for with wounds like that he had little chance of survival. There had been too much loss of blood, and if that didn't kill him then gangrene or disease certainly would. Still Jeannette was insistent so they would have to organise some form of stretcher to carry him.

A quick search found two discarded muskets and they slipped these into the late Thomas's greatcoat. It was a rough and ready affair but it would serve its purpose and they placed it on the ground and gently eased the wounded grenadier on to it. He whistled in pain as they lifted him and when Bernoit turned to the shattered legs the man gasped.

'Aagh!—Jesus, Sergeant—Be careful.'

Bernoit nodded reassuringly although there was little he could do for it was a horrible ruin of broken bone and torn sinews. There was no time to be gentle so Bernoit braced himself and scooped the tangled mess into his arms and bundled it on to the stretcher and, as he did so, the man began to howl in pain.

It was a heavy burden that they now had to carry and awkward to hold, but they struggled along somehow. They picked their route over the rugged hillside, doing their best to avoid the scattered corpses and the dark, twisted thickets. Several times they stopped and painstakingly lowered their bleeding load down to the cold, hard ground, and took a few precious minutes' rest before wearily staggering on their way. Once the widow stumbled and dropped the stretcher and the wounded grenadier screamed piercingly as he crashed down on his broken stumps. Bernoit ignored him because there was nothing he could do to aid him, although he asked the woman:

24

'Are you all right?'

She nodded assent, but he saw that her hands were unprotected.

'Have you no gloves?'

Her hands must be frozen and numb, he thought, for his own fingers were stiff in the cold night. Cursing himself for a weak fool, he took off his woollen mitts and offered them to her, and when she shook her head he said sharply:

'Here, take them—I can manage,' but he made a mental note to recover them when they reached the safety of camp.

On this occasion when they started off there was a sharp tug on the stretcher and the grenadier shrieked so that Bernoit felt the man's agony racking his own body. He looked to see what had caused this, and in sickening clarity, observed a foot trapped in the scrub and a long sinew drawn tight. Hoarsely he said, 'Wait,' and his hand was shaking when he lifted the thing and placed it delicately on the stretcher. This final shock had overcome the cripple and he fainted, and at long last they had peace from his agonised noises.

In time they came to the bridge and it was a great relief to see that it was still undamaged. The picket was there as before and the demolition party were still waiting, stamping their feet in the cold, impatient to do their work and be off. The sentries watched them curiously as they came through and the corporal of the engineers stopped them when they reached him.

'You took your time! Where's my bloody lantern?'

Bernoit grinned. It was good to be away from that gloomy place, to be able to smile again.

'Destroyed by enemy action,' he laughed.

'Bloody marvellous! You do a man a favour and . . .' The corporal looked at the body on the stretcher. 'You're wasting your time with him—he's a goner.'

Bernoit looked down on the grenadier's face and saw the unmistakable pallor of death. Their efforts had been in vain, after all. He gestured to his companion to lay the stretcher down but the corporal saw the movement and intervened.

'Not on my bridge you don't. The rearguard will be coming through any time now. Dump him over there.'

It was by the roadside that they laid him down and stopped for a moment to rest. Bernoit found that he was moved by the sad end to their little epic.

'A sorry business, Jeannette,' he said quietly. He rubbed his

25

hands which were now numb with cold and she saw and made to return his gloves.

'Let's see what he's got — he won't be needing gloves now,' and Bernoit bent to search the corpse. He soon found a pair of gauntlets and handed them over in exchange for his own mitts. There was little else worth taking so they collected their belongings and walked back up the road towards the battalion.

Their troubles were not over yet, for they had not gone far along the tree-lined road when four figures appeared before them in the darkness. Bernoit immediately knew them for what they were and was alarmed. They were marauding stragglers, driven away from the bivouac fires, hungry and ruthless, and he knew that they would be pitiless robbers. With growing dread he realised that he was not armed and as the men approached he looked around for a means of escape.

It was too late; burdened as they were, they attracted the rogues' attention and they were too encumbered to run. Bernoit was well aware that it was hopeless and his survivor's instinct told him to hand the men anything that they wanted, but he was carrying things that had belonged to Étienne Vernier and he knew that Jeannette Thomas would not lightly surrender her husband's possessions. He tried to challenge them.

'Why aren't you men with your unit? The Russians will be here at any minute!'

'It's "Old Valmy"!' one of them cried. 'I've got scores to settle with you, Sergeant,' and Bernoit recognised a delinquent from his own regiment. The men rushed at them then, and Bernoit threw aside the pack he was carrying and prepared to defend himself against their drawn bayonets.

'Here, Bernoit!' Jeannette shouted and she handed him her husband's sabre-briquet. It was a short sword and useless for anything other than cutting firewood, but it was better than nothing. He had not noticed that she had been carrying it and was grateful for her forethought. He saw that she too was ready to fight for her possessions.

'Come on, cowards,' he yelled and they were upon him. As he parried their hacking blows he began to bellow for assistance. One lunged at him and he side-stepped neatly, and stabbed viciously at another, causing him to yelp with pain and drop his weapon. The woman pushed forward and seized the discarded blade, and their assailants backed off.

26

'Come, cowards—are you afraid? Four of you against little me and a woman,' Bernoit snarled before raising his voice and yelling, 'Aid us, comrades! We are attacked by scavengers!' He sneered at them, 'Hurry now—you have little time left before you are caught.'

The marauders' blades circled cautiously, and then one of the men darted forward suddenly. Bernoit was too slow to defend himself but the man stumbled over their discarded belongings and the woman slashed at him so that he leapt back. Yet it could not be long before the men summoned up the resolution to attack jointly and overwhelm them. Then, from the road ahead, there was a shout and a clatter of accoutrements and men were running to their aid. The attackers broke off and turned to the woods. A shot was fired and a man screamed and then they were gone, crashing through the undergrowth. Their rescuers came to them; it was Necker with the gentle Chopart.

'What would you do without us, Sarge?' asked Necker, grinning from ear to ear, but Bernoit was in no mood for jokes.

'Where the hell have you been?' he snapped unfairly, but Necker was unabashed.

'Now if it hadn't been for the Sergeant-Major we'd never have bothered to look for you.'

Bernoit could imagine Garnard fidgeting with anxiety for his missing sergeant. He wondered how long he had been away, and found he could smile again.

'Thanks anyway—you're a lousy shot, you know.'

'That was Chopart—I wasn't going to bother.'

Chopart gestured in protest. 'At least I winged my man; the Corporal misfired!' He turned to gather up the woman's fallen bundles. 'Permit me, madame. Are you all right?'

Larguien looked exhausted. 'Where have you been, Sergeant? I thought we'd lost you.'

Bernoit spread his arms. 'Well . . . you know . . .'

'Yes, I'm very sorry. Sergeant-Major Vernier was a fine soldier —as are you. I can't afford to lose you like that, you know.' The officer changed the subject. 'Madame Thomas. The women have gone ahead now; she'll have to stay with us in the meantime, until we come up to our baggage again, or we can spare an escort. You'd better get some sleep now. We're standing to in a couple of hours.'

Garnard was still awake and was pleased to see him. He shook his head sadly when he saw Étienne Vernier's equipment, and when Bernoit showed him the medal he nodded, remembering. They had all been together then in that dreadful advance at Austerlitz. Neither of them felt able to say anything adequate. Instead Garnard spoke of other things.

'Your pork is there for you. I've packed it away in your pot. Oh! and La Sylphide left your brandy, Paul—there's only half the bottle left, the thieving bitch. The tobacco's there too, but there's hardly enough for a couple of pipes.'

'Thank you, Jacques. I appreciate all that.'

He could settle down now and eat a little pork and a mouthful of biscuit before going through Étienne's pack. It all seemed very distant now. He threw some wood on to the fire and it flared brightly for a moment. Slowly he began to sort out his dead friend's belongings into little bundles: the treasured mementos, the useful things like clothing, the spare socks which Émilie had knitted, and those various items which could be discarded, albeit reluctantly. He would have to go through his own things too, to see what he could throw away, because his pack would be heavy now. It would be a slow task but that did not matter, for he knew that he could not sleep.

The cold wind stirred the embers of the fire and men turned in their sleep on the frozen ground, and over at another fire the widow Thomas sat alone, sorting out her man's effects, unaware of Chopart who, in his compassion, came up from time to time to keep her fire burning through the bleak, lonely night.

3

The little knot of soldiers huddled into their greatcoats and stamped their feet in an effort to keep warm. The mist was thick and damp and it clung to their clothing in little beads of sparkling moisture, while on the trees it crystallised into wet globules which swelled to maturity and then, silently, dropped on them. Occasionally one of these ripe droplets would fall down someone's neck and run cold inside his clothing, to be welcomed by muttered oaths.

Nervously, the men stood in the forest and stared ahead, trying to penetrate the grey, wet atmosphere, to see what was out there, hidden in the dark blanket. Visibility was down to about twenty yards and it was simply impossible to tell whether or not the enemy was at hand, so they could only listen for the odd, distorted sound of movement and try to detect its source. At the moment there seemed to be no one there and they could only wait and wish that the weather was better. It was a considerable change from the recent wintry sun, and the morning had been overcast before they had marched into this all-embracing fog.

A trumpet sounded, its tone dead and flat.

'There's the Recall,' said Necker. 'Thank God for that. I hate these bloody picket jobs.'

Bernoit grunted. He felt very isolated here, in command of the hindmost troops in the rearguard. He looked round to where Andrieux stood alone, dimly seen among the trees behind them, providing a visual link with the rest of the company.

'That's it!' he barked. 'Let's get out of here. Make it snappy!'

They fell in behind him as he ran back through the forest and Andrieux was relieved when they joined him.

'God! I thought we were never going to move. It's bloody cold.'

Bernoit ignored him and ran on. The sudden exercise was pleasantly stimulating to his stiff, chilled limbs. It was also encouraging to see the main body of the company ahead, and the dim shapes take their own individual forms as they drew close. Larguien was sharp and businesslike when they arrived.

'Fall in your men, Sergeant. The flank and rearguards have been detailed. We'll have to push on if we're not going to lose touch with the battalion.'

It was all a familiar pattern now, hurrying along like this behind the rest of the army, turning from time to time to drive off the pursuing Cossacks. That was easy enough, for the Russians seemed to have no stomach for fighting. The Cossacks were content to pick off stragglers and take what they could in loot, but they shied away from the slightest resistance. God alone knew where the main body of the Russian army was. There had been little enough sign of that since Viasma. There were the usual rumours, of course, but only old Garnard worried about these.

The marching men hurried along the road, bowed under their knapsacks, while on the flanks and in the rear Yvel and Matthieu scurried from point to point in constant communication with the outlying guards. There was little talking in the ranks for everyone was listening for the first sounds of approaching cavalry, so they marched in near silence as their boots crunch-crunched across the long hard earth and they strode on through the ugly greyness of the forest.

The wind, when it came, was ferocious and it howled down from the north-east and the icy Arctic wastes. There was little warning, a slight stirring of the mist perhaps, and then it struck them with its full force, bending the fir-trees over before it. It buffeted into them so that men reeled under its pressure and were blown into collision with their comrades. Here and there a man, taken completely by surprise, was actually knocked to the ground and had to scramble stupidly to regain his feet while the rushing air pulled and dragged at his puny efforts. The marching column disintegrated and Bernoit braced himself against the awful wind to bellow at his disordered men, but his words were ripped from his mouth and torn away. They managed somehow to push the column back into formation and start moving again, but steady marching was now impossible. Every man had to fight his own personal struggle, to force one foot forward and then the other, and to retain his balance against the elemental fury. Yet they did achieve it and made their painful

30

way forward, but every one of them felt the cold rage of the wind.

Then it began to snow.

The snow came in large flakes, a few at first in flurried gusts and then more, and then in growing numbers until the air was filled with flying snow. A man could not breathe without drawing the chilled particles deep into him, and before his eyes the world became a white swirling mass. The snow did not fall but hurtled in frenzy across the land. It drove like ice into the marching men and sought out gaps in their clothing and tore at their exposed flesh. Appalled by this new horror the column staggered into disorder, more stricken by this onslaught than by any enemy guns.

Bernoit fought his way to Larguien. Already the ground was white, the snow lying treacherously on the ice below.

'Captain,' he shouted, but his words were whisked away and Larguien had to stoop to catch the broken words.

'Have to stop—can't go on—like this—extra clothing—blankets. Rest—a few minutes will do—wrap up—men—cannot—breaking up.'

He turned his head to hear Larguien's reply.

'Can't afford—stop long—Must—contact battalion—lost in this—organise—quickly as . . .'

Garnard was there now too, having come forward from the rear of the little column. Bernoit saw that the company had shuffled to a halt and men were already pulling off their packs to take out their spare clothing. Garnard was yelling something about the outlying guards and Bernoit nodded forcefully.

'No use out there—easily—lost in this. Enemy—own problems—these conditions—no danger—enemy action.'

Larguien appreciated the risk of losing the outlying men and turned to Bernoit. 'Get hold—Matthieu if—can't—find—bring in—pickets yourself.'

But now Matthieu appeared with Yvel and they could see that the guards had been brought in from the forest. Bernoit doubted if Matthieu had had the courage to make the decision himself. He imagined not, and wondered how much prompting he had required from Yvel. The men must have felt desperately alone out there, and as Yvel took a hasty roll-call Bernoit saw the corporal, Hélier, grin at him with relief.

He returned to his own men. They seemed cheery enough, wrapping themselves up in their blankets, binding scarves or shawls around their heads. Most of them had removed their tall

31

plumes and Bernoit nodded approvingly, for these were just extravagant encumbrances in weather like this. Necker had magically produced a fur cape from his overladen pack and Bernoit winked.

'I thought—keeping that—gift—your mistress.'

He went round them all, checking that they were properly protected. Most of them had ample to keep them warm, but young Gautier was a problem as usual.

'Have you—no scarf—son?'

The boy shook his head. He was shivering despite the blanket drawn around him. He could not even get that right and Bernoit helped him to adjust it. And his gloves were useless affairs; light woven things; ladies gloves, intended as a gift for his mother, Bernoit supposed. The soft eyes looked in gratitude for the gentle attention from this legendary old soldier and Bernoit felt sympathy. On an impulse he pulled off the scarf he had destined for Émilie, and wrapped it carefully round the youngster's head. Gautier smiled his thanks.

Bernoit glowered. 'Why don't—equip properly—campaign like this.'

Now Larguien and Garnard were moving down the column urging the men to hurry. Bernoit hastened to make himself comfortable before encouraging the others into some sort of order. At last they were ready and the little company began its march again, bent low before the dreadful blizzard, so that they, at the very rear of this mighty army, fought only one battle, and that against the weather, and they cared nothing for the whereabouts of their other less deadly, but human, enemy.

It was that day that brought the end of Napoleon's Grande Armée, as the wind drove the snow-chill through every man and caused him to draw deeper into his clothes and his private thoughts. They were strung out on a line of march fifty miles long, and as they marched they all dreamed of warmth and winter quarters in Smolensk. They made little sound for all their marching, for already the snow lay thick and muffled their feet as they fell, step after step, carrying the army on its way.

Division by division they passed, through the unfriendly forests. The long lines of infantry marched solemn and silent, each man wrapped close in his greatcoat and blanket, with one gloved hand exposed to clutch his musket, while the mounted officers struggled constantly to maintain their horses' footing on the icy, snow-clad surface. At the head of every regiment the band trudged with silent instruments, and little drummer boys bravely tried to keep the pace, encumbered by their swinging drums which remained unbeaten by hands too cold and stiff to do more than clench and withdraw into the scant shelter of their sleeves. The ensigns clung to their standards, the colours furled and cased, and felt the weight increase as the driven snow gathered on the eagles, blotting them from vision, a symbolic warning to them all.

The artillery had a miserable time. The wheels of the gun-carriages clogged with the snow and slithered round like mad things on the downward slopes. The gunners pulled and heaved to keep the guns steady, cursing and sweating in the knowledge that their heated bodies would soon tire and cool, and the wet sweat would chill, inviting the bitter wind. Yet they struggled on, spiking the wheels, hauling on traces, and their hands, bare to get a better grip, became first cold and painful and then numb, until they had to be chafed and beaten to start the circulation again, agonising but necessary to avoid frostbite. Carelessness or necessity would sometimes bring a naked hand in contact with the freezing metal of a wheel rim, and it would come away, leaving the frozen skin behind, the blood welling from the torn palm. The drivers, beside themselves, shouted and lashed at the patient horses, trying to get them to pull and stop at the correct times, but the animals were half starved, weak and cold, their delicate footing difficult in the deepening snow.

At intervals in the march came units of cavalry and they were in wretched condition. Bad horse-management had already reduced their mounts, and now the beasts were exhausted and feeble. Their unspiked shoes were inadequate for this weather and many fell, bringing their riders to the ground, in a thrashing of broken limbs. Each squadron had its growing group of dismounted men, striding unaccustomed in their heavy boots, the useless spurs balled with snow. Behind them was a trail of discarded cuirasses and lances, sabretaches and helmets and, above all, dead horses, to mark the increasing destruction in the army's finest arm.

From time to time the generals would pass with their staffs, or pause to watch their men go by, sometimes sending off solitary aides, moving carefully with the practised horsemanship of their kind, on some urgent errand. They, too, though better fed and housed and horsed than most, felt the cold. Sitting, perhaps for long periods, marshalling the endless stream of men, they were chilled by their inactivity. Their fine plumes and elegant uniforms could not bring warmth and they sat wrapped in their capes with scarves wound round their heads. It was ridiculous to see, perhaps, a woman's woollen shawl adorning such dignified and dashing warriors, but no one laughed and those who lacked such protection envied their more fortunate comrades with a vile envy and greed.

At times a coach would hurry past the marching lines bearing one of the great marshals, with his escort trotting behind as best they could. Recently such a passage would have called forth cheers and exuberance from the men, but now it was received with the bitter mood of the day which, if the occupants of the coach were sensitive, was more chilling to them in the warm interior than the weather to the men without. Together, they were harbingers of doom.

The mood of the men was not improved by the hordes of stragglers, and the baggage and camp followers blocking their way in undisciplined rabble. In the white tempest people were dying and, as wheels stuck axle-deep in the snow, despairing men began to abandon the waggons. The formed regiments could see this as they passed, all the litter and wreckage being left behind, derelict and unattended, save by the dead and dying. Villages which should have provided shelter were burnt empty shells, filling with the drifting show, barren, blighted places. Ominously now, there were corpses everywhere, each covered by a white tomb-like mound, left to lie untouched, except by the wolves that prowled in packs round the fringes of the dying army. The wolves brought horror to the most hardened veterans as they roamed among the carrion which had been old comrades and friends. The men were sullen and silent, the generals deep in worry. The Grande Armée was a long way from Smolensk.

Gradually, as the horses died and the weaker men dropped behind to die, units began to lose their form, and men looked to themselves and drifted away from their eagles. Unseen in the blizzard, whole regiments disintegrated, transformed by the onslaught of the weather into further mobs of stragglers, incapable of defending themselves, uncaring of others. The weaker corps crumbled away and generals found their entire commands

34

disbanded, and there was nothing left to them but to save themselves.

The rearguard was of better mettle than this, and it remained in good order as its men marched proud through the forest, sweeping the disbanded people before them. They were not afraid to discard waggons if these became over-cumbersome, but they held together in close, though disordered, formations and knew that they could turn and fight if by some unhappy chance the Russians made contact, in spite of the atrocious conditions. Ney was everywhere, encouraging and cajoling them to even greater efforts. He scorned to ride in a carriage, but rode among his men; often he dismounted and, like them, went his way on foot.

Bernoit's company came upon him by the roadside, waiting for them, alone with the Colonel.

'Well, Captain Larguien, is everything in order? Your men bearing up all right?'

'Yes sir.'

'Good. I'll have a word with your flank and rearguards if you'll take me out to them.'

'I've brought them in, sir. They were in danger of losing contact.'

'What! Can't have that, Captain. What'd you do if the Russian army came marching up your arse? Eh? Must get 'em out again. The weather's eased off a bit now.'

He looked around and saw Bernoit, who cursed silently, knowing what he was going to say.

'Here's Bernoit! He'll take charge of things out there. No danger of your losing touch, eh Bernoit?'

'It's an honour, Marshal.' Strangely he found that he meant it.

'Off you go then. Larguien, I thought you'd more sense than that. The Colonel's been singing your praises.'

As Bernoit's party organised to move out, Ney saw MacDonald and stopped him.

'Is that a rifle?'

'Yes sir.'

'Damned irregular, y'know. The Emperor doesn't like them. Can't say I care much for them myself.'

'I can kill at five hundred paces with this, sir.'

'Aye, no doubt. Damned accurate weapon. Takes too long to load for my liking. Still I must come and have a couple of shots some time. Carry on, Bernoit.'

Bernoit's men were encouraged by the Marshal's good spirits, and, illogically, delighted to be chosen for the unpleasant duty. Necker, of course, had to grumble.

'Why couldn't you keep out of sight, like me? "It's a sodding honour" indeed!'

'The Marshal wouldn't know you from a whore's tit. When did anyone but me detail you for anything?'

'Nobody ever gets the chance with you around.'

Bernoit grinned to himself. The Marshal knew a good soldier when he saw one. Despite his pride, Bernoit soon had reason to regret that he had been elected. The fresh-fallen snow was soft, and reached to his knees as he trudged round from picket to picket. It was worse in the forest than on the road, but worst of all was the ditch where he sank to his waist in the deep drifts and had to fight his way out time and again. Matthieu should have been with him on this lonely duty, but he supposed that he would be hanging around the Marshal.

It was not long before Ney himself came out, bringing the other officers with him. They came stamping and cursing across the snow and the Marshal stopped for a while and watched the flank guard moving through the dark trees, and called encouragement to them. Bernoit came up and saluted, and then they were off again, floundering together in the steep-banked ditch, then up to the road again to have a cheering word with the rearguard detail.

An anxious staff officer rode up, leading a horse, and they could see relief flowing through him when he found his missing leader.

'Thank God, sir. I must protest — this position. You are too exposed here!'

'Don't let these brave fellows hear you say that!' the Marshal roared. 'I'm safe when they're around me.'

The aide accepted the rebuke with practised ease, but his reply was urgent. 'Sir, there are dispatches from His Majesty.'

Ney was quick to take the proffered horse, but he turned to address the company before he left them.

'Comrades! My duty bids me be elsewhere. I leave you knowing that my rear is in good hands. However hard things get, remember that the honourable tasks are never easy. And know this — I do not forget that you are here, looking after things for me!'

When he rode off the men cheered him, and that on a day

when even Napoleon did not receive the cheers of his guard. But the Colonel had a rueful comment to make to Larguien.

'I wish someone had thought to send my horse back.'

The sky was turning through the various shades of grey from the gloom of day to the early darkening of night, the deep overcast denying the meanest starlight. It was still snowing. The 46th gladly handed over their rearguard duties to another regiment, and halted at last to sleep, and eke what comfort they could from the unfriendly land. The baggage, of course, was well in advance, and the usual little consolations could not be had. Tonight the regiment found itself bivouacking on a flat, unsheltered plateau with little firewood available, for fatefully they had marched out of the forest an hour before. There was no food other than the loaves carried by each man, and even Bernoit had eaten the last of his pork. The officers were quick to organise foraging parties and Bernoit caught the draft from the light company as they were leaving.

'Hey! Necker, make sure these bastards bring back everything they find. Anyone who returns with a fat belly will have to answer to me.'

'Sure, Sergeant,' replied the corporal, 'but there won't be many fat bellies in this mob tonight.'

'Necker, I don't want any bloody nonsense. You bring back everything. Another pig would do us all just fine.'

But there were no pigs in that freezing landscape, and Necker and his men returned with a pitiful handful of potatoes, just sufficient to give most of the company a mouthful or two.

Above all, ironically, there was a scarcity of firewood and the bivouac fires were tiny glowing flames whose embers afforded the slightest warmth. Even the skilled thieves and foragers of the 46th were trying to dig roots from the ground to throw on the miserable fires, knowing that the effort was wasted and that the roots would stubbornly refuse to burn.

As a matter of routine, Bernoit reported to Larguien and found him in discussion with Garnard and Rabinat, the quartermaster corporal.

'Ah! there you are, Bernoit. The Quartermaster has just been telling us that he has no idea where our baggage has got to.'

Rabinat turned to him. 'It's all mixed up with the transport from the other corps. Christ knows when we're going to find it.'

37

Garnard opined, 'It's going to be damned difficult. We foraged this road on the way out, and now the whole army has gone on ahead of us.'

'It wouldn't be so bad if the silly buggers hadn't burnt all the villages,' Bernoit affirmed, thinking of the smouldering ruins which should have provided shelter.

Larguien spoke firmly. 'The general opinion is that things are going to get worse. We're going to be caught by winter. God alone knows how bad it's going to be, but our duty is simple. We've got to keep the men together and prevent them from becoming disheartened. Still, we are only a few marches from Smolensk, and then we'll be snug for the winter.'

His eyes met Bernoit's, and in the flickering firelight both men knew that neither was deceived. He went on.

'It's a grim night and we'll have to watch out for frostbite, but remember, the Emperor too is sleeping in the cold.'

Necker was waiting for Bernoit when he returned.

'Well, Sarge, what's the news?'

'Oh we're all going to freeze to death, and then Cossacks will come along and spike us, and then we'll all be eaten by the wolves. But that won't happen till tomorrow. In the meantime let's have some more wood for the fire.'

Necker grinned. 'Oh well, so long as it's tomorrow, we might as well keep warm tonight,' and he sent a couple of soldiers off to cut more wood. Then he drew Bernoit to one side.

'I'm worried about Gautier—he's feeling the cold more than most.'

'What about the others?'

'They're all right—some cold toes—and no-one's enjoying it, but we don't have any problems for the moment.'

'Right. I'll take a look at Gautier now—where is he?'

The boy was lying wrapped in his blankets and looked up tearfully when Bernoit arrived.

'Well, son, feeling cold are you? So's the whole bloody army. The Captain tells me that the Guard are spending the night looking for the Emperor's balls—they fell off a couple of hours ago.'

Gautier tried to smile.

'Come on, son—you'll freeze to death, lying like that. Let's see if you can get any warmer. Necker! Go and find Boudin and bring him here. Now Gautier, we'll see if we can knock up some sort of shelter. Get up for a minute, lad — we'll try to build a dyke against the wind.'

He showed the young soldier how to cut snow blocks with his bayonet, and pile them to form a low wall, but the youth's movements were slow and clumsy, and Bernoit found himself doing most of the work. The effort was clearly tiring the boy, so Bernoit told him to stop, and made him jump and dance and keep warm, while he completed the rough shelter on his own. At last Necker reappeared in the swirling snow with the portly Boudin at his side.

'Right, Boudin, let's put some of that fat of yours to use. Get down behind the wall, with Gautier here, and wrap your grotesque body round him as if he was one of your Paris hags — God knows what they see in you. That's the stuff. Now we'll tuck you in like a couple of babes. Fine. Right, that's it. No buggery, mind — this is a respectable regiment, Boudin. Just keep each other cosy.'

Boudin swore vilely. 'Christ, Sarge, I'll keep the lad warm, but it's no picnic you know — I've got my reputation to think of. This chicken's got no tits.'

Young Gautier giggled, warm in the encompassing folds of Boudin's ample flesh.

Necker walked away with Bernoit.

'It's going to get colder before the night's out.'

Bernoit grunted in reply. He looked around at the huddled bodies of his men, sitting or lying stretched on the ground, dim in the flickering firelight, the snow already beginning to drift over them. It was going to be a long night.

Yvel loomed from the dark.

'You'll be pleased to know that my pickets are out protecting you from the Russians.' He flashed his white teeth in a grin. 'I'll have to keep going round to move them about in case they freeze. It's a lousy job in this weather.'

Necker said, 'There won't be many Russians about on a night like this.'

Bernoit growled agreement. 'Your lads would be better trying to get some sleep.'

'What, and wake up under three feet of snow? Oh! I have a message from the Captain — don't let your men get buried.'

He moved off leaving them alone. Bernoit turned to Necker.

'You should turn in now.'

'And you?'

'I'll prowl about for a bit.'

'Take care—we don't want to lose you.'

Later, when Bernoit had at last settled down in his own lonely bivouac, Garnard came to him.

'Just doing the rounds, you know. It's a bad night for the men.'

'Christ! Everyone seems as nervous as raped virgins tonight.'

'The Captain and young Matthieu have gone off to an officers' conference—he asked me to keep an eye on things.'

'My only problem is Gautier. Feeling the cold. I've bedded him down with Boudin—that should keep him warm.'

'Well, keep your eyes open. We don't want to lose any men this way.'

'They'll be all right tonight.'

'I hope so.'

'How's young Matthieu?' Bernoit asked.

'I'd be happier if he'd cheer up—he's even got me worried, with those sad eyes of his.'

I bet he has, thought Bernoit, irritated by the other's too apparent anxiety, but he said, 'Well Jacques, he's only a lad—hasn't seen much of this.'

'None of us have. Larguien's right, it'll get worse. I'd be happier if we had some of the older ones with us—like Marlot in command. Now there was a soldier!'

'Or Étienne,' Bernoit murmured.

'Yes, Vernier—we miss them now. Take Yvel—too damned cocky since he got his promotion. We need the steady old fellows now, you know.'

'Hm.' Bernoit was non-committal, thinking of Étienne Vernier, worried by Garnard's growing lack of control. But the sergeant-major was continuing.

'Mark my words, Paul, we'll start to lose stragglers after tonight—and the Cossacks will be on our heels all the time.'

'Well, we'll have to discourage both then, won't we?' snapped Bernoit and the other, taken aback, said:

'Of course, of course—but it won't be easy,' and then in the awkward silence added, 'Well, I'd better go and see how the others are faring. Goodnight, Paul.'

'Jacques.'

Bernoit nestled back down in his blanket, and watched the other disappearing into the falling snow. Garnard's depressing

words had disturbed him, but now, as he looked around at the
sleeping forms of his men, he drew comfort from them. The
bivouac fires spluttered and sparked in the snow, but all around
he could see the glow of other fires. He was among his comrades
in the midst of the mighty army. It may be cold and the Cossacks
might be close, great things might happen, but the army would
be all right; it always had been and it was no hardship to this
army to be on a difficult march.

It seemed to him that he had been on the march for ever,
sleeping in cold unfriendly bivouacs, or billeted in some pleasant
sunny village with laughing girls to chase. Long marches with the
scenery changing and the passing months bringing the seasons,
late or early, with new places and strange names. Between the
marches there were battles like Marengo or Austerlitz, or Borodino, and sieges like Saragossa, but mostly it was garrison duty or
lingering in camps, waiting for something, like the camp at
Boulogne, practising landing from boats, ready to invade the
British. Warm days where he and Vernier and the others had
such splendid times. Larking in the sun with those girls from the
village, growing flowers in the little gardens outside their tents,
and the day that Vernier discovered his girl was pregnant, and
what would Émilie say? And saved by the orders to march—all
the way across Europe to the guns at Austerlitz. Marching, always
marching. He seemed to have been marching all his days,
although once he could remember he had been a shepherd lad
near Millau, in Aveyron.

He awoke before dawn. The night was black as pitch and it was
snowing more heavily than before. Most of the fires seemed to
have gone out. Bernoit could feel the chill weight of the snow on
him, pressing through his blanket. It was very cold, and he knew
that he would not be able to get any more sleep. Bracing himself
against the wind, he stood up. It was going to be another
wretched day's march, if this weather continued.

He moved about, slowly in the dark, checking his equipment
and making sure that nothing would be lost in the drifting
snow. To his disgust he discovered that snow had found its way
into his shako, and he cursed himself for a fool. If he made
many more mistakes like that, his campaign would be short-
lived. He shook the shako out and saw to his relief that the
lining felt was not too wet. He pulled the blanket over his

41

shoulders and wandered off to check that all his men were well.

He had barely gone two paces when he was challenged.

'It's me, Bernoit. Didn't you hear me get up—move about?'

'No, Sergeant.'

'Where were you?'

'Right here, Sergeant.'

'You idle bastard—you were asleep!'

'No, Sergeant—I swear.'

'What's the bloody point of posting pickets if they keep their eyes and ears closed?'

'Sergeant—I swear.'

'Did you get a hell of a fright when I stepped on you?'

'Yes.'

'I bet you thought, "Christ, it's the Sergeant." You don't know how lucky you are. What would you have done if I'd been a whole regiment of Don bloody Cossacks, eh?'

'Sergeant'—a safe neutral reply. Benoit let it go.

'All right, lad—it's a lousy night, I know. But for Christ's sake, keep on your toes. You've seen enough in Spain to know this isn't a game we're playing.'

He moved on among the sleeping forms, stopping now and then to put wood on a fire which still survived the blizzard. He found Yvel on the company perimeter inspecting his pickets.

'Are you still up?' he asked.

'Could you sleep in this?'

'I did. I met one of your lads there—nearly frozen he was, and virtually out on his feet. How often are you changing them?'

'The usual, every two hours.'

'That's too long in this. No man can keep his mind active that long, when he's thinking about how cold it is. Change them every hour I'd say.'

'Can't, Bernoit. Garnard says he wants to maintain standards as long as possible, and Captain Larguien backs him up. A two-hour watch. That's orders.'

'That's balls!'

The other rubbed his nose.

Bernoit spoke angrily. 'Garnard I can believe. He has aged; not what he was, he's nervous and worries about things—and he spreads his worry.'

'He's a silly old woman,' interrupted Yvel.

'He's a damned fine soldier,' the other snapped, 'with a bloody good record. He was at Marengo when you were still drinking your mother's milk.'

'So was the Emperor.'

Bernoit whistled at the audacity. 'So was I.'

'Ah, but you haven't lost your touch,' Yvel replied with his easy charm, but making, at the same time, the clear implication.

Bernoit returned to safer ground. 'Anyway, Garnard is getting old—he fusses too much. Larguien is different. He's a good officer. Full of fire and ideas, and he knows what he's doing. I'm surprised he agreed with Garnard in this business of the pickets— unless it was to take you down a bit. That's no bad thing,' he added.

Yvel grinned. 'No, Sergeant, not me that worried him, but Matthieu. He really is worried about that little lad. The child was in tears when I saw him two hours ago. He ought to take off his silly epaulette and go home to mummy.'

'Watch what you're saying, Yvel. Lieutenant Matthieu needs all your support.'

'He needs a nursemaid. It doesn't amuse me either, Bernoit.' They were silent for a moment and then Yvel said, 'And now, I am going to change the pickets early. Thanks for your advice.' And he marched away into the dying night.

The camp was stirring and trumpets rang out, calling the morning. Drums rattled, the sticks harsh on the frozen skins, and men sat up in the dark and organised their own little bits and pieces. Bernoit returned to his own section, where Necker met him.

'Gautier is dead—frozen solid—Boudin's in a hell of a state.'

'Dead?'

The corporal nodded. 'You did your best. The others are fit enough—a few chilled feet but mostly we'll be all right.'

'What's wrong with Boudin?'

'You saw him wrap himself round the boy. All snug and cosy. Slept like a log. When he woke up the lad was lying beside him. Cold, stiff as a board. Boudin even had his arm round him.'

'I'll see him now. Everything else okay?'

'Sure—how about food?'

'Well, if you can't find anything . . .'

Boudin was dazed by the horror of his wasted guardianship and he poured out his heart to Bernoit.

'"Sarge," I said, "Leave it to me, Sarge. He's got no tits," I said, "but I'll keep him warm." But he's bloody well lying there like a block of ice, with his big blue eyes wide bloody open. First bloody think I saw when I woke up.'

'Come on, man—you've seen stiffs before—close mates in Spain. There'll be more. He was a nice kid, but he's dead. Forget him and let's get moving.'

'It's all right for you—you didn't try to keep him warm all night.'

Bernoit winced, in the knowledge that Boudin had been acting on his orders. He pulled out his precious brandy and handed it to the fat man.

'Take a drink. That should pull you together.'

Boudin drank deep, but his spirits did not revive. Despairing, Bernoit barked, 'Come on, Boudin! Snap out of it! Let's see you move!' and hoped that the man's automatic responses to discipline would heal some of the hurt.

Larguien came up. Bernoit saluted.

'Good morning, Captain.'

'Morning, Sergeant. Everything all right?'

'More or less. But we lost young Gautier during the night.'

'I'm sorry. He was a likeable boy. We're moving out immediately so you'd better get things moving.'

'The lads'll be ready in a minute—any chance of food?'

'You're joking, of course. I want the company fallen in within five minutes.'

The white plain was now alive in the growing light as the army gathered itself to begin another day's march. The men were stiff with cold, and here and there lay the frozen corpses of others who, like the boy Gautier, had perished in the night, and who were left there as the snows deepened, to lie till the distant spring. The tired pickets fell in with the others, cold and sleepy.

Before moving off, Bernoit went through Gautier's kit. He divided the useful items among his men, giving the clothing to those who most needed it, and rolled the blanket as a spare with his own before retrieving his scarf and collecting the few personal belongings.

The 46th fell in by companies and marched off behind its eagles, happy in the knowledge that the other division was now in the rear and there would be no repetition of the previous day's proximity to the enemy.

By now it was as light as it would be, and the sky was dark with hurtling black clouds. The wind blew strong and bitter, and the snow, thick and heavy, whipped across the marching columns in white swarms, lashing men's faces, clinging to moustaches and eyebrows, freezing on eyelashes. Icicles formed on their beards, and the white flakes clogged under collars, so that if a man turned his head they cascaded in icy softness down his neck, to melt and chill his inner clothes and skin.

The officers and sergeants marched beside their men, encouraging them in this dreadful day, a gentle word here, a harsh one there, keeping the wretched soldiers moving steadily. There were as yet few stragglers.

Bernoit was worried about Boudin. A gross cheery man who now seemed to have been broken by Gautier's death. There were others, too, who were having trouble—Privat had gone lame and was hobbling pathetically on frostbitten feet—but Bernoit was concerned at the suddenness of Boudin's decline, blaming himself. Boudin marched with a stubborn discipline, but his face was blank and his normal wisecracks were missing. The others, too, were aware of it, and there was a depressing gloom which all his efforts could not remove. Perhaps the gloom existed throughout the army.

4

Privat had fallen down, and the column marched round him. Bernoit went to his aid.

'Come on man, get on your feet—you don't want to lie here for the Russians, do you?'

'It's my feet, Sarge. I don't feel my bloody feet.'

'Come on, give me your gear. Let's try to get you walking again.'

He took the soldier's musket and pack and helped him to his feet. Privat could barely walk and Bernoit lent his shoulder as support. They staggered along for a while, but Bernoit was dismayed to see that the company was well ahead, and the second battalion was now marching past them.

'Try to pace it out, man. We're dropping back.' But Privat slumped to his knees again.

'It's no good, Sarge. I can't go on.'

'On your feet! Privat! I can't hang about here all day.'

The man looked at him pathetically, and shook his head. Bernoit saw that it was useless and, anxious to rejoin his company, he said sadly:

'All right then. I'll have to leave you. Try to catch up in your own time.'

He knew he would never see Privat again. Bernoit had seen too many stragglers fall out in other marches, including the dreadful journey to Moscow, to have any illusions. He said as much to Larguien when they halted briefly half an hour later.

'Yes,' the officer replied, 'I'm afraid it's going to get worse. The regiment's had a good record till now, but we've lost quite a few already this morning. Still, we'll be stopping in Dorogobuzh tonight.'

Dorogobuzh. Bernoit thought of the warm houses and the ample food which had been collected and stored by the garrison during the summer. Beyond that lay Smolensk and winter quarters.

'How many days, do you reckon, to Smolensk?'

'Five—maybe six.'

Encouraged, Bernoit returned to his men with promises of food and warmth tonight, and then Smolensk in another few days. Hope began to cheer the weary hearts as they marched. The snow would not go on for ever. Bernoit even managed to get a song going. It seemed a long time since there had been singing in the regiment and even young Matthieu looked cheered. Winter quarters in three or four days, comfortable billets tonight.

Then in the afternoon, as they approached the town, an aide-de-camp came galloping down the road and the regiment halted. The men looked at each other knowledgeably: a change of plan; trouble. Larguien was called away by the Colonel, and when he returned he brought ill news. They would not be billeted in the town after all. The Marshal had decided to make a stand at Dorogobuzh, and the division would be extended on his flank to spend the night on the open steppe. Depression settled on the men once more, and they despaired of ever sleeping in a warm bed again.

Yet when they marched through the little town they saw that there would have been little refuge for them there. As at Viasma, the uncontrolled pillagers had wrought their destruction and the few remaining buildings were burning. Flames crackled and seared at the marching troops, and glowing cinders were thrown into their faces by the vicious wind. There were sick and wounded everywhere, and over the stench of the fires and the mingled reek of the gallons of brandy which had been spilled in the streets was the prevalent odour of disease and the vile smell of death. The streets through this charred, stinking ruin were choked by abandoned waggons and guns, with their horses lying dead in the traces, and the men were demoralised to see this, the discarded impedimenta of the main body of the fleeing army. It was almost a relief to step clear of the foul decay and face once more the clean, wind-driven snow on the exposed steppeland.

The division spread itself out along the slopes beside the dying town and as night fell the 46th moved into a forward position to settle down for the long, dark hours. The fires were as miserable as before and the worn troops roamed far in their search for dry wood. There was still no food, and this was especially infuriating because the stores in Dorogobuzh had been destroyed, and the starving men were angry at the carelessness and indiscipline which had deprived them. Worse still, the foragers had failed to return. They might have deserted but the general opinion was that they had been killed by Cossacks, or by the vengeful townsmen or the peasantry that was beginning to prey on the army, along with the ravens and wolves.

Bernoit found himself on picket duty and had a wretched night. It began by his having a furious row with Garnard when the sergeant-major discovered that Bernoit was changing the pickets every hour.

'Sergeant Bernoit,' and Bernoit knew there was going to be trouble, 'Why did you reverse the Captain's express orders to keep two-hour watches?'

'Jacques, I don't want any troop of Cossacks coming riding through a line of frozen sentries, asleep because they've been on duty too long.'

'It's your job to make sure they stay awake!'

'Precisely! That's why I'm changing them so frequently.'

'Rubbish—this isn't a ladies' academy. A short duty like that is bad for discipline. The men will take advantage. You're too soft with them.'

'Have you tried keeping your eyes and ears open for two hours in this?'

'I know my duty. You can't tell me anything about standing guard.'

'And you can't tell me—only I realise that we've never seen weather like this before.'

'Don't be ridiculous! And don't you come the old soldier with me. I will not have the organisation of this company disrupted by you, or anyone else,' and he added pointedly, 'Sergeant.'

'Don't be so bloody pig-headed.'

'Don't you speak to me like that! You're being as awkward as you know how. There's another thing. MacDonald's still got that rifle. I told you he'd to get rid of it and take a musket. The Marshal didn't like it, the Colonel doesn't like it and, above all, I don't like it! He takes too long to reload. He's a risk to the other men with that thing.'

'You know perfectly well how good a shot he is,' Bernoit replied quietly. 'That rifle is very useful to me.'

'You're defying me!' Garnard was almost hysterical.

'Pull yourself together, man. You're like a frightened old woman.'

Garnard stormed off to find Larguien. Bernoit spat in disgust and, stepping out from the warmth of his watchfire, called Necker and set off to inspect the picket lines.

It was not long before Matthieu came to him.

'Sergeant, a word if you please.'

'Yes, sir, with pleasure. Necker, get out of earshot.'

'Sergeant, I understand you've reorganised the pickets.'

'Well, sir, we don't want the lads freezing to death now, do we?'

'Of course we can't have that,' said the youthful officer, his voice just broken, unsure of himself. 'The Sergeant-Major's very angry about it.'

'Well, we had a bit of an argument, but we've been together too long, old Jacques and I, for that to come between us. I'm sure if you have a word with him, he'll see the right of it, sir.'

'Yes, but . . .'

'And now, sir, if you'll excuse me, I must organise the next relief.'

'Oh yes.' The child was hesitant, not knowing how to handle the situation, then he opted for the easy course. 'Very good, carry on, Sergeant.'

Bernoit saluted the young officer and called Necker to rejoin him on his inspection. Just as they were walking away there were two sudden flashes followed instantly by the crash of shots. The nearest picket had fired. Bernoit ran forward, yelling for the quarter guard, and the other two followed him. There was more firing and he saw one of the sentries moving back.

'What is it, Chopart?'

'Dunno, Sarge—there's something out there.'

The other sentry came up. 'Cossacks—bloody hundreds of them,' he cried.

Bernoit said, 'Come on, let's have a look,' and led them forward and left Matthieu to command the quarter guard as it fell in. There was no movement ahead, no sound. Bernoit crouched behind the watch-fire and listened. Nothing. There could not possibly be hundreds of cavalry out there. He turned to the second sentry.

'Hundreds of Cossacks, eh? Just what did you see?'

'Shadows mostly, but when we fired I definitely saw mounted men. The second burst of shooting was from out there.'

49

'Have you reloaded?'

'Of course.'

'Right, you wait here. You'—he turned to Chopart, whom he considered the steadier of the two—'Come with me.'

With all the skill of veteran light infantrymen they went forward silently, stalking with infinite care, stopping occasionally to listen. Behind them was the clatter of the alarmed troops as they hurriedly formed up.

'Hist!'

Ahead someone was moving, clumsily—on foot. Bernoit challenged.

'Friend,' replied a voice with a marked German accent. 'I am wounded.'

'Come in slowly.'

Gradually the shadow took form. In the faint light Bernoit could see the man was a Württemberger light dragoon. He went to his aid and asked what was going on.

'Cossacks, hundreds of Cossacks,' replied the other in his thick French. 'I was on the patrol line but our vedettes were all overrun, suddenly, silently. I am lucky to be here. They are assembling about five hundred yards away.'

Five hundred yards! Bernoit was appalled and realised that it was essential to advise the Colonel immediately. He left them and ran urgently back to the lines. As he drew near he could see that both battalions were forming up, and was relieved that Matthieu, for once, had made the correct decision and had called an immediate alarm.

The Colonel came forward to meet him. 'Well Bernoit?'

'The bloody Germans have let the Cossacks penetrate the vedettes, sir. There's a large body of Cossacks about five hundred yards away.'

'Jesus!' and the Colonel bellowed the orders to form square.

The drums rattled, their tattoo stressing the urgency, and the lines of troops began the complicated wheeling as, urged by their officers, they hurried to adopt the complex formation. Bernoit rejoined his own company and danced with impatience as they went through the slow manoeuvre. There was no quick way to complete the difficult movement and the cold, sleepy soldiers cursed him openly as he emphasised the officer's commands with his own colourful oaths. In due course the square was formed and the men stood anxiously with their bayonets fixed, thankful that the Cossacks had not yet appeared. It was reassuring to see the close-packed men, grim and ready to defend themselves, their fringe of sharp, cold steel glinting dangerously, and to hear the other units of the brigade forming up on their flanks. It had started to snow again and the white flakes gathered on their shakos and settled in little mounds on their shoulders as they waited for the silent, unseen enemy. Larguien walked over to Bernoit.

'Did you see them?'

'No. There's a wounded Württemberger dragoon out there who brought the news.'

'Hm. Strange we can't hear them. I'd like you to take a patrol out.'

'For Christ's sake—they're there, all right. The German was running away from them.'

'Still . . .'

Moving quietly forward the six men advanced nervously in skirmish order. Bernoit in the centre was trying to retrace his steps to the point where he had left Chopart with the wounded dragoon. In the darkness with the snow falling it was difficult to find direction. A voice spoke quietly from just ahead.

'Sergeant?' and they found the two men huddled together in the snow.

'Well, friend,' said Bernoit to the German, 'where are all the bloody Cossacks? The whole brigade's standing to, and they'll have my guts if you're lying.'

Chopart said, 'They're out there all right, Sarge. I heard them.'

The German snarled. 'I bloody saw them—how you think I got wounded?'

'Probably fell off your horse, asleep, like the rest of your sodding mob,' said Necker.

'You bastard. My whole squadron's wiped out, I think. Our horses were sick and useless, because your bloody generals don't know how to look after cavalry. Murat—eh? I shit on him and your bloody Emperor and every other French bastard that got us here.'

Bernoit said, 'We're here too, mate.'

'Oh yes—so where's the French cavalry on vedettes, eh? Which division in the corps had to be broken up, because it had taken the brunt of all the fighting. There's bugger all of my country-men left—and you know it!'

Chopart intervened, 'Sarge . . . the Cossacks . . .'

Bernoit turned, annoyed with himself.

'Shush.'

Nearby, he heard quite clearly the rustle of moving cavalry and the tinkle of a bit; a horse snorted and someone coughed; the murmur of voices. They had either moved closer, or the freakish sound conditions had changed. There were very many of them.

'Let's go back.'

'No—listen.'

The horses were advancing and they could hear the subtle change as they gathered speed and cohesion. In the muffling snow the whispering noise grew to a thunder, swelling in volume and terror, bearing down upon them. They knew it was too late to move, and paralysed with fright they waited helplessly, to be trampled down, swept away. They could see them now and the powder snow, whipped up by the flying hooves, froth-like, rushed towards them, a breaking wave, unstoppable. Then from this hurtling force came a dreadful banshee wail. The Cossacks were yelling their outlandish war cries as they charged.

On and on they came and the world trembled under their hooves. The flying snow swirled around them and lashed at Bernoit's party, ice-balls thrown up by the pounding feet. They could smell the sweat of men and beasts, feel the dashing figures as they were engulfed. But no one touched them, none harmed them, and incredibly the horde swept past them, unseeing in their helter-skelter charge.

'Christ, they've missed us,' Necker whispered in awe.

Bernoit fought to assemble his thoughts, control his jangled nerves. He forced himself to concentrate. The Cossacks were throwing themselves directly at the regiment and there were hundreds of them. He hoped someone would hear them in time and knew that he should have sounded some sort of warning. It had all happened with such frightening speed. He did not consider that the square could stand before so fearful a storm and he thought of the ranks of men waiting; not knowing what to expect from the unknown enemy; listening to that awful clamour. Panic would grow like fire in the wind. The square would break and his patrol would hear the regiment being slaughtered and know that the enemy could pick them off after daybreak. He wondered what the time was.

Someone said, 'Sergeant . . . if they come back . . .'

52

If by some miracle the square did stand firm, the disordered cavalry would come back this way, marauding and killing off stragglers like his little group. He did not know what to do. They had been so incredibly lucky during the charge.

A rippling volley flared out, where the regiment stood, and then the roar of shots was drowned in the clash of weapons as the collision took place. For an instant they could see the scene, lit by the blazing muzzles, like some hell's kitchen of fighting men and rearing horses, and then everything was dark again. They listened to the tumult of battle, the screams of casualties and terrified animals.

'Come on, Sarge. Let's get out of here.'

Bernoit thought furiously. The cavalry must be in a frightful shambles after its charge in the dark. Their commander had taken a terrible risk, attacking formed infantry at night, and Bernoit wondered why he had not moved earlier when he still had the advantage of surprise. He supposed the enemy must have had difficulty in adopting formation, or perhaps had expected that the French would be unsettled by the long anxious wait. Certainly there had only been time for one quick volley before the cavalry had smashed into the square. Even the most seasoned men would have been terrified. However, when the square broke the Cossacks would be too disordered to organise a pursuit in these weather conditions. Most of the men should be able to escape. In which case Bernoit's patrol would stand a better chance of survival by withdrawing than by remaining isolated here to be picked off when it was light.

'We're pulling out,' he announced. 'We'll try to rejoin the regiment. Chopart, give Wolfgang here a hand.'

The others sighed with relief. It always seemed safer in the body of the regiment. Bernoit led his men in a long route round to avoid the fighting. The hubbub of the struggle was dying away and only occasional bursts of noise could be heard. The battle seemed to be static, Bernoit noticed, and then he realised with amazement and relief that the regiment must have stood firm after all. In that case, he reflected, the retreating Cossacks would be falling back in his direction.

They heard the sound in the nick of time; a group of horsemen galloping straight at them. Again, there was no time to evade and Bernoit hastily threw his tiny party into line.

'Come on, lads—there aren't very many of them. Just one

53

volley and they'll ride off home,' he said with more conviction than he felt. It did not sound as if there were more than a dozen riders and there was just a possibility that a show of resistance might deter them from investigating their opposition more closely. Still, seven muskets, assuming there were no misfires, seemed unlikely to stop any but the more irresolute. The alternative was to run away or hide, and be hounded like swine in a pig hunt. Bernoit stood in line with his six men, their muskets presented at the enemy. Behind them the dragoon slumped on the ground, swearing softly in German. The Cossacks drew closer.

'Wait for it lads, steady does it—any moment now—wait for my order,' Bernoit murmured quietly, while the others, tense and silent, prepared to fire. The enemy were almost upon them now, and he felt that he could smell the horses' warm breath and hear their rustling manes. Now . . .

'Fire!'

He squeezed his trigger and saw the flash of the priming powder, but his carbine did not fire. The blast of a volley crashed out beside him, and he grunted with relief that some of the others, at least, had managed to keep their powder dry.

In front there was the crash of falling horses, oaths, and then the sound of the riders pulling away. The ruse had worked. The unseen horsemen had turned away from this unknown enemy. But one man was on his feet, half seen in the dark, and he ran at them brandishing his drawn sabre. The man was enormous, a great bearded fellow, his size exaggerated by his loose-fitting blue uniform and his splendid fur cap. He raised his sword arm, encompassed in the thick folds of his sleeve, and came on at them, spitting fury through broken teeth. Their bayonets were not fixed and they swung at him with the butts of their muskets, but he thrust the blows aside in scorn and brave and in the violence of his rage they found themselves forced into defence against his slashing blade. Behind Bernoit a shot was fired, unexpectedly, and the Cossack spun in surprise and, with a stricken bellow, fell back, dead. The German growled, as he slipped his pistol back into its holster.

'One should always have one's reserves, Sergeant.'

Bernoit, shaken by the ferocity of this latest attack, scowled.

'Come on, we're moving.'

They did not take time to reload, but hurried back in the

general direction of the regiment. The night was now still and silent, and only the cries of the wounded told of the fighting.

'Who goes there?'

'Sergeant Bernoit and seven men,' he replied as the wave of relief swept over him. They were home and the regiment was unbroken.

Larguien was there and Bernoit made his report.

'Well, Captain, there were hundreds of the bastards.'

'So I saw. We thought we'd lost you.'

'So did I. What happened?'

'I've no idea—they just appeared, and the first volley knocked them into the most awful shambles. We didn't have very many casualties at all. The men did incredibly well, but we were very, very lucky.'

'Very. Odd thing to do, though, charge at night like that.'

'Hmm. The Colonel's afraid they might try it again. He wants to establish a strong picket line. God knows where our cavalry is . . .'

'That's it,' interrupted Bernoit pointing to the wounded dragoon, who was lying nearby receiving first aid.

'Ah yes—our gallant allies. We're better doing this ourselves. You'll be pleased to learn that the light companies have been elected.'

'Shit.'

'Quite. Get your lads organised—we're going out immediately.'

The night was lasting for ever for the weary picket line. It had stopped snowing hours before but the sky was still overcast and there was no light, for the watch-fires had died long ago, and there was no more wood. Dawn seemed far away, and nothing was stirring except the regular changing of the sentries and the constant inspections by the officers and sergeants.

Bernoit felt great waves of sleep gathering over him and knew that to stay awake he would have to keep on his feet. He forced himself to stand up again. One last look round and then he would be able to hand over to Garnard and Yvel. Matthieu looked up.

'I'm just taking a last look round, sir.'

'I'll come too, Sergeant,' and the boy manfully got to his feet.

They moved quietly along the picket line, answering the soft challenges, noting the reports, knowing nothing was moving, going to happen.

'You must be very tired, Sergeant.'

'That's war, sir.'

'Yes, it is tiring, isn't it?'

You poor little bastard, Bernoit thought, you don't know anything yet; you've done as many weeks as I've done years. It was wretched luck that he should be blooded in a campaign like this. Bernoit recalled their earlier conversation and grinned to himself. Garnard had accepted the revised guard duties as a *fait accompli*, and Larguien had expressed himself as satisfied with the new arrangements. Garnard bore him no resentment from the incident and had been comforted to see Bernoit on his return from patrol. He looked at Matthieu. The boy seemed to have grown up during the night. It was strange that he should have found the confidence to sound the alarm at the right time. Perhaps he derived his new self-assurance from that, for it was no small thing to rouse out an entire regiment. Like himself, the lad had had a sleepless night.

'You seem to spend all your nights on watch and all your days marching, sir.'

'Sergeant-Major Vernier once said something like that to me. You and he were great friends, weren't you?'

'We'd known each other twenty years.'

'I am sorry that we lost him.'

'Paul?' the voice had rung through the alehouse. 'Paul, you old bastard, where are you?'

Looking up from the table where he had been sitting with Garnard and a couple of grenadier sergeants, seeing the broad man against the light in the door. His hair is going grey, he had thought.

'Étienne.' And, running from the table, 'Étienne.'

The flowing mugs of German beer.

'First I've tasted since 1807. I hear vodka is better.'

'So you're coming with us.'

'First Battalion—it'll be like old times, Paul.'

'I'm flattered you gave up your cosy depot job for that.'

'Oh, the Emperor couldn't do without me! "Come on Cyclops," he said, "I need that eye of yours in Russia."'

'So it is Russia, then?'

'Tut tut—state secret—he wouldn't be scraping the bottom of the barrel if it wasn't. Look at us—you, me, young Garnard here—we should all be taking our leisure in some spa or other. Sergeants on active service, it's pathetic.'

Garnard had said, 'Come on Étienne. We're all bloody good sergeants. Look at our experience. We can keep the lads on the go.'

'Oh sure—look at the pair of you hiding in Germany from Lord Wellington. I'm telling you our little man wants too much cake. He'll get indigestion.'

One of the grenadiers had stood up. 'How dare you speak of the Emperor like that!'

Bernoit had said quietly, 'Unless you were at Valmy and Marengo you'd better sit down.'

'Sure, but tell Cyclops to take it easy, we're not all republicans.'

Vernier had growled, 'Grenadiers don't get calling me Cyclops —I lost this eye at Austerlitz.'

Garnard had said, 'Christ, Étienne, you're an argumentative bastard. Sit down and drink more beer. We're all responsible sergeants you know.'

'Yeh, that's a big consolation. Have you seen the young lieutenant I've been told to keep an eye on? Matthieu's his name. Still in his bloody swaddling-clothes. He'll probably get me killed while I'm changing his drawers.'

Bernoit looked at young Matthieu's eager face.

'Yes sir, Étienne Vernier was a good soldier. We fought together at Valmy.'

'I know.'

The night was around them in a quiet impenetrable blanket. Nothing was moving. There was going to be no more disturbance in the night. In the morning they might be fighting or marching. There would be no rest.

When Bernoit turned in after his watch he found that the sleep he had craved for so long now evaded him. He lay on the cold snow and strove to keep warm, restlessly turning to find a more comfortable position. Gradually day began to break, and the sombre dawn announced the persistent unbroken weather. Wearily Bernoit got to his feet. Around him men were stirring on the flat, unbroken steppe.

A new sound came to him, carried in the gusting wind, and he strained to identify it. It was the clamour of an army moving and he knew that the enemy had reached them, at last. Then, from

57

Dorogobuzh, he heard the guns and the tumult of fighting and as the noise grew in his ears he became aware that the town was attacked.

About him now drums were beating out the alarm, but he stood motionless, watching, and as dawn turned to day he saw that the white wooded slopes in front of the town were held by a great force. They had advanced through the night and had lit no fires, and as the cold light revealed them they commenced their assault on the lines of the other French division. Others, too were watching, knowing that the position could not be held, and they hesitated to join the ranks. They were cold and hungry and sick at heart that this fresh trouble should be thrust upon them.

Garnard was at his shoulder, and murmured, 'It makes you sick to think of all these disbanded bastards ahead of us. Why should we have to die here? To protect them?'

Bernoit looked at him sadly, and shook his head. He could give no answer.

It was the Colonel who saved them, and rode among them, exhorting them to recall their duty, their honour, to remember their behaviour during the night.

'Will you be cowards now? When the Marshal is in his greatest need?'

Ashamed of their despair the men rallied and returned to their ranks, sensing disgrace that they should have been so close to failing. But when Bernoit checked the roll-call of his section he found that Boudin, the fat cheery Boudin, was missing. He was distressed, for Boudin had been destroyed by young Gautier's death, and Bernoit felt guilt, remembering. He was becoming too old for war.

They spent the morning marching and counter-marching round the town, wheeling and manoeuvring in reserve while the generals endeavoured to save the hopeless position. By noon Razout's division had been pushed back and Dorogobuzh was in Russian hands. Ney saw that nothing could be done, that he had to withdraw if his little corps was not to be destroyed. When the orders reached them the men turned away from the enemy, and in the knowledge of defeat and pursuit, abandoning vehicles and guns and all who could not march, they stepped out once more on the road to Smolensk.

5

It was not till over a week later, fighting rearguard actions the whole way, that Ney's exhausted corps marched into Smolensk. By then Napoleon had withdrawn from the city. There were to be no winter quarters. The army would retreat across half Russia as the season's icy grip caught and strangled it. Ney and the rearguard would have to look to themselves; the Emperor could wait no longer.

The previous days had been dreadful. They had fought in two major engagements and had been skirmishing all the time. Cossacks had made regular forays into their ranks, while the peasants were killing off stragglers and foragers. The entire line of the retreat was littered with abandoned equipment and weapons, guns and waggons, and baggage and the clutter of loot and booty and corpses. Above all the corpses. Corpses of men and horses lying in every imaginable position; men sitting round fires, their faces and chests burnt black, and their backs frozen white; the horses lying stiff with great slices cut from their sides. Bernoit had been eating horsemeat for several days now. And then there were the human bodies with the slices cut from their naked loins. His mind shied away from those, to the memory of the woman suckling her baby at the roadside, both frozen, dead.

It had been terribly cold. Colder than man could imagine. In the bitter nights men died quietly, frozen and stiff, without making a noise to disturb the others. The ranks of Ney's corps had thinned terribly. As discipline eroded in the cold despair whole regiments had disbanded. Other units managed, somehow, to stay together, but with fearfully reduced numbers. The 46th was in the latter category but the regiment had only a fifth of its original strength and many of their old comrades lay behind them.

Frostbite, exhaustion and exposure had taken appalling toll

and the fallen men were abandoned where they fell. Garnard had gone that way, broken by frostbite. On the previous day they had left him behind, his frozen feet unable to bear him any longer, his mind deranged by exposure, his eyes blinded by the heat of watch-fires and the glare of the snow. Bernoit had marched past him, closing his ears to the pitiful cries, knowing the dangerous futility of stopping.

The company was now only some thirty strong and was the only light infantry available to the regiment, which had been amalgamated into one reduced battalion. The other light company had been cut off three days before, and none of its men had managed to escape.

None the less they marched steadily through the rabble of stragglers and deserters. Though there was no music, for the bandsmen had long since cast away their instruments, the soldiers still had their eagle to follow and their shoulders were square as, proudly, they were led by their colonel in through the gates of Smolensk. The Colonel was no longer mounted; his horse had been eaten days ago.

The city was little better than others they had seen, with the same disorder, and the smell of sewers and disease lying thick among the charred wooden buildings. Yet there were large areas which remained undamaged and there the citizens took shelter from the embittered soldiers, and it was in these districts that the weary troops were to be billeted. The weather was milder than of late and to the exhausted men the bleak unfriendly buildings and the stone churches on their commanding hills seemed gentle, mild places where they could rest awhile.

The billets of the 46th were in an older quarter on the slopes beside the river. Bernoit and Yvel found themselves a room in one of the old buildings which had not been totally plundered, and in which there were two beds. They collapsed exhausted on these and fell asleep immediately, enjoying the rare comfort, and the warmth which the shelter provided. At long last it was possible to lie in peace, knowing that other units were guarding the perimeter and that their sleep would not be disturbed by the threat of an enemy charge. The rumble of gunfire at the other side of the city caused them no qualms and they were too tired to feel the slightest pity for the unhappy men defending the city.

Bernoit's sleep was not peaceful. His dreams were dredging up the memories of the last two weeks. Things which his conscious mind rejected came flitting through in a jumble, piling horror upon horror. Again and again Garnard came to him in accusation, and it was Garnard as a young man, companion of his youth, drinking with Vernier, but Vernier has no head, and Garnard dissolves into a screaming horror writhing on the ground as half burnt, half frozen men eat his living flesh and rip the baby from his womb, and the baby is a Cossack, chasing him, screaming revenge and the snow is blood-red, with snarling mouths biting at him with yellow fangs and he cannot run, but can only march, slowly in the close-packed column, restrained by the pressure of the unknown men around him and the band playing 'Ça Ira' while the grapeshot cuts swathes in the ranks, and he falls, entangled in the dripping entrails to lie with blackened, frozen limbs, with maggots and worms running from the green, gangrenous mess that has been his body, and Garnard laughs as Étienne stands watching with his left eye running in a bloody mess from its empty socket . . .

He woke up screaming, clutching at the blankets, feeling the sweat running on his body. Beside him in the dark, Yvel's voice pierced the night.

'You too?' he asked.

Sleep must have come again, for it was light when he woke. The distant gunfire was still going on. In the street outside there were the sounds of people moving at ease, and occasionally of a body of troops marching past. Yvel was still asleep.

Bernoit arose. He saw the pock mark on his naked wrist and realised with irritation that his bed had given him fleas to keep company with the lice which seemed to have been with him for ever. He swore. Lice he had learned to tolerate. They were inevitable passengers on his body in any campaign, but fleas disgusted him. They brought real discomfort and frequently disease. He swore again.

He wondered if any of the others were moving about yet and, leaving the room quietly, he went downstairs. Half a dozen men were sitting round a table playing cards.

'Morning, Sergeant, you certainly got your beauty sleep.'

'What's the time?'

'About one o'clock.'

He had been asleep for almost twenty hours.

'Have any of the officers been round?'

'Lieutenant Matthieu was in here about a couple of hours

61

ago. He spoke to the Corporal—he's through there if you want him.'

Bernoit went through to the next room and found Necker sitting in the midst of a pile of assorted litter.

'What was Matthieu saying?'

'Oh, he reckons we're here for a couple of days anyway, with nothing to do. The Russians seem to be taking a hell of a time to catch us. The rest of the army have eaten all the bloody food, but I'm told the rats taste good. It'll be like Saragossa again. He didn't want to disturb you, but you'd better go across and have a word with the Captain. The officers are all in that house across the road, the one with the dead horse lying outside.'

'Fine. What's all this junk?' Bernoit pointed to the debris on the floor.

'Trophies of war, and it's not all junk. I got this little piece in the cathedral in Moscow—solid gold that is—and if I know anything that stone's a diamond. And this ring—now, that's a ruby.'

'Have you carried that stuff all this way?'

'Some of it, although I won most of it from the boys at cards— that candlestick, the clock there . . . '

'Jesus man—you'd be better carrying food, furs. Those trinkets aren't going to keep you alive.'

'Ah, that's the point. There's a regular little market in town. You can get anything there—even food. This lot'll see me okay. Seems some lads in the Guard started it, and it's been going ever since. Some of the mad bastards even stayed behind to keep their shops open! God knows what they'll do when we pull out.'

Bernoit viewed Necker's collection ironically. No wonder the army had been so laden with baggage when it left Moscow. The treasures of the Russian capital must be lying in a long, abandoned trail back along the whole line of the retreat. He shook his head sadly. The men never changed, but precious few of their baubles ever got home. Booty always encumbered even the best march which, God knew, this was not. Still, the market sounded promising. He thought of the diamond-studded coronet in his own knapsack.

'I'd better go and see the Captain. Tell Yvel to come across if he wakes up.'

He crossed the street to the house where the officers had established their quarters. The dead horse had clearly lain for days and it shocked Bernoit to note that slices had been cut from its rotten flesh. There must indeed be a shortage of food. What had happened to the great stores which should have been established?

Several of the officers nodded to him when he entered and on his inquiry he was shown into a room where Larguien sat alone with a bottle of wine.

'Come in, Bernoit—you've had a good sleep? Sit down, man—a glass of wine?'

Larguien poured the wine and, walking over to the door, called for Matthieu. He turned back and slumped into his armchair.

'Well now, here's health to us! Yvel is still asleep? Oh, let him lie.'

'I left orders for him to come across when he wakens.'

'Good. You've probably gathered by now that there's damned little left here in the way of supplies. It would appear that the main army is in a hell of a mess—indiscipline, food riots, even mutiny. The roads are blocked by thousands and thousands of stragglers. Things got completely out of hand—there's even a bazaar been established in the town centre. I shouldn't be telling you this, I suppose, but you'll know better than I how these things can get out of hand. The staff is very worried in case the same thing happens here. There's no rearguard to save us from the Russians. Anyway, we're stopping here for a day or two, so you'll have to be on your toes to keep the men in hand. Our brigade's all right just now and we want to keep it that way.'

Matthieu came in.

'Ah, there you are René. I've just been giving Bernoit the story. Pour yourself some wine. More for you, Sergeant?'

'Now it seems to me', continued Larguien, 'that a lot of the riff-raff trading at this bazaar must have quite a bit put away. They always seem able to produce food and clothing. I think it's time some of it was commandeered. I want every man in this company to leave here with a full belly, warm clothing and plenty of food in his pack. But I don't want anyone disappearing to join that mob at the bazaar. No one is to leave our lines without express orders.'

'The men won't like that, Captain,' said Bernoit.

'I know, and I'll tell you something they'll like less—I want to confiscate all the useless booty they are carrying.'

Bernoit whistled at this and Matthieu said, 'You could provoke trouble, Charles.'

'Well that's where you two come in—and Yvel. We're going to need all that junk if we're going to leave here properly equipped. It's not going to be easy to enforce, but from now on this company operates on share and share alike. We'll use what we have to buy the food and clothes we need. You, Bernoit, will go to the bazaar and negotiate on our behalf. You may take whom you wish to assist you, but no one else may leave our lines. Lieutenant Matthieu will administer our assembled treasures. Is that clear? Good—and now I think we had better start our collection.'

The men were furious and resentful at having their precious booty confiscated and even Bernoit had a pang of regret when he threw his coronet on to the pile. Necker's discomfiture did much to ease the general annoyance, and the men whom he had beaten at cards laughed and jeered at him as he was compelled to surrender his extensive wealth. The corporal was sullen and angry, but he cheered up considerably when Bernoit told him that he was taking him shopping in the market.

In all his years Bernoit had never observed such a scene as that at the market. There were men from every corps in the army crammed into the square and the side streets, bartering all manner of goods. It seemed that many of the treasures of Russia had not been lost on the march, but had come to Smolensk to become the ordinary currency of this ragged mob. Furs, blankets, cloaks were available and here and there were stalls selling food. It was extraordinary that the food had not been commandeered by headquarters for distribution, but things were so obviously out of control that Bernoit would envy no one the task of clearing away the ruthless mob. The stall-keepers seemed for the most part to be Grenadiers of the Guard, as Necker had suggested, still here though their units had left days before. These men were deserters and profiteers of the worst kind, and he was disgusted to see that senior officers were trading with them, as equals.

'Jesus!' exclaimed Necker. 'Look at that.'

A general was haggling with an ordinary fusilier over the price of a fur jacket. He proffered a sum of money and the fusilier shook his head. The general drew out his last coins in desperation, but the fusilier shrugged his shoulders contemptuously and turned to serve another customer. The general burst into tears.

'Christ,' growled Bernoit. 'No wonder we're in such a mess, with bastards like that running things.'

Necker said, 'Generals or sergeants—that's the way to treat them.' But he regretted it immediately as Bernoit turned on him in a blaze of anger.

An old Jew came up to them and said in astonishingly good French, 'Well boys, you look hungry—how'd you like to buy some flour, eh?'

'Where is it?' Bernoit snapped.

'Oh it's very expensive, you know. I'd have to see the colour of your money first. What have you got to trade with?'

'These,' and Bernoit showed him the treasure in his haversack. 'There's more where they came from—we're buying for our company.'

'No doubt, no doubt—that's what they all say. Still, I should be able to set you up nicely enough. You'll be looking for furs too, no doubt. But, you see, this is not much use to me, you know. What would Mother Russia say if she found these in my possession, eh?'

'Probably give you a medal,' Necker rejoined, 'if she ever got to see them. Come on, old man, I know what these should be worth.'

'Yes, yes, of course. But there's a lot around you see. Look for yourself. I won't be able to get much for this lot, you see. Still I might be able to do something for you. How much do you want?'

Bernoit specified the quantities of food required, and added, 'And warm clothing for thirty-three men.'

'Dear dear, we are ambitious, aren't we? I won't be able to manage that—not on this kind of stuff. However I'll see what I can do. Meet me back here at six with all you've got and we'll see what we can arrange. I'll have to hold on to this of course, as a token of good faith. Now gentlemen, don't get so alarmed—you'll have to trust me. After all, I'm not cold and hungry now, am I?'

The Jew turned and headed away from them.

'Get after him, Necker, but don't let him see you,' shouted Bernoit and shoved his way over to the fusilier with the fur coats. He pulled the coronet from his pack, threw it down and grabbed two of the coats. The fusilier shouted objections but Bernoit turned on him with all the authority of his experience and the other backed down, beaten. Now the general was pulling at Bernoit's sleeve.

'That coat is mine—I've just paid for it.'

'Get out of my way you snivelling bastard. You're not fit to command a squad of sewer-rats.' Again the general burst into tears. Bernoit pushed him aside with contempt.

Running up the side street he caught up with Necker waiting at the corner.

'He's just ahead of me, going down the main road here.'

'Good,' said Bernoit. 'Put this coat on—we won't be so obvious in these. Better ditch our shakos too.'

Thus disguised they followed the old man through the town. He looked round once or twice at the beginning but then he appeared to decide that he was not being followed and walked on without further hesitation, until at last he entered a large building about a mile from the square.

'So this is it. He could have a bloody great warehouse there, Sarge.'

'He'd better have.'

It had been dark for nearly two hours when Bernoit led his little group into the square for the six o'clock rendezvous with the Jew. There were six of them and they were all armed. Necker was with him, and Chopart whom he knew to be a good man in a tight spot. Yvel was there although Larguien had protested that this left him without any sergeants, but Bernoit had insisted. He had the feeling that he and Yvel could work well together. Bernoit had picked two others, the scar-faced Andrieux, a ruthless scavenger, and the pitiless MacDonald, still carrying his controversial rifle. Rabinat, the quartermaster corporal, was not far behind them, with the waggon and horses which they had stolen just after nightfall.

The market was still in business and although the crowd was somewhat less the tumult was as great as before. The scene was even more grotesque, with the torches casting flickering light over the struggling mass of people, and the voices rising and falling in their perpetual bargaining. There were other noises too, screams and yells, to tell of things that were happening which, even in this wretched company, could not be done by day. Bernoit felt the reassuring pressure against his body of the pistol stuck in his waistband, which Larguien had thoughtfully lent him. The Jew failed to appear.

'Right lads, that's it. Come on. Necker, make sure Rabinat knows the way.'

They moved quietly down the slushy streets, tracing the route which the Jew had taken that afternoon. Bernoit stopped at the corner just before the old man's house and waited for the waggon to come up.

'Right,' he said, assembling his little group. 'Necker and me'll go in first. The rest of you stay out of sight. Any trouble and you come in, Yvel, with Andrieux and MacDonald—Chopart covers the windows. Rabinat, don't bring the waggon up until Necker and I are inside—give Chopart a hand if you must but don't, for Christ's sake, let the horses bolt. There might be shooting, and as a carter's son you ought to know what that could mean to gun-shy animals like these. Now, it might be hot work, so I suggest, like me, you get off your greatcoats and chuck them in the back of the waggon.'

They ran forward quietly and the main party hid themselves in adjacent doorways as Necker and Bernoit hammered on the door.

'Remember, Necker—don't let the bastard close the door behind us. I go in first.'

There was silence; the house was dead. Bernoit brought up the butt of his carbine to beat on the solid door. An upstairs window opened.

'Who's there?'

'We've come for our flour—remember us, you old sod?'

'Ah! Yes, boys. How clever of you to find me, when I am so indisposed. I regret being unable to meet you.'

'Come down here, you old bugger, and open this door.'

'Yes, yes, in time. But payment, payment. Where is your—eh —currency, let us say?'

At a sign from Bernoit, Necker emptied the contents of his pack on the ground where they glistened, even in the dim light, the gold shining dully, the diamonds sparkling. The Jew paused, impressed.

'Come down,' Bernoit cried.

'Oh yes, I'm coming, I'm coming. Wait just one moment.'

Bernoit smiled to himself. Seen lying there, the collective pickings of his own seasoned company impressed even him. It was amusing to think of Larguien's expression.

'How do they do it, Sergeant? How do they do it?' he had asked. 'There's enough here for us all to retire on! Spain was never like this.'

'We brought our trophies home from Spain though,' Bernoit had replied.

There were noises behind the door now. The rattle of keys, the old man calling out that he was coming. Bernoit slung his carbine, then drew his pistol and cocked it.

'Watch him, Necker. This is bloody dangerous.'

The other nodded. His musket was cocked, ready to fire.

The door swung open and the old man stood behind it, grinning toothlessly. The hallway behind was dark against the spluttering torchlight in the street. The old man's eyes glittered on the rich pile of baubles at his feet. He looked up and scratched his beard.

'Of course, you see, my problem. My failure to meet you—eh—my entire warehouse has been requisitioned. There's no question of selling it. I have to answer to the commissariat. Think of the penalties.'

'We haven't even seen it yet. Let's go inside and discuss it, shall we?'

'But you can't leave those lovely things lying here. They're no use to me, of course, but strangers passing—might—eh . . .'

'We'll take that risk. Let's see what you've got to sell.'

'I can't let you have very much, I fear. The risks, the penalties, but come in, come in, do.'

He turned to close the door behind them but Necker caught it and said, 'We'd prefer to leave it open. You know—strangers in the night.'

The old man shrugged and led them inside. He beckoned them to follow him into the next room and opened the door suddenly, to cast the light into their eyes. The shadow moved, just a fraction too soon, and Necker fired immediately. Bernoit threw himself at the old man, but was too slow, and the other dived through the door and rolled to safety.

Necker cried out as another man ran from the shadows to leap across Bernoit's prostrate body. Bernoit fired the borrowed pistol vertically into the passing body and, with a terrible shriek, the man crashed to the floor. Bernoit felt the hot splatter of blood cover him.

Yvel and his two men were there now. He could hear Necker reloading in the dark. Glass shattered and there was a shot from the next room. Yvel shouted to Andrieux to get outside and help Chopart. Chopart seemed to be coping on his own though.

'Paul,' he shouted, 'there are three of the bastards in there. We can pick them off from here.' And then, for the benefit of his targets, 'Why don't you bastards throw it in?'

Bernoit got to his feet. He was pleased to be called Paul again. The last man to address him thus was Garnard. His mind shifted hastily. That Chopart was a good young fellow.

Another shot and Andrieux yelled, 'Now there's only two and the Jew, Sergeant.'

Behind them, on the stair, there was movement. Bernoit was struggling to reload the pistol. MacDonald fired, blindly, and the ball plucked splinters from the staircase.

'Sergeant,' a cold aristocratic voice pronounced, 'I am Major de Saint Louis of His Majesty's Imperial Guard. I know not what brings you here, but this is a requisitioned storehouse which has been placed under my charge by General Charpentier himself. You have already killed several of my men in this unprovoked attack. You will leave at once, in which case I will allow circumstances to rule the matter as never having occurred. Otherwise, you are traitors to the Emperor and shall be dealt with accordingly.'

Yvel said, 'Hey, Bernoit, I thought . . . '

Bernoit fired his pistol at the dimly seen figure, but missed.

'You fucking shit!' he shouted. 'You fucking hypocrite. You fat-bellied fucking aristocrat . . . '

Necker shot the man square in the chest; MacDonald ran forward with his bayonet drawn to catch the falling body.

There was more shooting from the room next door and a wounded man screamed in agony. Andrieux shouted that the occupants of the room were busy reloading and if Bernoit wanted to rush them now was the time. Then there was a hail from Rabinat, trying to control the frightened horses, and wondering how much longer they were going to be because the street was filling up with the curious. Bernoit drew his sword.

'All right, we go in now. Yvel, you've loaded, haven't you? Fine. Keep your eyes on the staircase. Okay, you two—let's go.'

With a warning to the men at the window, Bernoit leapt into the brightly lit room, closely followed by Necker and MacDonald. Their adversaries were running to another door. The old man had disappeared. Bernoit jumped over the wounded man on the floor and charged the length of the room. The two men turned to defend themselves and he recognised one of them as the fusilier stall-holder. This man swung his musket viciously. Bernoit ducked underneath it and heard a crash as Necker went down beside him but the fusilier was too slow to recover and Bernoit thrust up into the man's belly. He felt the man's weight push down on his arm and he had to twist round and bring his foot up into the fusilier's chest to wrench his sword free. The fusilier fell back with a fearful scream as Bernoit's blade slipped free, spilling the wretched man's entrails on to the floor.

He looked around. Yvel and Andrieux were coming down the room. MacDonald was on guard at the door with his bayonet fixed and Necker was slowly picking himself up.

'Are you all right, Necker?'

'Yes. He just clipped my shoulder. It's hellish sore, but I'll live.'

MacDonald looked round.

'Sergeant, there are two or three of the bastards down there. There's a staircase down to the cellar. My man jumped down. It's going to be fairly difficult.'

'Yvel, is anyone left upstairs?'

'Chopart is checking just now.'

'Right, we'll reload and go down together when Chopart joins us. We'll start by throwing these two down first.' Bernoit indicated the dying fusilier and the wounded man in the middle of the room.

The device was successful. The two bodies thrown down the stairs drew their enemies' shots, and then Bernoit led his men in a wild charge into the cellar.

There were three soldiers there and they did their best to defend themselves but Yvel, firing from the hip, shot one of them and Andrieux cut down another. The last man turned to run and Chopart dropped to his knee and fired. The soldier ran on blindly into a wall and then crashed back to lie sprawled on the floor, motionless. Of the old man there was no trace.

In the gloomy cellar they could see that they had found a very well stocked warehouse. There were sacks of grain and flour and boxes of vegetables. Sausages were hanging from the beams and on one side were furs and blankets and warm clothing. There was also a most remarkable collection of assorted treasure and other valuables. This clearly was the headquarters of a syndicate which had been trading in the square. It was extraordinary that they had been able to hoard so much when the army was desperate for just these very things. Probably the dead Guard officer had been able to secrete much of it away and it seemed likely that the group had made full use of his influence.

Bernoit and Yvel began to organise the loading of the waggon, carefully sorting out what they required. They were busily working among the furs when Necker called.

'Hey, look what I've found!' and he pulled the old Jew from behind a pillar where he had been hiding. The old man was whimpering with terror.

'Well, you double-crossing old devil,' growled Bernoit, advancing threateningly. But MacDonald was closer and still held his rifle. He thrust his bayonet through the man's throat, and then, as the old man rolled his terrified eyes and screamed soundlessly with the bayonet grotesquely sticking through his neck, MacDonald squeezed the trigger. The blast blew the neck apart and the body fell decapitated to the ground. The head landed at MacDonald's feet and he kicked it brutally so that it spun back, behind the pillar.

Bernoit had wanted to question the Jew and he said quietly, 'That was unnecessary, MacDonald.'

The other looked at him with his cold brown eyes, steady and expressionless.

'He was a shit.'

'Come on,' said Yvel, breaking the tension, 'let's get the cart loaded.'

It was not the easiest or safest of jobs to take the loaded vehicle back through the streets of Smolensk, and the entire party had to be constantly on watch against the bands of marauders who were prowling the city. Bernoit was very relieved when he brought his little procession back into his own lines.

Larguien was most impressed by their acquisitions and, when Bernoit explained the size of the hoard, he suggested that the entire regiment might be equipped. Bernoit grimaced: 'It's not very pretty.'

'I didn't imagine it would be — I noticed you'd fired my pistol. Still, nobody will be asking any questions. I'll tell the Adjutant immediately.'

'Ehem — there was a major of the Old Guard — I'm afraid he got in the way.'

Larguien whistled. 'You really did things in style, didn't you? But he was no doubt killed by one of the deserters, eh? We can't have the story going round that you took the law into your own hands. Not with a major of the Guard involved. But don't worry. So long as we all have full bellies no one will be bothering about how you got the food. I'd better get the parties sent out right away. Rabinat can take the waggon back and show them the way.'

Bernoit was sitting on his bed, meticulously sewing the double gold stripes on to the sleeve of his coat. Stitch by stitch he worked along the red edging, ensuring that the badges would be permanently attached to the faded blue serge. He worked carefully, and with satisfaction, because he had carried these stripes in his pack for a long time, since that day in Spain when he had surreptitiously picked them from the dusty parade ground where they had been cast by the officer who had torn them from him in his disgrace. He had vowed then that when he replaced them they would never be removed. On the floor his sergeant's insignia lay, discarded. He was a sergeant-major again.

The Colonel had been highly delighted at the supplies of clothing and food which had so mysteriously appeared and had summoned Bernoit to his presence. He had been affable and cheery and had spoken of the campaigns in which they had served together. He had expressed his regret that he could do no more for Bernoit than restore his rank but, as he had pointed out, he was avoiding knowledge of the whole circumstances and felt it better not to advertise the story.

'I understand, for example, that it would be tactless to recommend you for appointment to the Guard,' he had remarked in his oblique reference to the incident.

Beside Bernoit, his greatcoat was stretched open and on it he had spread out the contents of his pack. Item by item he had been examining all his possessions in preparation for the next stage of the march. They would be leaving Smolensk in the morning and it would be a perilous undertaking for they were two days behind the main body and the Russian armies were concentrating. Yet as he looked around at his bits and pieces he decided that, all in all, things could be worse.

His equipment, the pack and cartridge case and the crossbelts, was holding out well enough, although it had been necessary to repair the stitching on the buckle of his bayonet frog. His weapons were in good order; he had replaced the worn flint in the lock of his carbine, and had spent the morning moulding bullets and parcelling up fresh cartridges—pleasant relaxing tasks. Later he would sharpen his bayonet and sword, but he would eat first, once he had crammed as much food as possible into his knapsack.

His uniform was beginning to fall apart and prior to his present employment he had applied his tidy needlework to the decaying seams and requisite patching. He had even managed to fashion some new buttons since the old ones were crumbling in the cold. There was a rumour that the buttons had been manufactured in Britain and smuggled across despite the blockade, which, if true, left Bernoit unimpressed by British workmanship, making buttons that disintegrated when it became too chilly. His trousers had been virtually replaced by fragments of a stolen blanket and should last until he found a corpse whose trousers fitted him.

His pride and joy was the fur coat which reached down to his knees and had sleeves wide enough to tuck his hands in, like a muff. The collar turned up high so, with the woollen scarf wrapped round his head, he should be warm enough. Over the scarf he would have to wear his forage cap and he regretted the lost dignity of his shako. Somehow Necker had contrived to find himself another.

Bernoit's most serious difficulty concerned his feet. He had been issued with new boots in Moscow but the soles were wearing through and the uppers were beginning to go. Unhappily, it was impossible to obtain replacements because everyone had similar problems. He had already had to substitute cloth leggings for his dilapidated gaiters and now foresaw that he would have to bind his feet in similar fashion. The idea filled him with distaste for bindings were always unsatisfactory, with a tendency to come undone, and, in the present weather, it would be nearly impossible to avoid wet feet, with the attendant danger of frostbite. He would have to be very careful.

His new insignia were now sewn on to his satisfaction and he inserted the last stitch and tied a neat knot before biting the thread and placing the needle in his housewife, which he then rolled up and laid on his greatcoat. He scratched the stubble of his beard. The fleas were very irritating and he saw a bleak flea-bitten and lice-ridden future until he reached decent quarters and obtained a complete change of clothing. Then he would shave, although he was grateful for the thickening growth for he was certain that the present mild weather would not last long.

Bernoit decided that things were as satisfactory as he could expect. The regiment was in far better condition than when it

73

entered Smolensk two days before. The men had warm clothing and all were well fed and had food to carry away. They had been fortunate in having had no duties during the entire period and everyone had been able to rest. By confining the men to quarters the regiment had avoided desertions and their numbers had actually been increased by returning stragglers, including eleven from Bernoit's own company.

He put all his little bits and pieces in his knapsack, carefully packing in his food and the jug of vodka which he had purchased at the market. He also slipped in the miniature jewel-encrusted crucifix acquired during the raid on the warehouse. It was not heavy and he might be able to buy boots later on.

He placed the pack at the foot of his bed with his haversack and cartridge box and laid his sword and bayonet on top. Everything seemed to be in order. He took his pipe from his pocket, stretched out on the bed, and drew the greatcoat round him. It was good to have tobacco again, to roll in his fingers until the texture was right, and then press firmly into the bowl of the pipe. He opened his tinderbox and nursed the spark until he could get a satisfactory light which he applied to the pipe, and took the first two or three rapid draws until he was sure that it was lit. His head spun pleasantly with the nicotine for it was a week since his last smoke. He lay back and watched the clouds of smoke gently rising and drifting across the frozen window-pane where the grey light filtered into the room. He was rested and had no duties until tomorrow's muster. There was nothing to do but eat and sleep. He scratched himself slowly and looked up at the blue smoke rising above him. Sergeant-Major Paul Bernoit was a deeply contented man.

6

Larguien shook his head sadly and handed the telescope to Bernoit.

'Look at that,' he murmured.

In the ravine below them, only half visible in the fog, Bernoit could see the remnants of Ricard's division fleeing back from the Russian guns. He sighed heavily. This, probably the best division of Davout's corps, had reinforced them at Smolensk and now was ruined, broken by Russian artillery.

It had been a depressing afternoon, on the second day out from Smolensk, for this place had been a battlefield, the snow bloodied red and littered with corpses and shattered guns. They were able to identify the units which had taken part by the scattered cap badges, and deduce that the main army had been engaged three or four days before. The silent slain could not tell them of the outcome of the battle and they remained ignorant of the fate of their comrades. Then as they entered the ravine of the River Losmina at Krasnoe they had blundered into a Russian army extended across the road and an emissary had come forward under a flag of truce.

A tense scene had ensued for the Russian officer had called on Ney to surrender. It appeared that there were eighty thousand of the enemy present and the insult of the summons to the Marshal was tempered by the fact that there were, perhaps, only seven thousand French. But before the Russian could finish his speech the enemy cannon opened fire and Ney had personally to intervene to save the officer from the swords of his angry staff. Even under the wicked hail of grapeshot the story had been spread in the ranks and men were steadied by Ney's reply.

'A Marshal of the Empire will never surrender. There can be no parleying under an enemy's fire. You bring dishonour, and are my prisoner.'

The soldiers were ready to die for such a man, although the swarming stragglers had cannily melted away. Ricard's division, a mere fifteen hundred strong, had been advanced in challenge, and now as Bernoit watched he knew the gambit had failed.

Ney himself came hastening up to their position with Ledru, the divisional commander, and a bevy of grim, anxious staff officers. He threw himself from his horse, telescope in hand, saw Bernoit standing near and called him over.

'I see you got your second stripe back. Good man. I require your shoulder.' And Bernoit had to stand motionless with the heavy glass pressing on his collar-bone while Ney examined the withdrawal of Ricard's battered division. The Marshal grunted to himself and then spoke to his officers.

'A broken egg! So, we'll have to make another omelette. I must go down and rally these fellows. General Ledru! We advance across the ravine, line companies and grenadiers in brigade columns; group all your light infantry as skirmishers. Colonel Dalbignac! My compliments to General Razout; columns and skirmish line; the Illyrians to feint on the left. And then, gentlemen, we'll go straight across the smash their centre! I'll be back shortly to show you the way.'

He closed his glass and handed it to an aide-de-camp. As he prepared to remount, he turned back, the reins in his hand.

'Thanks for the shoulder, Bernoit. Good luck in this business. I know you'll do your duty.'

He swung himself into the saddle and, accompanied by his aides, rode forward into the ravine to rally the broken division. Behind him the remaining officers hurried away to attend to their various duties and Bernoit discreetly returned to his post. Larguien looked at him inquisitively.

'Well Bernoit, you seem to be in the Marshal's confidence. What are we about to do?'

'Go straight up the muzzles of these fucking guns. The Marshal wished me good luck; I'll need it. His fucking telescope stand is not looking forward to this.'

'Ah Bernoit, we must all serve the Emperor, each as he can.'

'Fuck the Emperor. I'll wager even the Marshal's thinking that now.'

'Doubtless. My own feelings are not dissimilar at being cut off like this. I must pass the Marshal's witticism on to the men. What was the phrase? "Up the muzzles of the fucking guns"?'

76

'I think the actual words were "straight across and smash their centre".'

'Quite. I rather think that would be more encouraging.'

Ney was soon back among them, having secured Ricard's reduced division behind in reserve. He placed himself at the head of the columns and the advance began. It was a bold enough plan: attack down the narrow defile of the ravine and then up the facing bank where the Russian batteries waited abreast the road. With the skirmishers out in front the French columns marched slowly along the bottom of the valley and under the growing weight of gunfire and musketry they started to climb up the slope to the enemy line. On the flanks the horse artillery moved forward in support, stopping to unlimber and fire off a couple of rounds before hurrying on to catch the solid columns again.

In Ledru's division the light companies, as ordered, had been combined in one skirmish line commanded by the Colonel of the 24th Light Regiment. Bernoit's company had its own sector of this line and advanced in alternating half-companies until they found, not far in front, a wooded knoll.

Larguien examined the copse through his telescope and Bernoit, seeing that the Russian skirmishers had fallen back again, turned and signalled to Matthieu to advance his half-company. Then he walked over to stand by Larguien and stamped in the snow, flapping his arms against the cold. The advance was going well with the entire corps moving at a quite satisfactory pace despite heavy casualties. Extended on either side of him, Bernoit's own half-company seemed steady enough and maintained a constant fire on the withdrawing Russians.

Now Matthieu's men came striding up, and passed through them to skirmish forward, each man holding his musket at the ready. As Bernoit watched they manoeuvred into their advance position below the little hill, the men moving with practised caution. Thus far the company had sustained few losses. Beside Matthieu, Yvel turned and signalled that his front was clear and Bernoit cocked an eye at Larguien expecting the order to advance. But the captain was worried by the knoll. The enemy appeared to have established a redoubt of sorts and from it marksmen were firing steadily at the French lines. There were signs of a substantial body of infantry prepared to fight strongly in its defence.

Larguien decided to halt the company and send his men

forward in twos and threes to take up firing positions, in the hope that eventually the little wood might be infiltrated. On either flank the adjacent companies were moving on, but engaging the copse in enfilading fire as they passed. Behind, the brigade columns were advancing up the slope, drawing closer, and bringing with them the fearful sounds of the cannonade, hurtling overhead.

Bernoit turned to look at the columns where Marshal Ney rode in front and the eagles led the battalions into battle. A ball smashed into the side of a staff officer's horse, throwing man and beast aside in a bloody welter, and then raced on its mad way whipping a current of red death through the close-packed soldiers. A gap appeared momentarily and vanished again as the sergeants urged the men to close up their ranks. Still they came on and the firing from the wood increased, concentrating now on the nearest column, sending the odd man tumbling in the snow.

Larguien growled, 'We're going to have to clear this bloody copse, quickly and on our own.'

Bernoit nodded. The knoll lay directly in the line of advance of the right-hand column and if the enemy were allowed to remain they could deflect the whole advance. At the very least there would be confusion and delay; at worst the brigade would lose its impetus, break and fall back, endangering the entire venture. The other light companies appeared to have moved on in the fog and the commander was somewhere over in the centre, hidden from the problem in the growing clouds of smoke rolling down from the Russian position.

Bernoit moved forward cautiously with a couple of others to a little hummock about fifty paces from the enemy position. Over on the right Matthieu and Yvel were deploying round the wood and Larguien was slowly coming up in the centre with the rest of the little company.

Beside Bernoit, Andrieux fired and grunted with satisfaction as one of the Russian skirmishers pitched forward and slid down the face of the hillock. Bernoit saw an officer in the trees and fired, just missing him to judge by the way he flinched. He hurried to reload and watched Hélier, the young corporal, run forward with Chopart to take up better positions. Just ahead he could see a dip in the ground which would afford better cover and from which he expected there would be a wider field of fire.

'Come on,' he shouted to his men and began to run, half

78

crouched, over to the dip. There was a terrific rush of wind which knocked him from his feet and he fell in a flurry of snow. He heard screaming and wondered if he had been hit and it was his own voice screaming. Then he realised that the cannon ball had passed between his legs and had hit one of the others. He rose and ran the remaining few steps to leap into the hollow.

Andrieux was beside him and turned, grimacing.

'I thought you were away, you old bastard,' he said. 'Fantin lost his legs.' Bernoit followed his gesture to see Fantin lying shrieking in the snow, his lifeblood ebbing out, turning the white to bright, beautiful red. He shuddered involuntarily.

'So did I. It went between my legs.'

Hélier and Chopart jumped in beside them and began firing immediately. Bernoit was struggling to clean his carbine which had been clogged with snow when he had fallen. He became aware of a growing intensity in the firing and looked up. A formed company had moved to the front of the wood and was firing rolling volleys down the hill. Larguien and his men were pinned down by the steady fire. He could see Necker, bareheaded, trying to lead some men round to the left. There semed to be very few of the company surviving on this flank. On the right he noted that Matthieu and Yvel were still fairly strong and were probing round further in an attempt to find an exposed flank. The smoke was now intense on the left, and he presumed that contact had been lost with the light companies in that sector. Partially obscured, the nearby brigade was still coming on, but more slowly. He wondered if the General realised what had happened here on the right.

The other three were firing regularly now and Bernoit swore at his useless weapon. He wondered how many men were available to him on this flank. He could see two men further up the hill and there was someone shooting from some dead ground just below. MacDonald perhaps; it sounded like a rifle. That made seven, so Fantin could not be the only casualty. With just seven men he could not do much on this flank, unless he moved further up the hill. It was just possible that the Russians had left an opening there, where fire from their rear could have a demoralising effect. On the other hand, it would be dreadfully easy to be cut off in such a situation. Perhaps it might be as well to have a look first, before making any irreversible decision. Anyway, it should not be his problem. The generals were paid to think out things

79

like this and he cursed the Colonel of the 24th for dashing ahead into the smoke, without first securing his flank.

He pushed his ramrod viciously, turning the worm to twist the blocked snow from the muzzle of his carbine. He expected that the snow would have run down the barrel and his powder would be wet. He swore vilely and the snow in response broke up and trickled out. Perhaps he could have fired it out after all. He wiped the firing pan, replaced the priming powder and checked the flint. All seemed to be in order and he looked for a suitable target. The officer he had seen before was standing in the open, gesticulating to his men. Bernoit took careful aim and squeezed the trigger. To his surprise the carbine did not misfire and he felt the reassuring thump of the recoil as smoke obscured his view. He stepped aside just in time to see the officer drop to his knees, his head in bloody ruin. Bernoit reached for his ramrod, stuck in the ground before him, when it disappeared in a black whir of angry metal. If he had not stepped aside from the smoke, the ramrod, plucked away by a passing shot, would have impaled him like a spinning arrow. Andrieux, grinning grotesquely with his torn face, slapped him on the back and said, 'By God, you're in luck today.' Another whir, and Andrieux was looking stupidly at the shattered stump that had been his arm. Blood spurted out over Bernoit who stepped back only to jump with horror. He had trodden on the severed hand. Andrieux fell to his knees, his eyes bulging as he watched the blood run from his body. He still made no sound but the scar on his face was now deathly white. Bernoit stood watching, badly shocked. He had barely felt the ball pass between them. He was very, very tired.

Chopart pushed forward and tried to make a tourniquet with his handkerchief, but Andrieux pushed him away in panic and tried to get to his feet. He began to swear in a high-pitched voice, then tumbled forward in the snow to lie writhing, and shriek the terror of his dying.

Hélier said, 'Leave him, you can't help him now,' and they left him lying, his voice becoming weaker and higher until at last it stopped and death brought him its own peace.

Chopart wrenched his eyes away from Andrieux's body and seized Bernoit by the shoulders. He was speaking gently, with understanding, his face drawn, anxious. 'Paul, are you all right? Pull yourself together. Are you wounded?'

What gave a boy of twenty the confidence to call him Paul?

Fear mutually shared? Trust? It was good to be called Paul. All the others, his old friends, were dead. Nothing seemed to matter but to be left in peace, with no decisions to make, no more men to kill. He tried to remember Chopart's Christian name. He had seen it on the company roll, trying vainly to pretend to be able to read it. All the meaningless, jumbled squiggles. He wished he could have remembered. Perhaps if he had been able to read; but then he might have been an officer. That was what Étienne had said, that being unable to read meant you stayed as cannon fodder. But then Étienne was dead, with all his attempts to spell out the difficult words in his books. Émilie would be sad. He would have to talk to Émilie. But he would not be able to because Andrieux was dead and Fantin, and all because he was having a lucky day and the Russians would catch him in the end, after they had killed young Chopart and all the others and Chopart was looking at him so intensely. Hélier had such a harsh voice; he seemed to be making so much noise. If they would only let him go to sleep. What was Hélier shouting? Who was talking about him. Chopart was looking concerned. What was that Hélier had said?

'Come on, Chopart! For Christ's sake the Ivans are coming out. Come back here. Leave him alone—it's useless. Can't you see the old bugger's had it?'

Like cold water the words flowed over Bernoit, waking him, bringing him to himself. Hélier yelled again.

'Leave it, Chopart. Can't you see the bastard's done for?'

Something broke in Bernoit's mind. A spring. A release.

'I'll decide when I'm done for, Corporal,' he barked.

Hélier was unabashed and shouted back, 'Thank Christ for that! Come and have a look at this.'

About a dozen Russian soldiers were advancing from the wood in an obvious attempt to clear Bernoit's men from their flank. A shot cracked, toppling one of them. That had been a rifle, so MacDonald must still be alive. Bernoit shouted encouragement ot the others.

'Come on, lads! We'll shoot a few more—chase 'em away!'

Two more of the enemy fell, and the remainder, discouraged, withdrew to the safety of their trees. At that range, Bernoit thought, it had been fairly easy. It would be folly now to move up the hill.

He turned to look at the brigade and was shocked to see that its advance had now virtually slowed to a standstill. Grapeshot was cutting great swathes through the column like a scythe in corn. The officers were shouting to the men, urging them forward again, and hesitantly the advance began once more as the cannonade ploughed gaping furrows in the crowded ranks.

On the left it seemed that things were going better. Razout's division had disappeared into the smoke and from there came the sounds of hand-to-hand fighting. Perhaps they were breaking through. Certainly they would require all possible support.

Larguien and his party began to move forward but a tremendous fusillade met them, throwing men down like ninepins. They turned back, cowering from the dreadful fire, while Larguien ran up and down, urging each man on, but without success. The brigade continued slowly up the hill. It was desperately important now to clear the knoll but Bernoit could see no way of achieving that from his present position. There were too few men available. He saw that he was shaking badly as he bent to pick up Chopart's ramrod. From the other flank was a sharp increase in firing.

Chopart exclaimed, 'Jesus, look at that.'

Bernoit looked up. Matthieu had somehow scraped together some two dozen men and now, waving his sword, he led them, charging, into the far side of the copse. Bernoit was appalled. There were all of one hundred and fifty foes in the wood. The Russians had seen their danger and were firing at Matthieu's gallant band. Here and there a figure went down, but they kept on going behind their youthful leader until they disappeared into the trees. He wondered if he should support Matthieu in his brave, futile attempt and looked across at Larguien. The captain had again managed to get his men to their feet and was driving them up the hill. He was shouting something and gesturing violently and although Bernoit could not hear he guessed that he was being commanded to give support.

Bernoit yelled to his men to fix bayonets and then ordered them forward. He hoped that everyone had heard in the fury of the battle. His own immediate group struggled up out of their hollow and began to advance. Bernoit saw MacDonald closing up on the right and two other men moving forward further up the hill on the left. They were under fire but the shooting was irregular and inaccurate. Beside him, Hélier was hit and staggered forward before sitting down suddenly in the snow. They strode on past him, leaving him there. The sound of clashing steel was now quite distinct and there was obviously a desperate struggle going on in the copse.

Russian soldiers were beginning to break into the open, running for safety. Clearly Matthieu was achieving some success. One man broke from cover just ahead and, throwing his weapons away, tried to run across their front. MacDonald cold-bloodedly shot him dead from no more than fifteen paces. Bernoit clicked his tongue impatiently. MacDonald might need that loaded rifle at any moment. Bernoit felt his sword to check that it was free in his scabbard, and tightened the grip on his carbine. He took a last look down to where Larguien was striving with the remainder of the company, up the steep incline on that side, and then turned to plunge in among the trees.

Immediately, he saw a formed line of Russian infantry with their muskets at the present. He knew at once that it was hopeless. There must have been at least thirty of them. They had waited there, concealed, until they had their target cold. The others, too, had stopped, only Chopart running on a few paces before he realised he was alone. Bernoit felt panic grow within him; these silent muskets were about to fire. There was only one escape. He threw himself back and to the right, landing in a snow drift and rolled over and over, downhill, away from that dreadful volley. In his frenzy he heard the shots crash out.

Above him he saw a shadow tumbling, slithering down, and he went for his sword. It was MacDonald, still clinging to his rifle, swearing vilely. They heard the Russians break line and charge. As they watched, huddled together in the snow, Chopart came running blindly out of the wood above them, blood streaming. He stumbled and fell on his knees and the Russian soldiers, pursuing, pinned him to the snow with their bayonets.

'Let's get out of here.'

They threw themselves down the steep lower slope of the knoll, rolling and and sliding until at last the ground evened out slightly and they were among friends. Necker was there with a handful of others, and Larguien, looking sad and beaten. He cast an arm behind him to draw Benroit's attention to the brigade. The column had ceased to exist. The confused mass of men was struggling back across the valley with the cannon still ripping great gaps among them. Behind them they left a litter of heaped bodies and smashed guns like the debris left by an ebbing tide.

Further over, Razout's entire division was streaming back in

flight. There was no semblance of order among the broken
regiments. Some troops remained to form a rearguard and he saw
that they were from his own division. He wondered if the 46th was
with them. Now, from the smoke above, the other light companies appeared, hurriedly withdrawing. Of the company which had
been on their left there was still no trace.

Above them the crescendo of killing and dying had sounded its
last chords. There could be no hope for the men in the wood.
Larguien looked at him and Bernoit shook his head sorrowfully.
The captain patted him on the shoulder. 'Let's go back,' he said
and the few survivors started to walk down the hill.

Then, behind them, they heard a voice screaming bitter abuse.
In French. They turned to look and saw Yvel standing on the very
crest of the snow slope, dancing with rage and shouting at them,
at the whole retreating corps.

'Come back you bastards, you fucking yellow shits, come back.
We've captured your bloody hill! Captured, d'you hear! I've only
half a dozen men left and I'll lose it if you don't come back.'

They stood amazed, shocked. But it did not matter any more.
There was no support. The Russian pursuit would be under way
already.

Larguien yelled back, 'Yvel! It's no use — it's too late! It's all a
bloody waste. Come back. Save your men. Withdraw. Do you
understand? Withdraw!'

They stood there waiting anxiously, listening for the sound of
enemy cavalry, while the little band of brave men came scrambling down the snow slope and ran to join them. There were only
four of them and one was unknown to them, a straggler from the
24th.

'Is this all?' Larguien asked sadly.

Yvel snarled, 'What do you expect? We thought you at least
would support us. Matthieu said the battle depended on it. Poor
little sod.'

Larguien shrugged. 'Perhaps he was right. Come on. We'll
have the Russian cavalry round our ears.'

They hurried back down the hill, catching up with the
remnants of the 24th Regiment. It too had clearly suffered
casualties. All around them the corps was in total confusion,
literally running away from the persistent cannonade. There was
no sign of movement from the Russian lines. Larguien looked
round the mass of terrified men. It would take a miracle of

organisation to rally them into any sort of defensive formation. Only the fusiliers of their own division seemed to be in any sort of order, but they were further over, deprived of light infantry. They were formed in line, a rearguard to be sacrificed to cover the retreat. Among them Bernoit could see the eagle of the 46th. He should be there, he felt, with the regiment, preparing to die, but he had no heart for it. Larguien too, was looking at their comrades awaiting their doom. But he merely said:

'I think we'll find our own way back, don't you?'

Bernoit nodded in relief. He was in no mood to face the Russian lances. He found that he had lost his carbine and supposed that he had dropped it in the snow, back there.

Freed from the restraint of formation the small band withdrew quickly through the terrible ravine. It came as a shock to Bernoit to realise that they were back where they had started, not fifty paces from where he had stood with Ney. It seemed a lifetime away. They stopped to look back. Where Ricard had been before, now was the entire corps, routed and broken, guns lost, generals dead.

Yvel, tears streaming down his face, pulled at Bernoit's sleeve and pointed into the smoke. There was Ledru's division fighting hard, but falling back, swamped by overwhelming numbers. On them, the whole hammer-blow of the enemy's assault had struck. They were almost surrounded now and could not last for long. Bernoit turned away. His regiment, his home, was down there and he had no wish to witness its destruction.

Night was setting in and at the front the guns were falling silent. The attempted breakout had failed. The corps was ruined, smashed against the anvil of Russian artillery. Tales and rumours began to spread of ruined, exterminated units, of lost guns. There was no one left to fight. They could not force through and there was nowhere to retreat. Bernoit and his few companions settled down behind the battlefield and built a lonely bivouac fire, to sit huddled against the cold and greet the odd straggler coming in wearily from the bloody ravine. There was a rumour that the Russian General Miloradovich had sent yet another summons to Ney, requesting his surrender.

Bernoit sat by his fire, watching the flickering flames and the embers glowing bright and red. Perhaps the Russians would put him in a warm room. He doubted it, and hoped that the stories told of what they did to prisoners were not all true.

85

7

The guns had been silent since nightfall. The huddle of men sat round their fire trying to get what warmth they could, leaning forward over it, as the flames darted from the burning timbers. now and then, one of them would throw a log on to the embers and this would send sparks rising into the air and eventually the blaze would brighten, but the heat was superficial, and men facing the fire felt their faces scorched by the hungry flames while their backs were chilled by the cold night around them.

Bernoit realised gloomily that sitting too close to the fire would cause its own problems and sat back a little, huddled in his warm clothing, watching Yvel who was bending right over the flames, his eyes screwed up against the heat, his face turning red and blackening with the smoke. Bernoit wrapped the long shawl which he had taken from a dying man tight round his head, and stared miserably into the red heat of the fire and waited for captivity.

Stragglers and wounded were coming in, trying to find their units in the dark, seeking warmth. A man shuffled towards the group and tried to push his way into the fire. No one made way for him and he spoke pleadingly in German. MacDonald looked up and said, 'Go to hell you German pig. Where were you today?'

'*Aber ich bin doch krank und mir ist so kalt,*' the German pleaded, but MacDonald drew his bayonet and brandished it threateningly. The German spat viciously and then turned, weeping, and moved slowly out into the cold. Few of the group had even bothered to look round to observe the incident and the others turned back to their dispirited contemplation of the fire.

Now they could hear the rumour of movement around them. Bernoit looked around him and could see figures darting about silhouetted against the starlit sky. Necker growled sullenly that they must be surrendering. They sat solemnly awaiting the inevitable orders.

86

At last Larguien appeared and began to speak to them and Bernoit, half listening, knew that it was all over. He would rot in a Russian prison if he were lucky enough to survive the onslaught of Russian vengeance. But then he noted that Larguien was not talking of surrender. The words 'withdraw from the enemy presence' penetrated to his mind. He felt a surge of hope. He began to listen to what Larguien was saying. Others too were hearing and stirring eagerly.

Ney had contemptuously rejected the summons to surrender. The corps would slip away quietly in the night, and march back towards Smolensk. The Marshal had some plan in mind and they would be saved. The Russians would not catch the old redhead and his eagles. The march might be impossible for lesser troops, but not for them, and he would return them somehow to the main army.

Larguien had stopped talking and now all the men round the fire were watching him, their faces excited, hope of survival restored. The prospect of a forced march did not deter them, although they had already marched some fifteen miles before the battle. Now Larguien spoke again. They would leave at once, the regiment (or what was left of it) to fall in immediately in one column of march. There were too few men to form up into companies, he added sadly.

The men began to stand up and move slowly across to the place where the scattered regiment was now mustering. Only Yvel sat still, hunched over the fire, uncaring. Bernoit and Larguien went over to him.

'Snap out of it, man. We're going back,' said Larguien. 'Get on your feet.'

Yvel looked round at them, scowling. 'There's no point. There's no point,' he repeated.

Bernoit took his arm and tried to heave him to his feet but Yvel pulled away. He crawled back from them, his teeth bared ferociously.

'Cowards,' he screamed, 'cowards.'

'For Christ's sake . . . '

'Cowards. You let him die. That poor frightened kid — you just let him die. He said you'd support us, said that it all depended on taking the wood, said you wouldn't let us down . . . '

'Yvel . . . '

'He's dead. Dead, and all the others too, and you didn't come and we took the bloody wood for you and you ran away. He was scared bloody stupid but he led us in there. Poor little bastard. And you . . .'

Bernoit seized him by the hair and slapped him hard across the face. Yvel's eyes looked up in amazement and Bernoit struck him again.

'You bloody fool. So Matthieu's dead. So is most of the regiment. All my friends are dead too. But you're still alive. Pull yourself together.'

He grabbed the sergeant by the arms and hauled him up. They stood facing each other, their eyes six inches apart.

'You're a big boy now, Sergeant. Your men are depending on you,' Bernoit snarled. 'Now get fell in.'

Yvel turned and left them and slowly walked over to the regiment.

Larguien shook his head sadly. 'He's about done for.'

'This isn't a bloody nursery,' Bernoit replied, 'and I'm not going to play nursemaid.'

For an hour they marched through the night, back along the road to Smolensk, back through the dead Italians of Eugene's corps and the guardsmen lying where they had fallen three days before. In silence they marched; no man could find words for their plight. It was Ney's presence alone which sustained them and he was everywhere, but most of all he was with their rearguard, fending off the pursuing Cossacks. Every one of them, from general to drummer boy, wondered what plan their fiery leader had evolved. And not the soldiers alone, but the ragtag and bobtail that had returned when the fighting was done, and the womenfolk, and the wounded in their lurching carts, all waited to see what the great man, Marshal Ney, Prince of the Moskowa, would decide.

They halted where a slight ravine traversed the road and those nearby watched as Ney stumped up to survey it. He turned to three grenadiers and commanded:

'Break me the ice on this stream.'

The crowd pressed forward to observe. The puzzled grenadiers plunged into the snow and, lit by flaring torches, they attacked the ice with their musket butts until they had breached a hole. The oldest looked up for fresh instructions.

'In which direction does the water flow?'

They inspected by the light of a blazing brand and one of them pointed. The Marshal nodded.

'There, this fellow points our way. This brook will guide us to the Dnieper.'

All could picture the broad river, deep in its wide meanders, torrential in its spate. How could they cross it? They had no pontoons. They would be trapped by its dark waters. One of them, a staff officer, voiced the thoughts of all.

'The Dnieper, Prince?'

'Yes. We will cross it. The river will be frozen.'

Another, more senior, asked, 'And if it is not?'

'It will be! We will be safe on the other side.'

The exhausted men set off once again, tracing the irregular course of the little stream as it hunted the mother river. With dull relief they accepted that they had turned aside from their retreat to Smolensk, were seeking some fresh escape, though in truth they sought only rest. And behind, Cossacks waited and watched where they went.

The march through the forest was a terrible experience. In the pitch black of the night the trees isolated each little cluster of tired men, disorienting them and causing delay while they tried to establish contact with the unit ahead, while the unit behind came up, colliding with their rear, and the bunching up caused men to swear and curse at each other. The more worn sat down to rest and fall asleep to be left lying where they lay when the march began again.

Each footstep was exhausting as they trudged blindly through the deepening snow and men stumbled and fell and were trampled over by uncaring comrades and abandoned to die. Most of the wounded were in the carts, but of the few who marched many fell out during the night, overcome by exhaustion, pain and despair. No hand was lifted to help those who dropped out, for each man was obsessed only with the need for his own survival.

The journey seemed endless. Bernoit did not know for how long they had been marching, nor how soon they would reach the river. He did not care. He was aware only of his aching legs pace after pace moving him forward. The only thing that mattered as one foot sank into the hard-packed snow and found his weight was to bring the other leg forward and thus yard by yard consume the pitiless miles ahead. The rhythm of his marching was steady, step following step, his mind blank, devoid of everything but awareness of the ceaseless movement forward, unknowing even of the purpose, the reason for this regular rhythmic pacing. He was, too, unaware of the comrades who marched beside him. They were slight shadows who haunted him and would not leave him. They also struggled in the hardship of the march, matching pace with his pace, steadily, like him, going forward. And the meaning of what they were doing was quite lost in the endless business of following step with step.

The forest raised its own difficulties for all that the trees provided some screen against the wind. The terrain was trackless and a way had to be forced through. Snow lay deep round the lower branches, but sometimes arched over in great hollow drifts. Incautious men who scrambled over those apparently sound drifts among the trees would plummet to the ground below and be imprisoned. They could scream and shout but no one outside would pay any attention, even if they heard. A man could try to dig his way out, but the snow was deep and impervious. So he would settle down in his snow palace, sheltered at least from the bitter cold, and if he had food he might live for a little while longer in his trap.

Occasionally the guns or waggons would strike against a tree and shake it, bringing the heavy volume of snow in the upper branches cascading down, an avalanche to bury and smother. The dying army carried on its relentless way, shedding men like a slave ship casting away its cargo, to lighten and gain headway on a pursuing patrol.

In time they came to a village and there the Marshal bade them halt and light their fires. The soldiers sprawled, exhausted, in the snow where they stopped.

Bernoit decided to eat and pulled off his pack to rummage for a meal. He looked around him and saw that there were others enduring this with him, and that they were more than just the empty shadows who marched beside him, but comrades, men whom he knew well, with whom he had served for years. It would be wrong to say that his mind went back to the regiment as it had been twenty-four hours before, reduced in strength, but still a cohesive unit. He merely knew that there had been a change. The horrors of the night march had dreadfully reduced the survivors of the battle. There was no semblance of military order. They were no more than a group of wretched, ragged survivors who had, long ago, it seemed, given up everything in surrender to the necessity (not hope, for hope had long ceased to be enough) of survival.

Bernoit took some dried meat from his pack and, clenching it in his gloved hands, began to gnaw at it. He became aware that the others had been watching him and were now searching their own packs. He thought regretfully of all the packs of food and warm clothing which lay behind in the long bloody trail from Smolensk that marked the regiment's ruin.

'How far is it now?' A voice penetrating, saying something, communicating. No one had spoken for hours, or if they had none had understood or responded. Bernoit turned to the source of that strange noise, his jaws still working as he chewed the meat. It was Necker, he saw, who had spoken. He struggled to understand and slowly saw that he was being required to determine the end of all this. His mind shied away from such speculation. The snow, the trees, the cold, death and weariness, were permanent, endless. He shrugged and turned away.

Others too were wrestling with the problem Necker had posed. They were sitting with anxious faces, looking concerned and trying to think, to see what Necker meant. Larguien was there, his face twisted in concentration. It was strange how they had stuck together, the nucleus of the light company, when everything else had dissolved. Yvel was there too and MacDonald and the man from the 24th whose name no one knew and who had been with Yvel in the wood. There were others too, familiar faces, but not many, and they were mixed up with the other units, sitting slumped in the snow, eating the food which they had stolen in Smolensk and there did not seem to be any other officers or sergeants, only their little band, somehow holding together unwittingly and careless of the fate of anyone else. The man from the 24th was watching them eating, avariciously, not pleadingly, but with cunning. He knew now that they all had food. He could wait until someone fell. If he did not fall first.

Larguien had been pondering Necker's problem, weighing it up in his mind, thinking of the maps he had seen. He looked at the ragged creatures around him, in their strange mixture of costumes, their singed and stained furs, shaggy dirty beards, faces blackened by powder and wood smoke and the eyes staring redly, like frightened rats.

'Midnight,' said Larguien, 'we should cross the river at midnight.'

The men absorbed this information without acknowledging it. They sat there as the knowledge seeped through them. They had

91

forgotten about the frozen river and now they had been reminded. They would be crossing the river at midnight. Midnight was inconceivably far in the future. How many hours more? A lifetime away, literally for some. But it was finite. They would reach the frozen river and they would cross it and escape.

Yvel finished eating his piece of black bread, carefully catching the last crumb and pushing it between his swollen, blackening lips. Slowly he enunciated the words, his voice croaking:

'Are you sure the river will be frozen over?'

'Of course,' Larguien gestured, 'in this weather . . . '

Bernoit watched Yvel. He had been sitting too close to the fires recently and his face was badly burned, hacked and pitted where the frost had broken open the blisters. Again he was nursed by the treacherous flames, searing the cracked sores. His eyes were inflamed, hurt first by the cold and the glaring snow and then by the scorching heat. They were puffed out and when he blinked there was pain, his eyelids splitting, the blood congealing, frozen and black. His nose and lips were also turning black where the half frozen, half burnt flesh was dying. Bernoit felt pity. Gangrene would soon set in and spread rapidly. He wondered if Yvel knew. How long could he survive with his face dying on his living body?

Larguien had spoken of the weather, emphasising that the Dnieper would be frozen. Perhaps it would, but on the other hand it had been relatively mild of late. Bernoit reflected. Despite the bitter nights there was a marked thaw. He doubted whether the Marshal's faith alone would bring thick ice to the heavy waters.

'Listen!'

There were guns firing, back whence they had come. Hearts surged. Had Davout come back to rescue them? They strained to hear the uproar of two armies locked in battle. They could not. It was the Russian batteries alone that were firing, in regular, celebratory salvoes. Advised by the Cossacks that the French had bivouacked, they were prematurely rejoicing at the forthcoming surrender of Ney's corps.

Necker spat into the fire.

'Confident buggers, aren't they?'

The Poles who had been sent out to forage were returning. One party alone had found anything of interest, a peasant too lame to run away. They took him before the Marshal. When the man's awe was overcome by his fear he became voluble enough.

'Your honour is but one league from the great river, but there is no ford. Your honour must understand that with the thaw the waters will not be frozen.'

Those in hearing bristled at this and looked to the Marshal. His senior staff began to protest but he waved them to silence.

'The Dnieper will be frozen. It must be. We will cross; there is no other refuge left to us. Let the enemy think we sleep. Come, we will march.'

The worn, haggard people rose from their fires and resumed their miserable journey. In the silent, empty village they left the signs of a bivouac and the Russians, duped, waited for dawn unaware that their prey had slipped away. It was as well that there was no pursuit. Harassment would have destroyed them in that terrible forest. Wearily they followed the lame peasant as he guided them along the twisting ravine.

Gradually companions reverted to meaningless shadows and humanity surrendered to the elemental instincts of survival. Decently protected by the darkness from sight and memory, the weak continued to drop from the march. Even a close friend could founder or die without occasioning thought or action.

So wretched was their condition that they barely knew when the ravine opened out to the snow-clad banks of the River Dnieper. When they halted their dulled minds were slow to absorb that they had achieved a blessed period of respite.

There was no semblance of an army in the men assembled on the river bank that night. Groups and units had disappeared. The cavalry had all but vanished and only remnants of the artillery retained the meanest cohesion, bound together by the guns which they had valiantly refused to abandon. The infantry was no more than a rabble and as commanders tried to bring order the extent of the disaster became apparent. Of the entire corps, regiments which had fought at Austerlitz and Jena and over the dry hills of Spain, and which had marched into Russia forty thousand strong, there were but three thousand feeble, exhausted souls crowding towards the river. Of the wounded and the women and children pitifully few remained.

They built fires and waited for the stragglers to catch up. At first Bernoit thought that only the vanguard was present. There were no more fires, no more men than had been in his own regiment when it crossed the Niemen five long months before.

Then as they reorganised he was appalled to realise that only the scattered strays were to come in. His original brigade was barely at company strength and a mere handful of the 46th survived. His few comrades from the light company still managed to hold together.

They now faced a new problem, a further depressing difficulty. The ice was not strong. Only in one place, where the floes had jammed in the river's bend, had the surface frozen completely. By the light of the moon an officer went forward to investigate and they watched him step on to the ice. It creaked ominously. Cautiously he walked forward and they could hear the ice cracking and settling on the water and the ripping noise as the stresses ran out to the banks. The solitary figure walked on, unhesitating in the moonlight and the ice creaked and groaned in complaint while the waiting men held their breath, expecting him to disappear taking their hopes into the chill, sluggish water. At last he achieved the distant bank and dimly seeing, they cheered him as he turned back to report.

He brought ill news. It was unlikely that the cavalry could cross and the ice would not support the vehicles. The guns would have to be abandoned and the wounded were to be deserted. The officer urged an immediate crossing but Ney remembered the trailing stragglers and refused to forsake them. They would wait a while longer.

Strangely conforming to Larguien's prediction, the evacuation commenced at midnight. The crowd moved down to the river where marshalling officers sent them across in single file. The ice complained bitterly but there was no panic. Ney stood among them, watching, encouraging. At first there was no incident and hope began to rise among the patient men.

Bernoit and his companions were now moving forward. Larguien had been silent and despondent for some time and Bernoit found himself carrying responsibility for them all. He had managed to push them into the queue. Necker stepped on to the ice and then MacDonald, walking carefully on the treacherous surface. Bernoit followed with Larguien behind and then Yvel and the others. Yvel was in a desperate condition. His face had broken up badly during the march and the charred sores were ugly and black. He could barely swallow and was virtually blind yet some inner instinct kept him going.

Over on the right the ice cracked ferociously and the splintering

94

ran rapidly so that Bernoit felt it start under his feet. In the dark he could hear splashes and cries and knew that the ice had weakened and was beginning to break up. The noise was terrifying and he was filled with a panic to reach the bank and safety and yet every step he took sent vibrations rattling off into the dark and the thin surface seemed ready to splinter and cast him into the dark, cold water to drown.

There was a clatter behind him and he glanced round to see that Yvel had fallen. The nameless man from the 24th regiment was directly behind and did not have time to stop. He collided, falling over Yvel, and the ice opened up beneath them. The crack ran straight at Bernoit as the two men slithered into the water. Larguien went in up to his waist but somehow managed to throw his arms out and brake so that he was slipping slowly, his hands clinging to the surface, gradually being drawn back. He looked up, met Bernoit's eyes and piteously cried for help.

Bernoit went back and caught the officer's hand, but the drag was too great and he felt his feet slipping. MacDonald was there too and they nearly had Larguien safe when a hand wrapped round his leg and Yvel's broken face appeared from the water, his mouth open, screaming in supplication. The ice began to give under the extra weight. MacDonald freed one arm and in a simple flowing movement unslung his rifle and swung it fero- ciously down on the black inhuman face. Yvel slipped back soundlessly, his arm relaxed, uncoiling like a tentacle and he sank down into the swirling water. MacDonald then, using his rifle as a crutch, pulled back with his full weight and they drew Larguien away from the hungry river and over to where Necker waited to help them on to the bank. Behind they could hear the ice shattering and the cries of the drowning, and they sat down to watch and listen. No one made any reference to Yvel's murder. There were only four of them now and they felt isolated, alone despite the people all around them.

They were gazing at a dreadful scene. The breaking ice was crowded and those wretches who were not thrown into the water were carried away on the drifting floes. There were many, too many, women and children out there and their cries came to the unhappy men and pierced their hearts. Bernoit wondered if Jeannette Thomas was there, perishing in the sinister abyss. He had not seen her since Smolensk.

A block of ice drifted close to the bank and clinging to it was a wounded officer calling for aid. Most of the miserable men ignored him and it was Ney himself who reached out a hand and brought him safely to the bank. Bernoit, observing, felt something akin to love for the old soldier.

Larguien was shivering badly. The water must have been fearfully cold and the wind was now cutting knife-like through his wet clothing. Necker unrolled his blanket and wrapped it round the officer, who sat hunched in a ball. The corporal stood up and clicked his tongue.

'If the Captain doesn't get dry clothing he's a goner.'

Bernoit growled sarcastically, 'Splendid! Why don't you go and scrounge some?'

But it was MacDonald who stood up. 'Wait here,' he said, and slipped off into the night.

Necker opened his mouth to speak but changed his mind. Bernoit shrugged. 'Let's get a fire going and build some sort of shelter.'

He remembered the hollow drifts in the trees which had made the march so difficult and he and Necker managed to find one nearby which they broke into easily. They helped the frozen Larguien inside and then lit a fire in the entrance. As they were doing so MacDonald reappeared carrying a bundle of clothing.

'I hope the Captain doesn't mind German lice,' he said sardonically and Bernoit, taking the bundle, noted that there were warm sticky patches. MacDonald noticed and said, 'Oh, don't worry, I didn't cut the clothes.'

They stripped Larguien and dressed him in the dead German's clothing. Then all four huddled round their fire and Bernoit, remembering the vodka in his pack, drew it out and passed it round. Larguien coughed over it and then took another long drink. He began to show signs of revival and shook his head sadly.

'Thank you, thank you all. I owe you my life. Those others . . .' He broke off and then added slowly, 'MacDonald, you are a ruthless man.'

MacDonald looked at him calmly, and then spat in the fire. He watched the spit sizzling and turning to steam, and then said quietly, 'It keeps a man alive, sir.'

Bernoit, to change the subject, asked, 'What's going on out there?'

'Oh, the usual shambles. Officers running around everywhere

trying to find out what to do. One thing's sure, no bloody Russian is going to get across the river.'

Necker said, 'Well in that case I'm going to get some sleep. It's a long time since some damned sergeant-major woke me up in Smolensk.'

It was dawn that woke them, oddly a fine clear day, with sunlight streaming through the gaps in their branched roof, sparkling on the hard frost which must have set in during the early hours. Bernoit rose stiffly and climbed out of their shelter. It was strangely silent, he felt. As he stepped into the open he expected to see the usual signs of camp breaking up, the smouldering fires, the bustling men, but there was nothing. He stood, appalled. There was no trace, no sign of Ney's corps, nothing to show that they had been there but frozen corpses and the trails of footsteps coming up the river bank and then merging and heading west. On the opposite bank the abandoned waggons and guns, dead horses and men, and the wounded left behind to their misery. Everywhere, on the banks, in the river, in the silent trees, was death and loneliness. There was nothing else.

He realised with horror that he had been guilty of the most abominable negligence. He had assumed that once safely on this bank Ney would allow his weary men to rest, but clearly he had pushed on without bivouacking, leaving Bernoit behind asleep with his three companions. Worse, there were the tracks of horses all around, spiked hooves he noted. Cossacks. There would be marauding Cossacks and peasants everywhere.

He stood transfixed for several moments before diving back into the hole to tell his companions.

8

It was about three o'clock when they found the woodcutter's cottage. They had been marching all day since Bernoit discovered their isolation and it was hours since Platov's patrolling Cossacks had forced them to turn west from Ney's line of march and seek refuge in the forests. The scent of a wood-fire had drawn them cautiously towards the cottage and they lay in the snow, silently watching. Here they could have shelter and a fire and defend themselves against any small body of the enemy. In the open they would be helpless and could not risk a fire.

There was little activity. They saw the woodcutter come out and walk round to the side of the house, returning a few minutes later, but there was no other sign of life. Bernoit was certain that there were no troops present and probably only the woodcutter and his wife lived here. There were no tracks in the snow showing the presence of any other.

Slowly they moved towards the cottage, Necker going round to cover the rear while the others carefully advanced up to the wooden walls. Keeping down to avoid the window they edged quietly up to the door and then Bernoit and MacDonald burst inside. The interior was gloomy in the setting day and what light there was came filtering through the single window and from the smoking fire. A woman sat motionless, looking at them with patient cow's eyes. There was no one else in the room and the woman said nothing, made no sound and did not reply when Bernoit, trying to adjust his eyes to the darkness, asked roughly:

'Where's your man?'

There seemed to be only the one room to the hovel, with straw strewn on the floor. To Bernoit, brought up as a peasant, one thing seemed to be missing. He tried to think. A storehouse, of course. It must be in the loft. He looked up just in time. An axe was swinging down towards the back of MacDonald's head.

Bernoit threw himself at the big man to bring him down. Falling back he twisted round and saw the blade rush past, inches from his face. As the two men tumbled to the floor, Larguien at the door fired his pistol and a lucky shot brought the woodcutter crashing on to the other two. The woman began a high-pitched wailing.

MacDonald picked himself up from the tangled heap on the floor and, seizing the fallen axe, advanced white-faced on the shrieking woman. Larguien, watching the trapdoor for another attacker, saw the movement. 'No! Don't' he bellowed. But MacDonald remorselessly swung the great axe down. She was staring at him with her sad, still eyes. Horribly, her screaming was stopped.

Necker called from the door; he hoped no one had heard the shot. His eyes were straining in the dark, taking in the scene.

Larguien said, 'We'll have to check the loft,' and Bernoit felt their eyes all turn on him, as he struggled to his feet. He scowled but slowly began to climb the ladder. He was ready to drop to the ground immediately there was any movement in the loft, but he knew that anyone there would wait until his head appeared. His head felt light and enormous. As he eased through the trapdoor he winced against the blow that would split his skull, or perhaps a pike to pierce his eye. The loft was empty. Relief surged through him. He found he was shaking and thought that he was getting too old for this sort of thing. If only they would let him lie and sleep without risk of disturbance or dreams. Heavily he climbed into the loft. It smelt musty and stank of the rodents infesting it. He leaned against a rafter to get his breath and called out.

'It's all clear. I'll break a gap in the thatch and take the first watch from here. You'd better hide the bodies somewhere good. If we get caught . . . '

No Russian would show any mercy to the men responsible for those two deaths. If they saw the woman the Frenchmen would be denied even a quick death. Bernoit hacked at the thatch with his sword. From here he should be able to see all around and if he kept his head well enough wrapped he would not be too cold. It was getting dark now but the moon would rise shortly. He shouted to Necker to bring him up some hot food from the pot which the woman had been stewing over the fire.

He did not know how long he had been on watch. The others

were all asleep below and he could hear Necker's deep relentless snoring. The moon had been up for maybe half an hour, casting weird shadows in the forest which strained his eyes and made him nervous as he thought he identified movement and then grinned to himself at being afraid of shadows. He altered his grip on the musket which he had salvaged on the bank of the Dnieper. Was that a noise? He tensed. He could hear horses. He strained to listen. Not cavalry, he decided, horses in harness and that hissing noise indicated a sledge. It was coming this way.

Bernoit leapt down the ladder and roused the others, urging them to grab their belongings and climb into the attic to hide. It was a desperate rush and they could now clearly hear the sleigh drawing nigh. Bernoit climbed quickly back to his post, just in time to see the sleigh glide out from the trees. It came to rest in front of the cottage. It was a troika with its three fine horses and there were five men, a driver and four Russian officers.

The officers climbed down and began to walk to the door. He could hear that they were speaking in French. The language of the Court, he remembered. Bernoit looked round and saw that the others had all managed to get into the loft in time. The door below opened and moonlight flooded into the cottage.

One of the Russians shouted, 'Vladimir Alexandrovich!' and his voice left silence rippling loud in the still night.

'That's damned odd. I've never known him to be away before—and Ninotka isn't one to go out at night.'

'There's a pot on the fire . . . '

'Perhaps the French . . . '

'This far west? My dear Count.'

'Deserters perhaps, Colonel.'

'I said we should have an escort.'

'Gentlemen, I do not think we want an escort as witnesses to this night's work. Would you not agree, General?'

'The Colonel is right, Count, I fear. But perhaps Captain Mikalovic will check the loft for us. Old Vladimir maintains his storehouse there. But first let's have some light.'

Larguien crawled over to Bernoit and whispered in his ear, 'There's something damned funny going on here. They're plotting something. If we could take prisoners . . . '

'Stuff it. There's a sledge out there that'll take us home. We'll leave these fellows to walk if they can. Necker and I can jump the driver from the roof while you two hold him.'

100

'But . . .'

'Forget it!' and he summoned Necker over while MacDonald waited to strike down the Russian captain when he investigated. Bernoit and Necker slung their muskets and wriggled out on to the roof. The driver was sitting with his back to them about twenty feet away. Together they slithered down the roof and dropped to the ground. The startled horses jerked forward and the driver struggled to hold them as the two Frenchmen pounced on him. Necker seized the reins. Bernoit bundled the Russian from his perch and slashed him across the face with his own whip.

Inside the cottage a shot was fired. The door opened and a man stood silhouetted against the lamplight. Bernoit had unslung his musket and he fired at almost point blank range, sending the Russian colonel pitching back into the room. Mac-Donald leapt down from the roof and scrambled into the sledge.

'Where's Larguien?'

'Just behind me.'

But Larguien was shouting to them, 'I've got them covered, the general and the other. They're coming out as prisoners. Keep your muskets trained on them.'

'Christ!' exclaimed Necker.

Bernoit was dismayed. It would be impossible to guard two high-ranking prisoners in the troika, leaving alone the problems of survival. Larguien was asking them to risk their lives for the doubtful prestige that might result from the general's capture. Bernoit did not consider the risk worthwhile. MacDonald beside him was pointing his rifle at the general and the count who were now walking helplessly out of the cottage. Bernoit thought furiously.

'Larguien,' he shouted, 'come out by the roof—the door is too dangerous,' and he seized Necker's musket. The driver of the troika had been writhing on the ground holding his slashed face, but now he drew his pistol. Bernoit saw and fired immediately and the Russian dropped back in the snow. Then MacDonald fired and one of the Russian officers screamed and toppled back, crashing into the door, and slithered to the ground where he sat howling in pain. The other darted back inside.

'You bloody fools—what the hell's going on?' Larguien shouted from within the thatched roof.

'Come out for Christ's sake,' Bernoit yelled back, and then added quietly to MacDonald, 'Have they got any firearms?'

In answer a pistol shot was fired from the window but the Russian must have been wounded or panicky for they did not even hear the ball. At last Larguien appeared, scrambling down the roof and leaping for the sledge. As they helped him aboard the Russian general began to shout.

'Captain Larguien! Is this French honour? Are your men so indisciplined? Would you leave wounded men like this—in this place?'

Necker swore and cracked the driver's whip. Larguien tried to grab his arm as the sleigh moved forward.

'I gave my word of honour,' he protested.

Bernoit pulled him back and said, 'We told you—no prisoners. How do you think we'd feed them, guard them?'

A parting shot was fired from the cottage where the general stood gesticulating at their departure.

MacDonald growled, 'There are plenty of our lads wounded, dying in the cold, without worrying about shit like that.'

Larguien was heated in his protests. 'They were involved in something. Planning something. They had papers, documents. It could have been important . . .'

Bernoit interrupted. 'Look, all that's important to us is getting out of this bloody mess. We've had our bellyful of heroics.'

MacDonald said, 'Bernoit's right, Captain, so just forget about it, eh? And if you're worried about your honour, it was me that shot the bastard. I thought he might try something.'

Now the troika was lurching madly, heaving them from side to side. They threw into one deep snow drift and for one dreadful moment they clung on to the sides for dear life, thinking that it was going to capsize. Then with a sickening crash the sleigh fell back on an even keel, tossing them into a heap.

'For God's sake Necker . . .'

But Necker was screaming, some nonsense about it being more difficult than he had thought and never having driven horses before and should they be going so fast? Bernoit felt the panic rising inside him. The trees were rushing past now and surely the horses thrashing along at this pace would smash the sleigh against one of the solid trunks. They were moving at a quite incredible pace, far faster than Bernoit had ever travelled. He knew that he could never bring the horses under control. He looked at MacDonald but there was no hope there, for he was clinging white-knuckled to the sides of the sledge

102

and there was clear terror in his normally expressionless face.

It was terrifying. The frenzied horses stampeded beyond control, throwing a spume of frozen snow from their dashing hooves. Hard ice lumps pounded the fear-paralysed men. On they hurtled through the thick forest. Black firs and naked birches were flying blurs whipping past, smashing back the echoing thunder of their riotous career. The hiss of the runners had become a high-pitched whine.

A stream crossed their path. Necker shrieked in terror. Undeterred, the horses leapt across and the sleigh bounced into the air, throwing them together. Necker was nearly cast away and grabbed desperately to save himself. Then, with a bone-shaking crunch, they crashed into the other bank.

The sled slewed round and they saw a birch blocking the lurching swing. Someone screamed. Collision was inevitable. They smashed into the unyielding tree. Wood splintered and then in a mad kaleidoscope of stars and snow and breaking branches they were hammering on. The trees were hurtling missiles and the moon-cast shadows lashed at them in their fear.

It was Larguien who saved them. He pushed away from Bernoit and MacDonald, freeing himself from their clutches. He stood up perilously in the tossing sledge and clambered forward. He reached the driver's box and pushed the stricken Necker aside. The corporal was glad to release the reins. Larguien had to fight hard to control the frightened horses. His efforts to draw the reins forced him to his feet and he was almost dragged under the heaving sleigh. But gradually his skill won over and the dreadful momentum eased. The mighty trees ceased to be terrifying obstacles and became identifiable, gliding gently past. Slowly the sleigh came to rest.

Necker lay over the driver's seat, retching miserably. Bernoit gasped with relief and slumped back into his seat. He could feel his body trembling in reaction. He noticed that MacDonald had fallen forward and was heaving in great sobs of pent-up fear. Only Larguien seemed to be unaffected as he climbed down and went to steady the lathered horses, talking soothingly to them, and stroking them. Bernoit tried to summon his voice to speak, but it sounded nervous and distant.

'Jesus, I thought we'd had it then.'

Larguien replied, trying to sound jocular, but they could hear the strain in his voice, sounding as it did when they were in action. 'Just like driving a coach and four.' But no one laughed and Necker swore vilely. Larguien climbed back into the sleigh. Bernoit saw that he was sweating heavily and his face was pale, almost blue in the moonlight. He met Bernoit's eyes and grimaced expressively. Berniot tried to smile but felt his face collapse in a lop-sided grin.

'Well...'

'We'll have to wait a bit. The horses are very tired.'

Bernoit said, 'We could all use a break. I think we need some vodka after that.' He rummaged in his pack until he found the precious bottle. He passed it to Larguien, who took a grateful drink, and then he pulled MacDonald up and handed him the bottle. The soldier was still shivering and spluttered when he drank.

'God, that's good,' he said hoarsely, and then turned to Necker still lying over the driver's box, gasping for air. 'Necker, you bloody idiot! What the hell were you trying to do?'

The corporal looked up and tried to grin. 'Rabinat always used to say it was dead easy. I'd always wanted to try! Thanks.' And he tipped the bottle back and took a long, long drink, and then began to retch again and, leaning over the side, vomited into the snow. Bernoit caught the bottle and, taking a warming sip, noted sadly that there was very little left.

'I wonder what the Russians have left us,' he said. 'Let's have a look, but first we'd better reload.'

The sledge was well equipped as no doubt befitted a Russian general. In the first place there were furs and blankets in abundance. Although the weather seemed not quite so cold as before, it was nearly a week since they had left Smolensk and already the warm clothing which they wore was showing the signs of the abuse it had suffered. Secondly they found a hamper of food and a jar of vodka. Then there were two muskets to supplement their tiny armoury. Finally Larguien found a sabretache containing maps and papers. There was a lantern in the driver's box and they lit it to inspect their finds. The papers were in Russian and so could not be understood but the maps were a godsend, more particularly as one of them showed the main Russian dispositions and accordingly they knew which areas to avoid.

Larguien was especially anxious to get these documents to the French headquarters and the others cynically expressed their agreement. So far as they were concerned the maps would help them personally and that was enough. When they reached the French lines that would be time enough to worry about the purposes to which the documents could be applied.

It was Necker who identified a major problem which they had quite overlooked. He found a bag of fodder and it was only then that they saw that its contents would not sustain the horses for long. That was a problem which would certainly require attention but which would have to be postponed. It seemed likely that they would pass another cottage or hamlet and could forage from the roof thatch as they had seen the mounted units doing. Bernoit remembered his friend Vernier's salty comment that the Lithuanian serfs would be duly grateful to their French liberators when it snowed. He looked at the map again. They had not been very far from here when Vernier made the remark, but then they had been marching east and it had been summer.

Larguien was thoughtful, poring over the map in the lamplight. 'I wonder where the army is,' he said. 'The last I heard the Emperor was going to establish a line along the Dnieper and Dvina to the north.'

'He's had that,' Bernoit replied, pointing to the map. 'Look at that Russian army coming down from the north.'

'That's Wittgenstein, and Chichagov is advancing up the Berezina. However, if the army is still at Orsha it becomes very urgent to get these documents to the Emperor.'

'Forget it. If the army was in Orsha we'd be behind our own lines now. Do you think Russian generals go playing hide and seek there? Anyway, your precious Emperor couldn't defend Paris with the army the way it is. He'll have run for the Berezina and that's where we'll go and hope to God we get there in time.'

'Well, my dear strategist, where would the Emperor be advised to cross the Berezina?'

Nettled by the sarcasm, Bernoit snapped back, 'You're the officer. That's your job.'

'There's the bridge that First Corps crossed during the advance,' Necker put in.

'Borisov,' Languien indicated the map. 'That could be the place. The Russians could be there first.'

'Yes. But it's right on the road from Orsha,' Bernoit pointed out.

'Very well,' said Larguien, 'we'll make for the bridge. I personally don't want to cross any more ice.'

They grinned in agreement, and Benoit added the rider that they should avoid the roads and towns in case they ran into the Russians. For all they knew the enemy might be close on the heels of the retreating French army.

It was difficult in that featureless country to work out exactly where they were and the map was not detailed enough to be of much assistance. However, Larguien managed to work out an approximate position and calculate broadly the direction in which they required to travel. He showed them the pole-star and they all solemnly noted the bearing they had to take. Navigation was a new problem to them all, accustomed as they were to the reassuring presence of a command which made all their decisions.

When the horses had been fed and they were ready to get under way, Larguien climbed up to the driver's seat and, as he pulled the furs round him, asked, 'Who wants to learn to drive this thing? We need a reserve driver.'

Necker shrank visibly and MacDonald said to him, 'Don't worry, no one was thinking of you.' But he seemed no more enthusiastic himself, so Bernoit reluctantly climbed up beside the officer as the sleigh began to move gently forward.

Larguien did not want to hurry for fear of tiring the horses and they glided at walking pace through the forest. He was finding the troika strange to drive and the harnessing of the three horses was an arrangement quite new to him. Bernoit watched with interest as Larguien got the feel of the gear and demonstrated what he was learning. It was good to travel so effortlessly after all that had gone before. In the back MacDonald and Necker were asleep already and even Necker's snoring seemed peaceful. Bernoit laughed out loud.

'This is the way to travel,' he said, and Larguien grinned back broadly.

Even the dismal scenery seemed pleasant in the moonlight as the trees cast shadows deep across the glittering snow. The sky was clear and filled with stars shimmering in the cold night, but it was not freezing hard and occasional cascades of snow crashed from the branches and thundered to the ground. Sometimes a night bird called eerily through the woods but otherwise there was little sound save the horses' breath and the jingling, creaking harness and the restful whisper of the runners carrying them over the snow.

They began to talk as they sat there on the driver's box, cocooned by their warm furs, watching the silent forest go by. In the security which the sleigh gave them it was easy to forget that only a few hours ago they were devoid of thought, mastered only by the instinct to survive. Now they felt companionship and friendship and the warmth of humankind which embraced the two sound sleepers behind them.

Larguien said suddenly, 'I've never understood why a man with your service isn't in the Guard.'

Bernoit grunted. He had often wondered himself.

'I'm an old Republican, you know. I was in Paris in '92 when we killed off the Royal Guard. I never thought much of replacing it. Oh, Étienne Vernier and I used to think about it — we joined the regiment at the same time, you know. Étienne used to say it was the best way to stay alive and get a full belly at the same time. He was right enough; look at Borodino. They've hardly done any fighting in the whole campaign. If Étienne had been in the Guard he'd be alive today. Anyway, we used to think about it and then we'd decide that the Empire was a load of shit.'

'But you fight for it.'

'That's different. Napoleon's all right if you're a soldier; at least he was until this do. Look, I remember the mess we were in before he straightened things out. I wouldn't like to go back to that. I think he's a good thing for France and there's no one else could do what he's done. But he's ambitious you see. We used to say that back in '97 after Italy. Look where it's got you and me. That and his being Emperor. It's France I've been fighting for and after twenty years I think I'm due a rest.

'You know, in 1804 a lot of us in the army didn't go along with the idea of an emperor. We'd spent too long fighting that sort of thing. Look at Bernadotte. Now he was an old Republican — commanded my brigade in the old days. A lot of us were shaken when he went over and became a marshal. Look at him now. Crown Prince of Sweden and sitting on his arse while all his old comrades are dying in the snow. That's what royalty brings; that and privilege. Like all those bloody aristocrats who came back to fat commissions and soft jobs on the staff.'

'Like me,' Larguien laughed. 'My father was an *émigré* bundled out by your lot in '93. The family came back so that my brother and I could rally to the Emperor's standard. I dreamt of victories like Austerlitz and a commission in the Guard.'

'I bet you never thought you'd be driving three rankers in a sledge.'

'No, and I didn't imagine anything like Borodino, either.'

They lapsed into silence and the sleigh continued to glide through the night. Larguien said, 'Why don't you turn in. You're looking tired.'

Bernoit replied, 'So are you.' But he climbed gratefully into the back of the sleigh and, after rousing Necker to keep a watch, wrapped himself round in rugs and settled down to sleep.

Later he wakened when Larguien stopped to rest the horses and he was vaguely aware of MacDonald moving over to keep the watch while the other two lay down to sleep. The motion of the sleigh was strangely missing and he could hear the horses stirring restlessly and noted that they were eating. They must have been fed what little there was in the fodder sack. He wondered how they were going to replace it and was still pondering the problem, mixed up and jumbled with other things, memories and queer fleeting thoughts, when he slipped back into sleep.

9

He was wakened by MacDonald just as dawn was breaking and he stirred reluctantly, realising that he was stiff and cold. Without the comfort of a fire he was not encouraged to leave the shelter of his furs, which now were hard with frost. Tentatively he moved his head out into the air and looked around. Night was being eaten up by the long glow of the sun reaching over the horizon and just beginning to pick out the tallest trees. The sledge was still in deep shadow and the horses lay asleep as yet undisturbed by the waking men. Necker was moving about quietly in the snow and Bernoit heard the crackle of burning twigs and smelt the sharp scent of woodsmoke.

He rose and saw that the corporal was heating up some sort of stew in his canteen. Seeing Bernoit's anxiety, Necker looked up and grinned.

'Don't worry, I'm not making any smoke. I thought we could use something hot.'

Larguien emerged from his own furs and said, 'That's an excellent idea.' And then, yawning widely, he stretched his arms.

Bernoit jumped down and stamped about to restore his circulation. He picked up a handful of snow and rubbed it on his face. The cold substance was refreshing and as it melted he used it to wash the sleep from his eyes. He slipped the tiniest piece in his dry stale mouth. The regimental surgeon had warned against this practice but Bernoit was sure that one little piece would not hurt and the sweetness as it melted when he wrapped it round his tongue was wonderful. A sharp pain stabbed him where the snow found a decayed tooth and he quickly sucked it to another corner of his mouth. He stamped again in the snow and flapped his arms. It was a beautiful morning and it was good to be alive. He grinned up at MacDonald sitting on the sleigh and the other smiled back, the cold brown eyes sparkling in momentary warmth.

Necker dished out the stew and the hot food was good to taste, burning his mouth, its warmth scorching its way down into his belly. He gobbled his portion quickly before it got cold, picking out the solid morsels with his fingers and popping them into his mouth. There was not much, however, and it was soon finished, with nothing more to be gleaned by further licking of his pannikin. He brushed his beard with the back of his hand and wiped his greasy fingers on his coat.

The horses were awake and moving restlessly, wanting to be fed. They would have to find some forage soon or the animals would die. Vaguely they had agreed that it would be safer to avoid travelling in daylight, but the problem of forage was now pressing. They decided to risk moving on until they came to a cottage and found something for the beasts to eat. There was certainly no sign of Russian troop movements in their immediate vicinity. An examination of the maps decided them. Larguien estimated that they had come twenty miles from the woodcutter's hut. If the Russians were advancing from the north on Orsha, deployed on a broad front, the sleigh was lying across their line of advance.

Accordingly, they harnessed up the horses and climbed back into the sledge to begin the second stage of their journey. As before Bernoit sat beside Larguien while the others remained in the back keeping lookout.

It was very different travelling by day. The forest which in the moonlight had looked strange and mysterious now appeared unfriendly and snowbound. The trees were tall and grim and the wintry sun merely emphasised the blackness of the trunks. They could see the visible signs of the wild life which roamed within the sheltered woodland and felt the secret eyes watching them. Glades which should have been lovely places were merely traps where an enemy could be waiting. The great banks of snow glared with the reflecting sun and wherever they looked the solemn lines of timber appeared to stretch sullen and endless. It seemed to them that the very forest was aware of being Russian and having enemies in its midst. The broad clearings to which they came from time to time provided little relief for there they were even more exposed. They crossed nervously, expecting at any moment to see a horde of Cossacks break from cover and come charging after them.

They came to a stream which, unlike others which they had

passed over, lay on the bed of a narrow ravine with its sides banked steep with snow. They were compelled to turn south and follow its tortuous course in an effort to find some place to cross. Till now they had seen few signs of man—occasional tracks in the snow, piles of cut timber, an abandoned waggon—but now they came to an isolated cottage, which appeared suddenly as they emerged from the forest into a sheltered glade. Larguien pulled the horses to a standstill and the others reached for their muskets. Everything was still and there was no sound.

There was to be no forage here for the cottage had been burned and the thatch was now black and charred, stirring dustily in the slight wind. They dismounted and advanced on foot. A blackening corpse lay in the drifting snow and they found another at the front of the building, impaled to the wooden wall by a French bayonet. Inside a charred body was stretched on the floor and they could see that it had been a woman and no imagination was required to identify her fate.

'Well, the boys have been over this place all right.' MacDonald remarked, looking back at Larguien who had waited by the sledge.

From inside the cottage Necker called out.

'There's nothing here worth taking. This all happened two or three days back.'

They returned to the sledge and climbed aboard. Larguien flicked the reins and set them on their way again. But they had barely left the clearing when a further grisly scene made them stop. Sticking up from the snow were seven heads which had been horribly mutilated. Around them lay clothing and rags which they could identify as French uniforms. With growing horror they realised that the tortured soldiers had been stripped naked and buried to their necks in the snow.

Appalled, they hurried on, feeling the heads watching them, feeling the woods alive with enemies, watching and waiting. They sat silent, filled with gloom and foreboding, their bodies tingling at the imagined touch of a peasant's knife, the icy weight of the snow compressing the body and the torn head sticking up exposed, hoping for early death.

Now they saw things they had not seen before, signs of life, the tracks of many horses, and men on foot, fresh dung. The woods were alive with their enemies and still the ravine turned and twisted, impassable. It was Necker who noticed that the sun had

111

been to their right for some time and whispered the first words spoken since they had seen the seven.

'The stream has turned, we're heading back east.'

With shock they realised that he was right and yet still the stream meandered relentlessly forcing them back. Their desperation was growing. They came to a spot where the banks eased slightly and Larguien drew up.

'What do you think?' he asked. It was no better than other places they had seen and decided were impossible. Their danger seemed more urgent and they were more anxious than ever to be across the persistent ravine.

'We'll give it a try,' said Bernoit.

At this point, though the snow lay steep on both sides of the gorge, it almost formed a bridge across the frozen stream and the gap was little more than a step across. They could see the obvious cornices but had no idea how strong they were or how deep was the crevasse. It looked dark and grim with the blue ice reflecting the harsh light. The surface of the snow was a hard, frozen crust with evil, gleaming ripples, treacherously slippy on the incline.

Despite the problems Larguien considered that the spikes on the horses' hooves would afford a satisfactory grip. He decided to attempt to jump the troika across. To ease the burden the other three climbed down and unloaded their equipment and supplies. Larguien would drive alone and they would make the perilous crossing on foot.

Larguien wheeled the sleigh back in a broad circle to give the animals the longest possible run. By the time he returned to pass the three men waiting at the edge, the team were thundering at full gallop. They launched themselves on to the snow slope heaving the jolting vehicle after them. Down they rushed, slithering on their haunches, their spikes slicing through the snow. Like a pendulum the sledge swung from side to side threatening to overthrow the racing beasts and roll them into the gully.

Yet they reached the bottom safely and leapt across the gaping chasm. For a moment all seemed well. The horses found their footing as the sledge rose into the air. Then the snow broke under the right-hand horse, a great block shearing from the cornice almost taking the animal as it fell. The horse whinnied in terror, but its forward hooves were on firmer ground. Somehow it struggled up in a tangle of harness.

But the sledge was off balance and it slewed round. Helplessly the three soldiers watched as it hurtled diagonally across the crevasse. It crashed with a violent lurch, throwing Larguien from his perch. He shrieked with fright as he fell, but his hands had released the reins and clutched at the wooden side. He managed to hold on, and hung there swinging over the cleft.

With a cry of despair MacDonald bounded forward. He tried to run, but there was no way in which he could stay upright on that wicked descent. His feet shot into the air and his back smashed on to the frozen snow. He tumbled over and over, slithering down the icy slope. His hands clawed desperately but his fingers would not grip and his palms were torn on the abrasive surface. Then he was gone, plunged into the abyss, and only the claw marks showing where he had been.

Bernoit and Necker looked at each other, appalled.

'We have to get down there,' the corporal said.

'Oh, that's really easy.'

Necker scowled at the irony and wrinkled his face in thought. Enlightenment came and he drew his bayonet.

'I'll give this a try.'

He flung his feet out on to the slope and slid down on his belly. Before he could gain too much speed he thrust the bayonet into the snow. Clenched in both hands it provided an effective brake on his downward rush. He fetched up against the sledge and clambered to his feet.

'Come on,' he shouted, 'follow me.'

Bernoit swallowed hard, and gathered his nerve. Reluctantly he leapt into space. At first he thought he was going to die for he was spinning down at a frightening rate. Yet when he stabbed at the flying snow he found his mad career come under control. His clothes were being ripped apart by the vicious surface. Then his feet hit the sledge with a breathtaking jolt.

'Jesus.'

Bernoit stood up nervously. Necker had already rescued Larguien and the officer was scrambling forward to calm the frenzied horses. Below him, at the bottom of the crevasse, some four yards down he could see MacDonald sprawled on the ice. The big man was moving, still alive.

'I remember seeing some rope,' Necker called, rummaging in the driver's box. He found what he sought and grinned.

'We'll have the Black Giant out of there in a couple of moments — you'll see.'

113

Bernoit started to climb into the sledge, but its balance was precarious and it wobbled sharply.

'For God's sake!'

Necker, nearly thrown off balance, was frowning at him. Bernoit felt he was a clumsy fool. He had to redeem himself.

'I'll go down,' he said.

No one tried to contradict him. He waited till Larguien had steadied the horses and joined them on the sledge. The officer nodded grimly. Bernoit tied the rope round his waist and climbed over the side. The sledge lurched dangerously but Larguien and Necker held on and lowered him into the deep, cold pit. He felt the rope bite into him but felt secure at first, pressing against the cornice faces. Then the chasm opened out and he began to spin. Round and round he whirled and the gloomy ice danced in grey-green menace. He had to close his eyes against the giddiness and thus was surprised when he suddenly felt the ice under his feet.

He untied the rope and looked around. The dismal scene made him shudder. This was an oubliette, ugly and chill, and reminiscent of his captivity in Austria. He shuddered again.

MacDonald was sitting up now, with his head in his hands.

'Are you hurt?'

'I don't know. Bit groggy. I'll live.'

The words were slurred and he was obviously concussed and badly shaken. Bernoit hoped that there were no broken bones. He knelt and tied the rope-end round the big man.

In the meantime Larguien had been preparing to employ the horses, but he nearly fell himself and was compelled to desist. Regretfully the two men above had to pull the heavy MacDonald up by hand. The effort caused them a dreadful expenditure of energy. To save their strength Bernoit tried to climb by himself, but after several attempts he failed, exhausted. Wearily the others hauled him up.

The tired men lay in the sledge and pondered their next problem. It was difficult to know how they were to get the vehicle out of the ravine. Again, it was Necker who had the solution. They would cut a platform in the snow and use it to lift the front of the sledge round. Another platform at the rear would enable them to push from behind.

It was a miserable business, hacking at the hard snow with their slender blades. At first there were only three of them, but in time MacDonald came to his senses. He seemed to be unhurt and

114

his recovery was a boon to them all. It was tedious work digging out the frozen, crumbling snow and sending it whispering into that dreadful pit, but eventually the work was done.

Without stopping to rest they turned their attention to lifting the front runners. The sleigh was very heavy and awkward to grip, but they managed to ease it up. Cramped by the great weight they shuffled across, drawing the vehicle on to an even keel. They gently lowered it into a position that would enable the horses to pull it clear. Yet even this brought its trouble for Necker had unconsciously placed his gloveless hand on the freezing runner. When he let go he felt the skin rip, and yelped with pain as the blood flowed from his skinless hand.

Then Bernoit remembered a further problem. All their equipment and weapons lay back where they had left them. They were sick with weariness, but had to rouse themselves to cut steps back up the slope. They began to carry their belongings to the sledge; MacDonald carried all the firearms in one cautious journey down the fragile staircase.

There was only the food hamper left now and Bernoit saw that the others were waiting to catch it when he slipped it down to them. Without warning a shot was fired. He whipped round. A patrol of Cossacks was riding down on him. He screamed in panic.

'Cossacks!'

Throwing himself at the hamper he lunged over the crest of the slope. But the hamper was a treacherous toboggan and capsized, sending him tumbling in the snow. He thought he was doomed, but MacDonald caught him at the very edge of the precipice. With horror he saw the hamper slide past and disappear with all their food.

There was no time to think of that. They heaved at the sledge and Larguien lashed the horses brutally. Then their luck changed and the stubborn vehicle broke free. It was a frightening scramble to climb aboard as they crashed over the crevasse. The cornice collapsed behind them, but they were all safe.

The horses were pulling well and they were climbing with increasing speed. Bernoit looked back. The Cossacks were gathering on the other side, preparing to follow. MacDonald's rifle cracked in his ear. The Cossack commander stood up in his saddle, astonished. Then he pitched forward and crashed on to the slope. Like a discarded puppet he slithered down, leaving a

115

red trail behind him and then he vanished into the icy oubliette. His men were discouraged and sat motionless as the Frenchmen made good their escape from the blighted place.

When they knew that they were no longer in immediate danger they stopped in the forest to rest. Larguien dismounted to inspect the animals. They were almost spent.

'We'll have to find them some fodder soon,' he commented sadly.

No one mentioned the lost hamper. That was too depressing to contemplate. Bernoit wondered how long they could last without food. Perhaps they would be able to raid a peasant dwelling. Necker was trying to bind his hand with a handkerchief and MacDonald in rare tenderness lent forward to help him. Larguien climbed back on to the driver's box.

'We'd better get on,' he said and nudged the tired beasts forward again. They had to find food very soon.

When they had been travelling for about an hour they came across fresh signs of human habitation and almost fearfully they turned aside to follow the tracks in the snow. They drove into a large clearing and saw a cottage about five hundred yards away. Immediately they reached for their muskets and held them ready. As they drew up to the building a tall Russian peasant came out with his family to watch them curiously. At first they had been mistaken for Russians, but now the peasants saw their identity and began to appear alarmed.

Bernoit spoke gently saying, 'It's all right, Ivan, we just want some of your roof for the horses,' hoping that his quiet tone would reassure the family. Under the cover of those three muskets the Russians were unimpressed by Bernoit's quiet voice. They started to look panicky. Fearing a bloody incident Bernoit decided that the family had better be hustled inside the cottage and he said as much to the others. They dismounted from the troika, Larguien too, carrying a musket after securing the animals. As they advanced the woman began to wail.

Bernoit shouted, 'Inside!' in Russian and pointed vigorously to emphasise. The family, at a signal from the patriarch, began to enter the cottage, but just before he turned to go the man, a great bearded fellow, paused and spat at MacDonald's feet. Ruthlessly MacDonald began to swing his musket but Bernoit was just quick enough to catch his arm.

'We don't need that,' he snapped and turned to the Russian,

in an attempt to look appeasing. 'Inside,' he repeated.

'You're getting soft,' MacDonald complained. 'D'you think he'd have left you alive?'

'You and Necker get on the roof and start chucking down the thatch,' Bernoit ordered, 'Larguien and me'll look after the Ivans.'

'Just you keep your eye on them, then. Remember that bastard last night and those seven lads this morning. We'd be a bloody sight safer if you shot the lot.' He turned and followed Necker, who was already on the roof, ripping out the thatch in armfuls.

When the Russian realised what was happening he began to shout volubly and only Bernoit's fixed bayonet presented to his chest prevented him from charging outside. Larguien too presented his musket and began to shout back at the man. They stood there, the three men in angry confrontation, and then a sudden movement broke the scene as a little boy ran between them and scampered round the Frenchmen's legs. Larguien drew back to fire, but hesitated when he saw the size of the child, and then the boy was round the side of the cottage. The officer turned to follow, and at the corner he again raised his musket, but paused again. He could not bring himself to fire and lowered the weapon. He shrugged and came back to Bernoit who had forced the furious father back inside.

'What harm could he do?' he asked with a rueful grin.

Bernoit cocked his head. MacDonald was shouting abuse at them, having seen the boy running away. He called them useless and assured them that they would pay for their mercy. Necker silenced him by passing him more straw to feed to the horses.

The animals were eating hungrily and the men piled more thatch into the sledge for subsequent use. While they were waiting for the horses to finish Necker noticed that there was a pot cooking on the peasants' open fire and asked the people for food. No one in the cottage moved and he repeated his demand forcefully. MacDonald reinforced it by bringing up his musket and the woman began to speak rapidly. They could not understand what she was saying but Bernoit could guess that she was pleading that this was all the food they had to feed the family. Well, the family would have to go hungry. He signalled to the peasants to move aside and held them at the other end of the hut while Necker scurried inside and removed the pot. It was a stew of sorts and they each were able to have several spoonfuls. The hot food was good to eat.

117

Larguien walked over to attend to the horses and as he did so glanced round the side of the building. For an instant he stood, horrified, and then bellowed, 'Cossacks!'

Bernoit dropped the pot he was holding and ran with the others to the sledge. Already Larguien was getting the beasts into motion. They jumped aboard the moving sledge and began to organise their little armoury. Bernoit looked up and saw that the enemy were about half a mile away, just within the clearing, and they were moving very rapidly.

'That bloody boy...' said MacDonald, and Bernoit nodded grimly. He was appalled at their carelessness, first in letting the boy escape and then in not keeping a watch. It was incredible luck that Larguien had moved when he did. There were about twenty Cossacks. There was just a chance that escape might be possible.

Larguien had whipped the horses to breakneck speed and was heading for the nearest part of the forest. There was no alternative. They could only hope that the woods would provide some form of refuge. The Cossacks had swung round on an intercepting course, and were slowly drawing ahead. Larguien turned the sledge in a broad circle to move directly away from the horsemen.

Bernoit watched the Russians carefully. They were travelling perceptibly faster than the sleigh. They were riding in a formless swarm with the swifter beasts bringing their riders ahead of the rest. Gradually the leading riders began to draw close, as the racing sledge bounced over the open snow. Bernoit muttered to the others, poised with their muskets.

'Wait until they're so close you can't miss.'

The plunging sledge was an erratic platform from which to fire. The leading Cossack was almost alongside, his lance lowered at Larguien's back, bravely ignoring the raised muskets. Bernoit and Necker fired together and the Russian toppled back over his mount's withers. He crashed to the ground and was trampled by the others following. MacDonald fired and Bernoit started to curse him for wasting a shot. Then he saw one of the horses slowing down and crumpling to the ground. It was quite remarkable shooting. He hastened to reload, standing in the rolling sledge while Necker and MacDonald picked up fresh muskets and waited for suitable targets. Bernoit glanced over his shoulder and saw that they were still very distant from the cover of the trees. He bleakly hoped that the horses would hold out.

The leading group of Cossacks were almost up with them. Necker and MacDonald both fired and another horsemen fell. Bernoit passed the loaded musket to the accurate MacDonald and began to reload the rifle. The riders drew alongside but were met by a small volley. Two more men went down and the others had to swerve to avoid them. One horse could not make the tight turn and fell in confused collision. Furiously they began to reload. Thus far they had been shooting well and the Cossacks, seeing their heavy casualties, decided on different tactics. They now rode abreast of the sledge, overhauling it but keeping clear of the accurate musketry. They were on both sides of the sleigh and obviously planned to swoop down together from the front and sides. Larguien could do nothing but drive straight into the trap. The Russians tactics did give Bernoit and his comrades the opportunity to reload all the muskets. MacDonald tried another long shot with his rifle and yet another horse collapsed. Bernoit swore in satisfaction and handed the marksman another musket.

He was reloading when the Russians charged down on them from both flanks. Their agility as horsemen was quite remarkable. Bernoit heard the others firing as he rammed the powder home. Then a horse collided violently with the sleigh and he fell, spitting out the ball in his mouth. As he looked up he saw a Russian closing fast, his lance aimed directly at Larguien. Bernoit fired and the ramrod flew like an arrow to pierce the Cossack through the breast. The lance fell from the astounded man's fingers. He brought his hands up to the steel rod impaling him and then fell over sideways into the sleigh. Necker fired Larguien's pistol. Now all their firearms were empty.

However, the Russians were losing their enthusiasm. Even as Bernoit reached for his sword they wheeled away and dropped back to follow the sleigh. Perhaps that last shot had killed their leader. They appeared to have lost their previous sense of direction.

They began once more to reload and Necker complained to MacDonald about the time taken to load the rifle. In answer he received an oath. MacDonald wanted to throw the dying Cossack from the sledge, but Benoit suggested that they hold on to his body to throw under the hooves at the next charge. Larguien shouted that the horses were flagging and that he would have to

119

ease up. Simultaneously the Cossacks began firing pistol shots at them. MacDonald spat contemptuously at their folly. It was virtually impossible to hit the bucking sledge at that range from the back of a horse, especially with a useless weapon like a pistol. Necker grinned and shouted to Larguien, exposed on the driver's box.

'Don't worry, Captain, these fellows couldn't hit the Kremlin at that range!'

There was a chopping noise like an axe on wood. Necker pitched forward in surprise and shock, his breath forced from him in one long moan of pain. His right arm hung limp. Blood was beginning to seep through the layers of clothing where the bullet had smashed his shoulder. It had been incredibly good and lucky shooting, but there was no time to attend to Necker. The Cossacks were beginning to close again.

Bernoit shouted to Larguien for more speed but the sledge barely accelerated. The Cossack horses were fast, ugly little brutes and they were gaining very quickly. Bernoit swung his musket up and carefully aimed at the nearest man. For one moment his eyes met those of the Russian and he saw the man looking at the death that faced him. He lowered his sights to the man's chest and it dissolved bloodily as his bullet gouged open the Russian's lungs.

MacDonald rolled the impaled Cossack from the back of the sleigh and the horses behind reared in fright. The two Frenchmen fired into the confused mass and a horse fell. For an instant the chase abated but then there was a rider alongside brandishing his sabre. Bernoit was just in time to draw his sword and defend himself. He was hopelessly disadvantaged by his difficult balance while the Cossack seemed to be at one with, a very part of, his horse. A pistol fired by his face and the concussion of the blast deafened him and scorched his eyes. But the Russian was gone, his horse shot dead and they were in the forest.

The enemy were so discouraged by their losses that they made only a token show of pursuit in the forest. They stayed a little distance behind, and Bernoit watching estimated that there were now no more than eight. Soon they dropped right back and eventually disappeared, presumably to attend to their fallen comrades, or possibly to seek reinforcement. For the moment at least Bernoit and his comrades could relax a little. Larguien allowed their exhausted horses to slow down and the motion of the sleigh became easier and less erratic.

Necker's shoulder proved to be a gory mess when Bernoit cut open his clothing. He had lost a lot of blood and was in great pain. Bernoit examined the wound. He could see no sign of an exit hole and concluded that the bullet must be lodged somewhere under the wreckage of the corporal's shoulder blade. He did what he could to staunch the bleeding, and tied rags from Necker's shirt round the shoulder to strap up the broken bones. He made a sling and bound the arm up and then, his inexpert work done, he pulled furs round the wretched man and tried to make him as comfortable as possible. Necker was suffering abominably, his face drawn and grey, and Bernoit forced him to drink some of the raw vodka. Eventually the jolting of the sledge caused him to faint and he passed into merciful unconsciousness.

They drove on for the remainder of the day without further incident, stopping occasionally to rest the horses. From time to time Bernoit took over the horses from Larguien while in the back MacDonald kept a nervous and constant watch. Occasionally Necker came round and they did what they could to help him, but clearly the endless motion of the sledge was causing him discomfort. Despite their earlier decision to move as little as possible during the day, they kept going for fear of Cossacks and gradually moved into more open country, where the woodland was becoming less predominant.

Towards nightfall they stopped in a wood to rest and await the rising of the moon. Fear prevented them from lighting a fire and they huddled together for warmth under the furs as the chill of the night began to seek them out. Later, cold and stiff, they drove on while the moonlight lasted and gradually they found themselves drawn into a relentless pattern of movement and rest as day succeeded night and in turn gave way to the dark. The horses became slower and weaker from the incessant movement and the poor fodder. The men, constantly watching for the enemy, starved and sickened.

Again and again they were turned from their route by steep-banked ravines like the one they had encountered on the first day, and only by considerable effort could the three unwounded men get the sleigh across. Frequently they saw signs of man's habitation and they took wide detours to avoid these, watchful always for Cossacks. The novelty of the early part of their journey became a hideous monotony as they sat, stiff-limbed and cold, in constant terror of a further attack. Their dread of lighting fires turned long-awaited rests into periods of abominable cold when even the furs and the huddling warmth of their comrades' close bodies could bring no relief.

If it was bad for the others Necker was in even worse case. He was racked by persistent pain and the motion of the sleigh was agonising. Time and again his wound opened and they had to repeat the whole business of binding it up, exposing his naked flesh to the elements and fumbling with numb fingers to replace his bandages. Loss of blood had weakened him badly. The torment of shattered bones and torn flesh gave him no ease. He was in wretched condition. He seemed unable to sleep, but lay in a sort of stupor, wincing at every bump, until the sweat stood out on his haggard face. By nightfall on the second day he was feverish, suffering respectively extremes of heat and cold.

By dawn on the third day the condition of them all was desperate. Suffering terribly from the intense cold and their exhaustion, kept awake during the night by Necker's delirious cries, gnawed by starvation, they moved slowly and clumsily, their limbs numb and unresponsive to the demands made on them. They did not know it, but they were all suffering from exposure. Only the stubborn will to live kept them alive as they set off blindly, unconscious to anything except the need to keep moving. There was no communication among them as they sat in the sleigh, forcing the wretched horses on, almost unaware of each other's presence. On that third morning as they thoughtlessly pushed the sledge further west they did so from instinct alone, imbued by the pattern of previous days. Death hovered like a spectre around them and they were unmoved by it, for on that morning they were dying.

10

Bernoit heard the noise vaguely, prodding the levels of his forgotten brain, slowly permeating through, forcing him to think, to remember. It was difficult to bring his mind to order, back from its animal state, to rationalise. Memory flickered briefly, telling him he was a man and that the forms beside him were his comrades. He remembered different things, faces of men he had known, the warmth of a good billet, queuing in kitchens for hot food, the smell so strong that his nostrils wrinkled at it. There were lines and lines of soldiers and the noise was familiar, heard before a thousand times bringing its memories of smoke and the acrid smell of burnt powder.

'Guns,' he said slowly, painstakingly enunciating the word. 'Guns.'

Muddled thoughts of marching over the hills into battle and all his comrades with him, like Étienne Vernier, and the sun beating down on the Spanish hillside as they sat together watching the blue, blue sea, drinking wine, while the white-sailed frigates locked in mortal combat, and they left the camp in Boulogne where the British sails sat on the horizon, and marched endlessly across Europe to hear the guns at Austerlitz, and knowing the army was just ahead as the rolling drumbeat of the cannonade announced the battle. Of course, that was it. The army. He screwed up his eyes to concentrate, to organise his muddled mind. Yes, there it was again, the deep rumble in the distance, ahead.

'Guns!' he shouted. 'I can hear guns!'

He seized MacDonald's arm and shouted it again and looked into his eyes, cold, dark eyes vacant at first and then puzzled, annoyed at being disturbed from their quiet dying. And Mac-Donald was dredging in his mind for the meaning of it all.

Bernoit clambered over Necker where he lay mumbling

stupidly to himself and scrambled up on the box beside Larguien. He shook Larguien's shoulder and the officer turned and looked at him, vaguely, wondering what the fuss was about, wanting to be left in peace, to die. Bernoit laughed aloud at Larguien, comical with his white frostbitten nose.

'Guns!' he repeated. 'Listen—not far ahead.'

Larguien thought about this deep in his inner recesses, turning over the meaning of the extraordinary behaviour. Bernoit was grinning and giggling with glee.

'Can't you hear them?' he asked. 'The army must be just ahead.'

Larguien found the problem too difficult and turned back to his horses. Again Bernoit tugged at him and shouted the words. He had to make the officer understand. Slowly he saw the flicker of recognition in Larguien's eyes as the thought troubled the quiescence of his mind. Then Bernoit saw that Larguien was so exhausted that the thought was only sketched in his awareness.

'Go back and rest. I'll drive now,' and he gently took the reins. The uncomplaining officer climbed down and snuggled under the rugs, his eyes open, listening to the thunder of the battle ahead.

Bernoit forced himself from the euphoria of his discovery to concentrate on its realities and implications. There was some sort of action going on ahead though it was difficult to estimate how far away. From long experience he knew the strange vagaries of travelling sound but he supposed that he could work on an estimate of three leagues. He imagined that at their present rate of travel they could reach the scene within the next two or three hours. He listened to the guns again. It did not sound like a major engagement. The firing was sporadic with occasional intense outbursts, more in keeping with an orderly withdrawal or a rearguard action. In that case he presumed the French must be retreating before a Russian advance from the north, probably led by that fellow—what had Larguien called him?—Wittgenstein. The Russians must be pushing down to try and cut off the army from crossing the Berezina. Presumably the allied troops engaged here were the northern wing of the Grande Armée, led by St Cyr perhaps, or Victor.

He could see that considerable care was going to be required if they were to avoid running into the Russians. The thing to do was to swing further south and hope that they did not run into any

124

outlying enemy patrols. If they did, Larguien and MacDonald had better come to their senses. Well, he could deal with that problem later; in the meantime he could afford to let them sleep.

For the next hour or so he drove on and still the guns roared in the background. He listened carefully and thought that he was able to detect the crackle of small arms fire. Perhaps he was mistaken but if he was correct the fighting must be fairly close. His route was taking him round the scene of the action and he had as yet seen no signs of troop activity. He thought that it would be dangerous to proceed any further without rousing the others. The prospect of the effort involved dismayed him but he drew the sleigh to a standstill. It was going to be difficult to get any response from his spent comrades. If only he could rest for a while, or find something to eat. The horses, too, were weakening on their indifferent fodder. He threw some straw down for the animals and then dragged himself into the back of the sledge.

At first he thought they were all asleep, but then Larguien opened his eyes and smiled. 'Do you hear the guns?' he asked weakly. Bernoit nodded and passed the officer the vodka. Larguien said earnestly, 'The army must be very close.'

'So are the Russians — we'll have to be on our toes. Do you think you'll be able to drive?'

'Give me a few more minutes.' But he slipped back lethargically.

Bernoit turned and shook MacDonald, who awoke and stared hostilely. 'What do you want?'

'We're near the army, but there are Russians nearby. You'll have to keep a watch.' He was concerned that unreasonable hostility was MacDonald's only reaction, other than his listlessness.

'Pull yourself together, man.' But he saw that MacDonald only wanted to be left to die in peace and that he would be of no assistance to them. Next he looked at Necker, but he was in sorry condition and could not be helped. He lay back unconscious, but still murmuring to himself, turning his head restlessly in his fever. Bernoit shook his head sadly and looked back at Larguien and saw that he had fallen asleep again. He felt totally fatigued and wanted only to slump down beside the others. Escape from their plight was so near, but it required so much effort. If only the others would understand, try to help him.

Then Larguien opened his eyes once more and looked around. He raised his eyes to meet Bernoit and smiled wanly.

'We are babes in your care,' he announced softly.

Bernoit sat down, exhausted, disappointed.

'I'll sleep for just a moment or two.' But he knew that it would be difficult to arouse himself again. Larguien smiled warmly at him.

'Just a moment or two,' he reiterated.

Bernoit did not know how long he had been sitting there when he heard the horsemen. The sound came to him clearly through his muddled brain and washed over him like a refreshing stream. He realised that the riders were very close and in a panic he struggled up to the driver's box, shouting to the others to defend themselves. He could see the cavalry now and noted with relief that they were hussars and not the cruel Cossacks. He realised that it was hopeless to try to get away and he slumped back and watched the patrol approaching. He felt nothing but a great weariness. At least now as a prisoner he might find shelter and warmth, but it was a terrible defeat to have come so far in vain.

Then with a shock he realised that these men were not wearing Russian uniforms. They were in motley rags and he could just identify them, and the equipment on their horses. They were Italian hussars, a detachment from Victor's corps. He was among friends at last. In great excitement he leapt to his feet.

'Comrades!' he shouted hoarsely. 'Friends!'

The hussars rode up and looked curiously at the scene, taking in the patient horses, the three exhausted men in the back of the troika, the crazy leaping figure who welcomed them. They had seen many stragglers recently and were accustomed to and unaffected by the universal misery which they witnessed. This, however, was a strange sight and told of some dreadful epic. They were curious and the very companionship of the men in the sledge reminded them of their humanity and made them feel sympathetic. Their officer came forward.

'Who are you?'

'46th, sir, Third Corps—we were cut off four days ago.'

'You seem to have had quite a time.'

'Yes sir, we're all that's left of the light company. There's one man wounded and my officer and the other chap are in a bad way.'

'Have you seen the enemy at all? Which way did you come?'

'From over there. We didn't see anything, sir, but I wouldn't like to say we were up to keeping a careful watch.'

126

The officer nodded. 'Very well, you'll have to find your own way back I'm afraid. I have my orders.'

A surge of disappointment swept over Bernoit as he realised he was to be left unprotected to find the French lines. It would be so easy to drift off to sleep again, or run into a penetrating enemy patrol.

'Yes sir,' he said slowly, and then with a flash of insight he remembered. 'Only there's the papers, sir. Captain Larguien said they were important.'

'Papers? What papers?'

'Russian maps and dispatches, sir. We captured them from an enemy general when we took the sledge.'

'Did you by God? Give them here — I'll send a galloper off with them right away.'

'No, sir,' Bernoit said emphatically. 'We'll take them to headquarters ourselves.'

For a moment he thought he had overplayed, for the officer looked outraged and indignant. Then he laughed. 'Very well, soldier — your tickets home, eh? What's your name?'

'Bernoit, sir, Sergeant-Major.'

'All right, Bernoit, I'll give you an escort. Do you think you can continue to drive — it's about two leagues away.'

'I'll be all right now, sir. Thank you, sir.'

So with his escort of three troopers Bernoit drove his sledge with its pitiful cargo across the remaining distance, through the outlying pickets into the heart of the French corps. Despite his exhaustion he was able to note the activity all around him. It appeared by the look of things that his assessment had been right. This was a corps in retreat, however orderly, but he saw that the troops were generally better equipped and in higher morale than the dying scarecrows to whom he had become accustomed. He remembered that Victor's corps had not marched any further than Smolensk, where they had spent a leisurely autumn. They had not experienced the rigours of the march to Moscow with its attendant battles, and had been spared the misery of the retreat. He recalled the rabble of men he had seen in Smolensk and the broken wretches of Ney's shattered corps. It was good, very good to be back among order, where soldiers looked and behaved as such, and where units still seemed to be intact.

Larguien too was clearly encouraged by what he was seeing and Bernoit was surprised to feel his arm being pulled and see his officer staring around with wild eyes, grinning broadly. 'It's good to be back, eh Bernoit?'

They passed through a village and on the outskirts the corporal commanding the escort signalled them to stop before a wooden building. It was a large house, incomparably different from the squalid hutches of the hamlet. It was possibly the residence of the estate owner or his agent, but now it housed Marshal Victor and his staff.

'There you are, Sergeant-Major,' the corporal said, in his Italian accent. He had said nothing during the entire journey.

'Thank you, Corporal. I don't think we'd have made it without you.'

'Thank *you*,' the hussar insisted with a wink. 'If you hadn't come along we'd still be out there looking for Russians. Me, I've seen enough of the bastards in the last two or three days.'

He pulled round his horse and with his two troopers rode off, leaving them stationary at the entrance to the Marshal's headquarters. Around them was the usual bustle of aides coming and going and the presence of the sleigh with its disreputable looking crew was causing some congestion. A harassed lieutenant came up to them and spoke officiously.

'You can't stop here! What do you think you're doing? Move on at once.'

Bernoit looked at him coldly. This was one of Victor's staff, still dressed immaculately in his fine chasseur uniform. It was clear that in this corps they had no idea of what had happened to the rest of the army. This indignant officer had seen nothing and was outraged that four tattered vagabonds should sully the dignity of the headquarters. Bernoit looked at the smart young man, an aristocrat, he guessed, and remembered Ney clad in his filthy rags, crossing the Dnieper.

'Shit,' he said.

The lieutenant became furious at being so addressed by a ragged straggler.

'What did you say?' he snapped.

Bernoit remembered that Victor's corps had been garrisoned in Smolensk, charged with the duty of communications and supply, and he remembered the shambles that Smolensk had been. Victor's staff had failed abysmally in their task and at that moment this elegant, privileged non-combatant embodied the object of his hatred and contempt. He spat and began to reply

128

but Larguien, at last aware of his surroundings, had brought his weakened body and mind under control and spoke first.

'My Sergeant-Major said "Shit". He's quite right. We have here important captured documents which must be brought to the Marshal's attention.'

The lieutenant was unabashed. He knew how to treat stragglers.

'Well, you'd better give them to me then,' he snapped.

'No, little man. I won't do that. I'll see the Marshal or the Chief of Staff personally.'

'Indeed? And who are you?'

'Charles de Fezenque Larguien of Mejean, Captain of the 46th Foot, and I repeat I require a personal interview.'

'Oh, Ney's corps—it's very irregular.' The lieutenant hesitated.

Bernoit could not resist a rejoinder.

'Look, when we last saw our corps it was only about a thousand strong. That's fucking irregular too. Now get a move on. It's urgent. Sir.'

The aide stood appalled. There had been rumours, but nothing definite. Here was fact: the destruction of an entire corps, catastrophe. He looked at Larguien and saw the confirmation in his eyes and then looked back at Bernoit. Perhaps the latter's seasoned face and authority reminded him of his youth and inexperience, and he glared at Bernoit with resentment.

'Wait here,' he said and ran inside.

They chuckled at the aide's discomfiture. The confrontation had pulled them together, dispelled their exhaustion for a few precious moments. Bernoit looked round at the other two, both lying unconscious in the back.

'I'd like to get those two to a doctor,' he said.

Larguien nodded. 'I thought you would come in with me but God knows how long this will take.'

'I'll come back for you with the sledge.'

'Don't lose it.'

Bernoit grinned and said 'Shit' and they laughed together. Then Larguien gathered together the captured documents and climbed slowly down. His legs almost gave way under him. Bernot saw and bellowed at an orderly to come and lend his support. Larguien winked up at him and said, 'I hope these bloody papers are of some use in here.'

'Perhaps they'll give you some coffee,' Bernoit replied, and saw a wistful look come into the other's eyes.

129

'I'll try to scrounge some for you,' he said.

'See you later—with the sledge.'

'Shit!' And they giggled insanely as Larguien turned away with his supporting orderly and entered the building.

Bernoit called to a passing aide for directions to the nearest casualty station and the officer looked sympathetically at them before instructing an ugly little orderly to guide them there. The soldier climbed up beside Bernoit and gave him instructions. They moved off.

The man was a chatterbox and spoke with a distinct Marseilles accent. 'You've had a time of it, haven't you? What's your unit?'

'Third Corps. A fucking shambles. Who was the officer?'

'Oh him? Van Eyck, a Dutchie—yeh he's all right. They're all pretty soft though—useless lot of bastards really. Turn left here. Was you in Smolensk? Well you'll know what it's like then—you want to have seen the waggons the commissaries came away with. All right for us of course. No one's ever short in headquarters in this corps. Can't have been nothing left by the time you got there.'

'We were with Ney in the rearguard.'

'Yeh? Well you'll know then won't you? I've got a brother in the Fourth Chasseurs. They were supposed to be foraging. No bastard could get it organised. Last I heard half their fucking horses were dead. The staff in this lot couldn't organise remounts for a troop of whores. You said you were in the rearguard?'

'That's right.'

'Yeh, well that's what we're going to become—I bet you. You want to turn right here and follow the tracks. Bloody rearguard. We was supposed to be keeping the lines of communication open—nice cushy number compared to most in this do. Know what's going to happen? We're going to be the last poor bastards to get across the Berezina.'

'Don't be. We were last across the Dnieper. It's not funny.'

'Yeh, well, normally with headquarters you wouldn't worry, would you? But with this lot—well look at us now, fighting an ordered withdrawal for three bloody days now. Ordered, by Christ, that's a laugh. You want to pull up here; they'll see your lads all right—no, like I said the staff in this corps couldn't organise the storming of a maidenhead.'

Bernoit drew to a halt before a little church which had been pressed into use as the central hospital for the corps. It was

130

obviously a busy place but could not have been in operation for long to judge by the comparatively small heap of frozen corpses lying outside. He turned and thanked the talkative Marseillais.

The little man wrinkled his squat, unpleasant face. His ears stuck out like sails.

'Don't mention it, mate. First time I've travelled in one of these. Hear you took it from a Russian general. If I was you I wouldn't let it go—from what I hear you're going to need it.'

If he was like others of his kind, Bernoit knew that his assessment would be accurate. It related closely to his own feelings and he had not failed to note that, whereas the chasseur lieutenant had, with his initial ignorance, treated them like vermin, the orderly by keeping his ear to the ground had discovered the story of the sledge.

Now there were hospital orderlies hustling around to help him carry his unconscious companions inside. He was anxious to see one of the surgeons to explain their condition but he suddenly realised that this would mean leaving the sledge. In an area like this he would lose it the moment he turned his back. He saw the orderly from headquarters talking to some of the medical staff and instantly took a decision. He called and the ugly fellow turned round and came back.

'If you're in no hurry would you like to keep an eye on the sledge?'

'Oh, don't tempt me, mate—I'll be back home before you could blink. Yeh, it'll be a pleasure. You're right enough, can't trust any bugger around here.'

Bernoit nodded his thanks and went inside to see to the others. It was not as busy as he would have expected. Clearly the casualties from the day's fighting had not yet filtered this far back. He was met by an understanding surgeon-captain who assured him that his friends were in good hands, adding that he suspected that MacDonald only needed a little warmth and attention. They were lucky to have arrived at this time he said, for otherwise everyone would have been too busy to spare the time. It seemed the captain had done over thirty amputations on the previous day.

Then, as Bernoit moved to go, the captain said, 'You're looking pretty rough yourself, Sergeant-Major.'

'I'm shagged out.'

'I'm not surprised. From what I hear you've had quite a

131

time of it. Well, there's a spare bed here for you if you want it.'

Weariness spun round Bernoit's mind and he craved that warm bed. He remembered his promise to Larguien and shook his head ruefully. The captain listened to his refusal and smilingly told him to come back later.

When they reached headquarters there was no sign of Larguien and Bernoit realised that he might have hours to wait. His new friend was appreciative of the position and managed to inveigle one of his cronies into allowing Bernoit into an orderly room while he discreetly moved the sledge round to the transport park. Bernoit was now too tired to resist and meekly succumbed to the other's almost conspiratorial assistance. They found him a chair and someone brought him hot coffee which he drank with drowsy appreciation. It was incredibly good but he was too tired and he fell asleep even as he drank, spilling the hot liquid all over his clothes.

He was awakened suddenly, urgently, and at first he was in a panic until he saw his surroundings. They told him his officer was looking for him.

Larguien was pacing impatiently up and down in the narrow hallway and he looked very annoyed. When he saw Bernoit he said sharply, 'Come with me, I've got a billet,' and he led a wondering Bernoit out to the back of the building. There was a courtyard with the usual jostle of horses and orderlies, and an array of small outhouses and stables. It was into the latter that Larguien led him.

The building was empty, save for an old woman who welcomed them obsequiously. At the officer's imperious demand she showed him the stall which was to be his bed, a filthy place with stinking straw. With a rasp in his voice Larguien told the woman to bring them coffee and she left closing the door behind her. Bernoit was astonished by Larguien's conduct. This was a remarkable change from the exhausted, amicable man he had left.

However, Larguien was quiet enough when he asked gently, 'How are the others?'

'In good hands. They're keeping Necker. They seemed quite worried about his condition. MacDonald's going to be all right. Plenty of warmth and rest's all he needs.'

'Like you and me. Have you got any accommodation fixed up?'

'They say I can sleep in the hospital.'

'Good.' Larguien paused and Bernoit knew that he was going to hear what had caused the other's irritation.

'The maps were interesting but only showed old dispositions. On the other hand, the documents contained a complete break-down of the major Russian formations. You will appreciate that this is very important information.'

Bernoit was impressed. He had half suspected that Larguien's patent anger was caused by an outright rejection of the captured papers. The other hesitated almost guiltily before continuing in a burst.

'I am appointed to the Marshal's staff with the temporary rank of Major.'

Bernoit whistled in amazement. They must have been very impressed in headquarters, but he felt bitterly disappointed. He had assumed that he and Larguien would stay together and go on in the sledge to the Berezina crossings.

'It is not my wish,' Larguien began to explain apologetically. And then, in an outburst, 'It's a specific order! I tried to explain but the Marshal is a stubborn man. It seems that he is short of able staff officers. I can't even do anything positive for you—I might be able to arrange something but you know how it is.'

Bernoit understood only too well. He had not been betrayed; fate had intervened as it did so often in his soldier's life. Still, if he waited till MacDonald was fit, and didn't lose the sledge, he supposed he could cope. He remembered the orderly's gloomy prophecies and determined he would not risk being cut off in a rearguard again.

'I think I'll try to push on a bit with the sledge,' he said.

Larguien replied, 'Stick around for a day or two to see how things develop. It appears the crossings are contested.'

Bernoit nodded. It made sense for the Russians to contest the crossings and it confirmed his view that the sooner he got to the bridges the better. The rearguard could very easily be cut off. Until ordered otherwise his duty was to regain his unit which in the circumstances gave him virtually complete freedom. He realised that Larguien's appointment had removed the last formal restraint on his movement. Then it occurred to him that Larguien had lost that very freedom, together with the compan-ionship it had brought. Bernoit felt a wave of sympathy for the young officer. He had got his glory and it stuck in his craw. As the coffee arrived Bernoit found himself saying:

'It's a good job we didn't bring the Ivan general along. You'd make a most disreputable colonel.'

Larguien laughed but said, 'Seriously, I feel very bad about deserting you like this.'

'Don't. We'll muddle through, and I haven't congratulated you yet, Major; it's an honour. The others will be pleased too, when I tell them.'

'It should belong to all of us. I wish . . . I'll do what I can for you.'

They sat back in the soft, foul straw and drank the coffee which the woman had brought to them. Incongruously it was served in delicate china cups, and the aroma was sweet to their senses. Bernoit was content to listen to Larguien explain what he had learned of the current troop movements and outline the expected developments. Once across the Berezina the army was to fall back to winter quarters in Vilna. Amicably, Bernoit made it clear that for the moment at least he wished to remain independent. They agreed that it would be best if he stayed around the headquarters for a day or two to recuperate and await the outcome of the various manoeuvres that were taking place. By that time the emperor should have secured the vital crossings. In the present weather there was no hope that the river would be frozen.

At last Bernoit rose to go and as he left he looked at the new major.

'You know,' he said, 'if I were you I'd have someone look at that frozen nose of yours. You've no idea how funny it looks.'

He walked out into the night and made his way back to the hospital. He was desperate to lie down on that warm bed and sleep.

11

Necker tried to smile, but his cracked, hollow face would not comply and his sunken, red eyes merely grimaced.

'I wish I was coming with you,' he said.

'You're better where you are. You'll be evacuated today; they'll look after you better than we could. You'll be all right.' Bernoit tried to reassure him, but his eyes strayed to the flattened blanket where Necker's frostbitten feet should have been. 'I'll look you up in the Invalides when I get back to Paris,' he tried to joke, but he knew it sounded false and wondered if Necker was aware of the spectre of death waiting by his bed. It was not far away. Bernoit was anxious to be gone, his flesh crawling at the knowledge of the typhus which was now raging in the hospital, but he felt wretched at leaving Necker here like this. He took the corporal's hand and patted it gently.

'Well . . .'

'Take care of yourself.' Necker tried to smile again but failed and turned his head away to prepare for his lonely death.

MacDonald was waiting for him at the sledge, looking gaunt but remarkably well after his rest in the hospital. It was astonishing to realise that it was only two days since they had arrived here. All around them was the great bustle of activity signifying that the corps was once again preparing to withdraw. They had the horses harnessed up and were busily checking their equipment when the talkative Marseillais orderly appeared. Bernoit had learned that his name was Thirion and he had been of invaluable assistance to them, managing somehow to protect their belongings which had been left in the sledge. Now his air seemed furtive, almost apologetic.

'Couldn't use an extra driver, could you, mate?'

Thirion had made his own evaluation of their situation and

135

wanted to take the opportunity to desert. He obviously considered that his best chance of getting across the Berezina lay with Bernoit's sledge. In view of Larguien's comments when they said goodbye, Thirion's appreciation could well be correct. Bernoit felt sympathy for the soldier, but more important, an extra driver would be of great help.

'Where's your gear?'

Thirion grinned gleefully and said, 'Half a moment.'

He scuttled off out of sight, but reappeared a few moments later laden with his equipment and carrying a sack of food.

'Thought this might be handy—eh?—never know when you'll get your next issue.'

Their drive that morning was very different from the long, lonely journey they had made from the Dnieper. The road was well marked and blocked with marching troops and vehicles. To avoid the congestion they kept to the right of the retreating columns, secure in the knowledge that even if Cossacks dared to appear they could run for protection in the midst of the army. All around them there were other vehicles in a similar position. Many were privately owned, containing officers' baggage and the like, and everywhere there were women and civilians, the camp followers, pushing ahead in swarms.

The troops appeared to be in reasonably good condition, stepping out smartly, and now and then the three men on the sledge heard singing as they passed. It was quite unlike the marches to which Bernoit had become accustomed with their long, shuffling lines of dying men. These troops had spent the autumn comfortably installed in Smolensk and for the last month had been maintaining a leisurely retreat before the hesitant Wittgenstein, enduring few of the hardships which the rest of the army had suffered.

Bernoit remembered what he had learned from Larguien and did not envy the marching men. The bridge at Borisov had been cut and Napoleon was going to try to throw bridges across at Studyanka, about ten miles upstream. Victor's corps seemed likely to find themselves forming a rearguard on the wrong side of an extremely perilous crossing.

He thought of Larguien, looking ridiculous with his nose bound up and bandaged where the doctors had removed the tip to prevent gangrene. The new staff officer had been philosphical about his position and assured an anxious Bernoit that he would be taking considerable pains to avoid being trapped by another Russian river. They had parted on the warmest of terms.

Bernoit found that he was missing the presence of Larguien and Necker. It was strange to be back in the sledge without them and he felt that MacDonald too was experiencing this. He had indicated as much when they left, remarking that the light company could not even form one rank now. Necker's plight in particular had depressed them, hardened though they were to omnipresent death. It would have been a gloomy journey had it not been for the irrepressible Thirion, who chattered incessantly, amusing them with his endless fund of anecdotes and his professionally cheery pessimism. Even the dour MacDonald retaliated with banter.

They stopped at about noon and had a relaxed lunch. Thirion had done them proud and had scavenged the headquarters supplies ruthlessly. He even got a little fire going and brewed coffee over it. As they gratefully drank the hot liquid, Mac-Donald looked around at the abundance of food.

'If this lot had belonged to me, I'd be out to shoot you,' he said with a wry smile.

'Listen, mate, if they catch me they're going to shoot me anyway—a bloody deserter, aren't I? Christ, pissing themselves with envy they must be. Still, right enough though, if they find this lot they're going to shoot me twice, aren't they though, eh?'

'Bloody six times I'd reckon.'

'Yeh, that's about right—take that lot about six goes to get it right. No wonder they held on to your officer—he's bloody good you know. Been there one day and shaken up arses I never thought I'd see move—and that's with the vets sawing off his nose in the night. They dunno what's hit 'em in there.'

In the late afternoon they crossed a ridge where they saw the troops beginning to form a defensive line and settle down for the night. They moved on for a league or so and stopped by a large fire where a varied group of stragglers and civilians were making their camp. It was a luxury to unharness the horses and leave the sledge, and to construct a shelter secure from the threat of attack. They cut branches to form a frame over which they laid blankets, and lined the interior with their precious furs. It was snug inside with the fire nearby and Thirion cheerfully prepared their meal.

It was Thirion who found the woman with whom they shared

their meal and who lay with them in the cramped heat of their shelter in a wonderful release of entwined limbs and bodies, as, each in turn, they eased himself into her warmth, fumbling under her clothing at her full body in a furious escape. Later, she left with the food they had given her, to seek out and succour her husband where he stood with his regiment, protecting them.

Satiated, they slept until the noise of the dawn and the awakening army aroused them. They lay for a while in the cosseted heat of their huddled bodies and watched the early light slowly drowning the flickering firelight. In the gloom they stirred, companionably. Thirion sat up and rubbed the slumber from his ugly face. Bernoit, watching him with something akin to affection, said, 'You're a sordid bastard, Thirion,' and received a cheery grin.

'Ah, shut up,' MacDonald growled sleepily. 'That's the best night I've had for months.'

Lazily they rose and prepared a hot breakfast, which they sat eating while they watched the troops and their followers bustle to start the day's march.

'Still falling back,' Thirion commented.

'We've plenty of time to get to Studyanka,' Bernoit replied. 'Give them a chance to open up the bridgehead. We should be there by dusk.'

They harnessed the horses and loaded their sledge. Everywhere troops were moving in orderly formation, in the midst of swarms of stragglers and women with all their attendant vehicles. The three men set off with almost a feeling of holiday. They were free from the ordinary restrictions and, in the meantime at least, from danger. If they found their regiment, good and well. They would shelter under its protective blanket, but if they did not make contact they should, in four or five days, reach Vilna, where winter quarters and safety awaited them. They would have to look after their horses; forage would be a problem as ever, but Thirion's sack should keep them going quite happily over that period.

There was no hurry to get to Studyanka. At their present rate they would be there before nightfall and would take the first opportunity to cross the bridges. From then on it would be a straight uninterrupted drive to Vilna. Sitting companionably on the sleigh that morning it was easy to overlook or discount the hazards on the way.

Thirion in particular was cheery and light-hearted. Released from the tedium of his job in headquarters he found their independence exhilarating and he was exuberant at their adventure. He had seen none of the misery which the others knew so well and his merriment lifted them above themselves. He sang and they found themselves singing with him—gay, happy songs dragged from the wretched tombs into which their minds had been cast. His company was a boon to his comrades and together they watched the morning blossom into a beautiful day, oblivious of the sullen sky.

They became accustomed to moving round the columns of marching troops, avoiding the clogged traffic on the roads like other stragglers who were walking or riding in well-found vehicles. The route was being used by the numerous messengers passing to and fro but no one seemed to bother them in the anonymity of the crowd. Then in the middle of the morning they were overtaken by a staff officer leading a detachment of the gendarmerie, presumably to marshal traffic on the road. The officer slowed up as he passed and then pulled over beside them. Bernoit recognised him as the young lieutenant of chasseurs whom they had encountered on their arrival at Victor's headquarters. Thirion was in the back of the sleigh with MacDonald and desperately tried to render himself invisible.

'Well, it's Major Larguien's loyal sergeant-major. Leaving the noble Major behind now that he's taken all your glory?'

'Trying to rejoin our unit, sir.'

'Indeed—most commendable. We're not saying "Shit" today, are we, Sergeant-Major.'

'No, sir,' replied Bernoit, wishing to say precisely that, but anxious for Thirion's sake to control his tongue.

The lieutenant looked back at the other two men in the sleigh, and Bernoit saw a look of what might have been triumph flicker in his eyes.

'Ah, Thirion!' he said with a lethal quiet: 'We've all been wondering where you'd got to. How very considerate of the good sergeant-major.' He called over the sergeant of gendarmes and said, 'Sergeant Bro, these men are deserters. Disarm them and take them to headquarters. My compliments to Colonel van Roos and request a drumhead court martial. Escort of four. Retain the sledge as transport.'

Bernoit protested furiously. 'I told you, we're trying to rejoin our unit.'

139

'Deserters, Sergeant-Major—and thieves. If I can I will see you before your execution.'

Bernoit spat in the officer's face.

'Note that, Sergeant Bro. He assaulted me.'

'Yes, sir.'

The officer turned and rode off with his troop of gendarmes.

The sergeant of gendarmerie was no fool and the three men found themselves well guarded as they were efficiently disarmed. Bernoit tried to protest to the sergeant, but Bro looked at him with contempt, and spoke with venom.

'Silence, coward. I don't know why they need to bother with courts martial for shit like you.' And Bernoit found himself compelled to turn the sledge round and retrace their route under the unsympathetic escort.

For a while no one spoke, then Thirion burst out, 'Sorry mates, Christ sorry—if I hadn't come along . . .'

'That bastard would have got us for something,' growled MacDonald. 'He's got Bernoit for assault now.'

'That was worth it,' Bernoit muttered.

The gendarme sergeant snapped, 'Prisoners stop talking,' and MacDonald replied with malice, 'Go fuck yourself, Bro.'

Bro raised his riding crop but his eyes were met by those cold eyes and he saw reflected there perhaps some of the death which MacDonald knew so well.

'Just try it, son,' MacDonald hissed.

'Don't tempt me.' But Bro had seen his danger and lowered the crop.

MacDonald laughed harshly and Bro whipped his horse ahead to the jeers of the three men in the sledge. Somehow the incident made their plight less oppressive.

It was not a long drive back to the cluster of hovels which had become the new headquarters. They were flung into a hut with a sentry posted outside, while Bro went off to start the short process that would lead to their court martial. Bernoit tried furiously to persuade someone to deliver a message to Larguien but the gendarmes were cruelly uncooperative.

Thirion commented, 'Usual bloody business—bastard battle police. Make every other sod go into the line so long as they don't have to. Bastards the lot of them.'

They sat miserably contemplating their fate. Bernoit was desperately depressed and the irony of their situation was devastating. For what seemed a lifetime he had been living in fear of cold-blooded death at Russian hands and now for no real reason he was going to be killed by his friends. There was no doubt of the outcome of the court martial; it was a mere formality with no attempt at justice. The court would be too hurried to listen to any pleas he might make. Anger boiled in him at the futility of it all. It was infuriating to be unable to contact Larguien. He lapsed into a stream of vile obscenity.

In the brooding silence of the dark hut the three men waited for the noises that would tell them of the assembling court. They could all imagine the hurriedly assembled officers with their escorts. The firing squad would have been detailed and would be standing white-faced, nervous, discreetly out of sight until the court martial formalised the inevitable verdict. At every sound of movement outside the prisoners started and looked up, but still no one came for them. Bitterly, they waited and they lost all track of time.

Suddenly, without warning, the door was flung open and light flooded into their cell. They stood up with a start, nervously moving forward.

'This is it,' said Thirion, his voice drawn and strange. But he was wrong for the sentry shouted, 'Bernoit — outside!' and, puzzled, Bernoit stepped out into the daylight, leaving his companions perplexed as the door swung shut behind him. He screwed his eyes against the light and saw a figure standing, waiting for him. It was Larguien.

'What the hell's going on?'

'Christ! I'm glad to see you.' Bernoit's heart leapt in relief; hope flooded through him. In response to the repeated question Bernoit explained what had happened.

'Uh-huh,' said Larguien thoughtfully. 'Our friend, the little shit. I'll have a word for him when I see him.'

'I spat in the bastard's face. I understand that's part of the charge.'

'Great. That's of immense assistance.'

'It seemed worth it at the time. I've been trying to get hold of you but these bastards wouldn't let me.'

'You were very lucky. Someone recognised your name and drew it to my attention. Anyway, I'll go off now and square things with the Provost-Marshal. If he feels the way I do he'll overlook the assault thing. I'll have you both out of there in half an hour.'

141

'What about Thirion?'

'For Christ's sake—you don't know when you're lucky. I don't know what came over you, abetting a deserter. That's what he is and you know it. It was one of the coolest things I've seen. The bastard cleaned out the stores in the staff mess. You can't hide a thing like that. Every orderly in headquarters is thinking about trying the same stunt.'

'So they've got to make an example?'

'Bloody right—and you know that too! Honestly, you could have been in the real shits for helping him. Fortunately I think I can square things.'

Unchastened, Bernoit said, 'Well don't let me keep you back.'

In the cell MacDonald and Thirion were waiting for him expectantly. He felt wretched about Thirion and hesitated before speaking. He looked at MacDonald.

'That was Larguien. You and I are going to be all right.' He turned to Thirion. 'I'm sorry. He can't do anything for you.'

The little man hunched. His last, faint hope had gone and he was to be left alone to face his fate. He looked at his companions and saw their sympathy. They were distant now where a few minutes before they had all been together, facing the same miserable death. Bernoit felt helpless. There was nothing he could do or say to ease Thirion's misery. As reprieved men he and MacDonald had become remote from him, their future life creating a gulf that was impassable. MacDonald tried to express his regret, but it sounded false, and they could hear in his voice the soaring joy of his restored life. After that no one spoke for a while until MacDonald, impatient to be away, asked:

'When's Larguien coming back?'

'Shortly,' and for a moment they lapsed back into silence before Thirion spoke.

'Don't worry about me, mates. Chance I took. Glad you're out of it. Really worried me that did. Dragged you into this. Better if I hadn't come along. Really pleased they're letting you go—worrying me to death it was.'

MacDonald said, 'I'll promise you this, Thirion. If we run into that chasseur lieutenant again I'll get him for you.'

'Doing his duty, wasn't he, mate?'

'I saw fuck all sign of his work in Smolensk,' Bernoit snarled.

'Dead right there, mate. Useless little shit he is really. They're all like that, saving your man of course. Fact is, I'll be bloody

142

amazed if they can organise my . . . ' and he tapered off, unable to finish. Later he asked them to try to contact his brother and let him know, and gave them messages for him, but they all knew that such a contact would be nearly impossible in present circumstances.

Larguien came for them shortly afterwards and they left Thirion behind, alone in his cell. MacDonald had paused only to repeat his vow.

Relief at the fact of their release was considerable. As they walked away with Larguien they tried to express their gratitude, but the major stopped them.

'You'll never know how lucky you were,' he said. 'if I hadn't heard . . . Look, my advice to you now is to get the hell out of here. I wouldn't hang around. I'm going back to organise the next stage in the withdrawal. I expect they're screaming for me by now. It looks as if it's going to be the usual bloody shambles.'

'Oh well, we'll be off then. Just tell us where the sledge is.'

'You're joking! That's been requisitioned. You're back on your feet, Bernoit. Serves you bloody right for eating my dinner last night.'

'What about all our food though, our equipment? They took everything away from us.'

'That's a point. Try their quartermaster sergeant; tell him I sent you. You should get your personal equipment and weapons back all right, but you won't get anything else. Look, I'll have to get back.' He shook hands with them both and added, 'Good luck. Take care of yourselves.'

The gendarme quartermaster was surprisingly sympathetic, even to the extent of taking them to their sledge and inviting them to take what belonged to them. But all their vital furs and supplies had disappeared and they only managed to recover their own weapons and accoutrements. They were dismayed to discover that their packs had been ransacked and all their food had been stolen. They checked their weapons and found these to be in order and then, thanking the quartermaster, they set off to see what they could pilfer. They hunted around the area of the headquarters but without success.

They chanced to walk round a corner and found troops drawn up. They had just time to take in the scene and see the firing squad and Thirion, his arms pinioned, standing facing it. Then the volley ripped into the little man's body throwing him like a

143

rag doll to the ground, his blood running red on the snow. The two men stood, aghast at having witnessed this of all things.

'Let's get away from this bloody place,' said MacDonald, and they walked round the other side of the building and sadly began the long walk to Studyanka. Bernoit reflected bitterly on his optimism that morning when he had calculated that they would reach the crossing before dusk.

It was hard work, walking, after they had become so accustomed to the sleigh. At first they tried to follow the road, but the traffic had been so heavy that the surface was dreadfully broken up and had turned to slush, so that they found themselves up to their knees in the rotting snow. They felt the wetness beginning to seep through the rags binding their feet and knew that unless they could get fresh footwear they would be in grave danger of frostbite.

By mutual consent they abandoned the road and climbed to the broad snow fields where the surface was firm. Here they fell into their regular marching pace and it was strangely good to be swinging along in step together. It was as if the regular rhythm of their march was cleansing the misery from them and gradually their silence changed, subtly reflecting their easing sorrow and bitterness in the growing mood of healthy endeavour. They passed the scene of their arrest before nightfall and neither commented nor allowed themselves pause on the fact. It was a landmark, no more, by which they could assess the distance they had come.

When night fell they did not stop, but carried on through the lines of bivouac fires with their huddled owners sitting round, ignoring them. From time to time a wakeful sentry challenged them as they passed through the camps of the various units, sometimes passing horse lines in the dark, where the animals snorted at their disturbed rest and then, ignoring the silent, moving men, returned to champing and stamping their restless feet. Once, they tried to stop at a large fire, lured by the scent of cooking food, but the men there were German and chased them away. Only occasionally did they stop for rest, for they were determined now to reach the bridge as soon as possible, and seek the safety of the west bank of the river.

In wooded country they found they were stumbling around aimlessly until they came back to the road and were forced to follow it once more. The going here was exhausting and when, at a crossroads, they found an ordnance unit halted, with bright fires burning, they sat down to rest. The soldiers here were patient and moved over to let them in at the fires. Bernoit noticed that the waggons were all harnessed up and the officers' horses were still saddled and bridled. A troop sergeant saw his glance and grinned.

'Waiting for orders. Been sat here for two hours now nearly. It's the usual cock-up, you know. Someone somewhere needs ammunition. Somewhere there's a battery pissing itself wondering where this lot's got to. We're sat here not knowing where to go because some silly bastard at headquarters has forgotten all about us. Of course when he does bloody turn up we're going to go wandering off in the dark and get lost half a dozen times before we find the bloody place. Probably get there and find orders has changed and they want this lot somewhere else. Bloody marvellous. Seen it all before.' He spat into the fire. 'We're going to be up all bloody night and we've got a couple of moves again tomorrow. Wish I'd stayed at home.'

Bernoit laughed sympathetically and said, 'And I'll tell you what, when you do find the battery they'll be screaming for the guillotine. It'll be all your fault, you know.'

'You're dead right there, mate, dead right.' And in a generous gesture of comradeship the sergeant passed them both some food from the stewpot on the fire.

It was perhaps about half an hour later that the staff officer came walking up leading his lame horse and sought out the column commander. There was a short conference up near the head of the column and the friendly sergeant was called over. He returned as the unit started the bustle to get under way and sent his men scurrying to their waggons. He paused to throw a comment to the two infantrymen before moving off.

'Bloody marvellous. No bloody guide. We've got to find our own way. Whiskers and spurs from headquarters there says he's got to sit here and wait to direct other units coming up. We'll be wandering about all bloody night while he sits here frying his arse over our fires.'

The column moved on to the road and with the ponderous motion of its kind sorted itself into its marching order and moved away, along the dark torn road, in search of the mythical battery.

Bernoit and MacDonald watched it slowly disappear into the

night, leaving the sound of creaking carts and shouting drivers hanging in the darkness as the only signs of its presence. A horse whinnied nearby and they looked round to where the staff officer sat in the gloom not far away, attending to his mount's lamed leg. He leaned forward out of the shadow and in the firelight they recognised him as the despised chasseur lieutenant. Bernoit felt MacDonald go tense beside him and saw him reach for his bayonet.

'No,' he commanded, 'there's no need to kill.'

MacDonald grunted and relaxed, but Bernoit did not know what he was thinking. He, Bernoit, felt a deep loathing for the officer and watched him resentfully, but he knew that the man had duties to perform and that others were dependent on him. He thought of the cheerful little Thirion and felt his gorge rise. He remembered the sarcasm and the aristocratic arrogance and he screwed his eyes with hate. They would talk to this man, he decided.

The officer had seen them, two hunched figures silhouetted against their fire, and he rose to walk over to them, his voice confident and austere as he began to speak. 'You two there! I have duties for you. I require . . .'

He saw them now in the glowing flames and he knew them. He hesitated, unsure of himself, not knowing how to react. He looked at them, from one to the other as they sat there silent, watching him, and he felt their hatred. Without speaking he turned on his heel abruptly and began to walk away.

Bernoit shouted after him, 'Lieutenant!' and the man stopped for a moment but then continued walking. Bernoit shouted again, 'Stop, you shit!' and this time the officer stopped and faced them. He spoke and his voice was controlled, assertive. 'Well Sergeant-Major, I'm a shit again, am I?'

Bernoit forget his carefully thought out phrases, his verbal destruction of this arrogant, useless man and found himself streaming out foulness in long abuse.

The officer smiled sardonically and said, 'How very expressive,' and he turned and slowly walked away, and Bernoit heard his voice become a scream as the obscenities poured forth, and he felt the impotent outrage of his defeat.

Then MacDonald slipped silently from his side and, moving like a cat, approached the officer's back and Bernoit saw the glimmer of the bayonet's naked blade and fell silent. The steel flashed redly in the firelight as it darted with practised accuracy. Bernoit heard the soft thud and the wheeze of air escaping from the ruptured lungs. He saw the man's knees sag as his weight came back on MacDonald's rigid arm. The big man pushed his victim forward, off the blade, and sent him toppling forward into the snow. The chasseur twitched for a moment and then died.

Silently the two men gathered together their belongings and, without speaking, without even looking at each other, they moved quietly away, into the night.

12

It was still dark when they arrived at Studyanka. The whole army seemed to be assembling and as the two men marched into the village they passed through the lines of units from every arm of the service and heard the languages of nearly every nation in Europe. Stragglers like themselves were everywhere, swarming, seeking accommodation and food. There were thousands of non-combatants, civilians, clerks and servants, and above all the women. The women were in desperate straits, alone, separated from their menfolk, lost in this great mass where few hands would turn to help them.

Towards the river they could hear the rumour of the regiments crossing the bridges. Columns of marching troops passed on their way to join the queue and they passed long formations waiting patiently for their turn to cross. Both men were anxious to rejoin their own corps, but they were very tired and first they sought out shelter, postponing their search till daylight.

It seemed that every house was filled with refugees and at the first doors they approached they were chased away by the hostile occupants. Then MacDonald managed to force an entry into a house near the river and found a crowded room in which they could lie down. The condition of many of the occupants was pathetic. Cold and exhausted, they sat vacantly staring around them, or stretched prostrate on the unyielding floor watching the ceiling with open, sunken eyes. The fine uniforms which had once made the army so resplendent had all but disappeared. Soldiers could be distinguished only by the vestiges of their equipment, or perhaps, here and there, a forage cap or shako. Every man wore a different combination of motley furs and clothing, filthy and ragged, greasy from spilt fat or tallow, frequently clotted with blood, and invariably scorched and blackened by the campfires.

148

The women were in like condition, seasoned campaigners who had shared the trials and hardships of their men, clad in wretched rags, layers thick to shield against the weather. They too were exhausted from the march and many had seen their husbands or lovers lying dead on the field, or had watched them slowly perish in the cold. Occasionally, under the unseeing eyes of the men a mother would bare her breast to suckle her child and the infant would cling to the hollow, empty pap, striving for nurture which, from weeks of starvation, could not be there. In all this miserable crowd few people spoke.

In the midst of this company Bernoit and MacDonald settled down to sleep, warmed by the heat of the pressing bodies. They were aware only of their own weariness and the desperate need for rest, and ignored all else, even the cold damp of their wet footwear. They did not know that in upper rooms of the house men lay dying as plague corroded their weakened bodies. They lay there, careless of all this misery, content to forget it and all that had gone before, knowing only that they had at last reached the bridges and tomorrow they might be safe. And thus they slept.

They were roused long before daybreak. Men were smashing their way into the building, lighting their way with blazing brands. From outside came the crash of breaking timber. Some soldiers burst into the room casting their torchlight over the unhappy scene. A voice cried:

'Here's a beam that might do, General!'

'Yes, that's solid enough — let's have it!'

Crowbars appeared and the men attacked the flimsy structure in frenzied enthusiasm. The wooden walls cracked and splintered.

'Hey! What the hell's going on?'

The less apathetic occupants were rising in protest. Bernoit pulled at one of the intruders.

'Stop that! You'll have the house down.'

Someone caught his sleeve and restrained him.

'We need these timbers, soldier. We have a bridge to repair.'

Bernoit was about to retort but when he saw the speaker he stopped. The man was exhausted. His face was gaunt, skull-like with his balding head and sunken cheeks. His eyes were hollow and red-rimmed with strain. Yet the long nose gave the worn face distinction and Bernoit noted that the tattered coat bore the

149

insignia of a general. Bernoit wondered who was this officer.

The general spoke loudly, addressing them all.

'The bridge is broken. We need these timbers. You must look to yourselves. I am sorry, but my men will not be prevented.'

The general shivered and Bernoit saw that his uniform was sodden. His men's clothes also were soaked through. They were blue with cold; they must have been in the river, working on the bridge. It was astonishing that they could survive the icy water. The people in the room drew back in respect. These brave men were pontonniers and this man, their commander, would be . . .

'General Eblé! Is General Eblé there?'

'Yes. I am here.'

A staff officer bustled in.

'Sir, the Emperor is anxious at the delay. How much longer must you take? The artillery is kept waiting.'

'Then, sir, you must remind his Majesty that he watched my men toil in the river throughout yesterday. They continue to work without relief and will do so until the army is safe across. You will also tell his Majesty that had he not insisted on my destroying the bridge train this dreadful effort would not be necessary. The bridge will be ready soon, but only through the sacrifice of my men.'

'General, sir . . .' the aide protested.

'Go now, and convey this to the Emperor.'

There was silence in the room. The tight-lipped emissary paused as if to object again, then changed his mind, saluted and left the house. The pontonniers returned to their work.

It was obvious that the front of the building would soon collapse and the stronger occupants were starting to drift away. MacDonald laid a heavy hand on his shoulder and Bernoit looked round. The tall man whispered.

'Let's try a back room. We should be able to get in all right. It's better than wandering around in the cold.'

The room they found had all the misery of their previous refuge. There was a vile stench of vomit and excreta but they ignored it and settled down. Their rest was disturbed once, when Eblé's men demolished the front wall, but their shelter was unbroken and they soon slipped into sound sleep.

Bernoit was wakened by MacDonald shaking him, his voice penetrating the dreamy screen of his mind.

150

'Come on. Wake up. It's light now.'

He sat up and muzzily strove to collect his thoughts. His whole body was stiff and sore, his face crumpled from lack of sleep. Above all, his feet were aching and bitterly cold. MacDonald persisted anxiously.

'We'll have to get on the way. God knows where the corps is.'

Bernoit nodded. It might take all morning to find the corps, assuming that Ney had not already crossed the river. Yet his feet needed urgent attention. Those wet bindings would bring frost-bite, and that would kill him. MacDonald's feet would also be wet.

'We'll have to find dry rags for our feet first.'

'Help yourself.'

MacDonald cast an arm round the room and Bernoit saw that it was filled with the corpses of men who had died during the night.

They found that they were alone in the room, bar a few wasted souls who watched them with sad cunning as they sat awaiting death. The two men began a methodical search of the bodies stretched on the floor. At one body MacDonald leapt back with a gasp of horror. He drew away in disgust and fear and the eyes of the watching men gleamed with triumph. Now Bernoit saw that others had the same purpled faces and smelt the running excreta on the floor. He and MacDonald backed to the door in terror of the silent, deadly enemy.

MacDonald, stricken, whispered, 'We've been lying among this for hours.'

Bernoit nodded, but he could feel his feet protesting at the cold. He replied slowly, 'We'll get bindings for our feet then. It won't make any difference now.'

'Go ahead. Just be careful whose you choose.'

Bernoit controlled his panic and forced himself to examine the corpses until he found one he considered safe to touch. He stopped to strip the man, anxious to find rags suitable for his purpose. The man's white linen trousers were almost intact and would do well enough. With these in his hand he left the room. He could see no sign of his comrade, so he sat down on the broken stairs and used his sword to cut the trousers into long, broad strips which he laid out carefully beside him.

When this was done and the material would yield no more strips he turned his attention to the damp bindings on his feet.

He delicately cut the knots and unwound the wet bandages round his feet. He had worn them since his boots had fallen apart almost ten days ago. As he undid the yards of cloth he wondered what he would find. The rags fell away from his right leg and he found himself looking at a white, wrinkled foot. He was relieved to see it still looked healthy. His left foot, too, was in good condition.

He took each foot in his hands and rubbed vigorously. The tired old skin peeled off but otherwise there appeared to be no problem and his feet responded to the treatment. He lifted one of the strips and, carefully folding it over his toes, wound it round his foot until he came to the end. He then laid the next strip over to hold it firm and continued the binding in this fashion, up round his feet until he could tuck it under his puttee-like gaiters and then down again to cover the toes. When he was satisfied that his foot was sufficiently protected he sliced the end of the linen and in a series of neat knots made the binding secure. He repeated the whole process meticulously on his other foot then, content at his handiwork, he gathered the old bindings together and put them in his pack against an emergency. While he was collecting his equipment MacDonald came down the stairs. He had wrapped his feet in similar fashion with lengths cut from a blanket which he had found in a room above. The brown eyes looked down at him and wrinkled anxiously.

'There are stiffs all over the place. This house is rotten with fever.'

Bernoit's flesh crawled and anxiety gnawed at him. He felt contaminated and he looked at his feet and imagined the disease creeping into him from the corpse's shredded trousers. It was with considerable relief that they scrambled over the ruined frontage and departed from the house and its dead and dying occupants.

Once outside they asked passing soldiers for the location of Ney's corps, but their requests were either ignored or met with shrugs and denials of knowledge. One man did point to the south of the town and as they headed in that direction they found others who confirmed this. However, when they reached the place where they had been told to look for the corps, people told them that it had moved west, or east, or even north. The search was becoming fruitless and frustrating and they returned to the centre of the town to acquire more positive information. The natural flow of the crowds drew them towards the river and the

152

bridges. They found a staff officer with a detachment of grenadiers trying to marshal the mob. Bernoit went up to him and
managed to attract his harassed attention.

'Sorry to trouble you, sir. We're trying to rejoin our unit. Third
Corps.'

'They crossed during the night, I'm afraid. You'll have to get
across on your own.' And he turned back to direct the movement
of his grenadiers.

'If we hadn't kipped down we'd have caught them,' said
MacDonald bitterly.

Bernoit nodded. It was the foulest luck and now they would
have to take their chance among the disorganised rabble crowding towards the two slender bridges.

'Come on,' he said, and the two friends stepped forward to
mingle with this unruly advance. The closer they approached to
the crossing the thicker became the crowd, and in the consequent
jam movement ahead decreased to a slow and irregular shuffle.
There were thousands and thousands of stragglers, deserters,
civilians and women in the striving mass of humanity.

There was a disturbance behind, shouting and the whinnying
of horses, and then the blare of trumpets. People moved on
regardless but the press thickened, slowing them, and a new
pressure was asserting itself. All movement ceased and they
craned their necks to identify the cause.

A body of cavalry was forcing its way through the masses.
Bernoit recognised them at once by their high bearskins with the
tall red plumes and golden cap cords, ridiculous to see on a
cavalryman. Yet there was nothing ridiculous about these men
for they were horse grenadiers of the Guard, resplendent in their
blue riding-cloaks. Their grenadier uniform was known in every
capital in Europe, with its broad white lapels and red epaulettes,
and every man displayed a long pigtail and sported a gold ear-
ring. Proud men these, the grenadiers, both horse and foot, they
were the symbol of Napoleon's might and were feared in every
land.

At their head rode Marshal Lefèbvre, Duke of Danzig, the
tough old Alsatian commanding the Old Guard. He was undismayed by their adversity and ruthlessly ordered his men to cleave
their way through the rabble. On they came, and Bernoit
distinctly saw a sabre hacking down at some poor wretch who had
not moved aside with sufficient dispatch. Behind the grenadiers

they could see the gleaming helmets, with their horsehair plumes, and the green coats of the Empress Josephine's Dragoons.

MacDonald said, 'The Guard must be crossing now.'

The mounted grenadiers drew nearer and the people pressed tight to open a passage for the Guard. Regiment by regiment they passed, the cavalry with its guidons and kettle drums; the infantry, with its honourable eagles. A panoply of glory in decline. They were all there; the bearskins of the Old Guard, the shakos of the Young; the lancers and hussars of the light cavalry, the cuirassiers and dragoons of the heavy; the artillery in red and blue with its guns and caissons.

They saw the green-plumed busbies of the Chasseurs à Cheval and knew the Emperor was approaching. The crowd surged to see him but the escort forced them back. The staff was passing, dressed in blue and gold, the civilian secretaries in their drabs. There was Duroc, the Grand Marshal, there Caulaincourt, the Grand Equerry. There rode the black-faced Roustem, the faithful Mameluke. And then they saw Napoleon.

He looked small among the others, the man who had brought them here. He seemed to have shrunk into his long fur coat and the fur on his green velvet cap was drawn down over his eyes. Those eyes, which had fired a nation's dreams, stared straight ahead, as if the stout little man feared to see the ruin he had caused. This gaunt, exhausted fellow was not the leader whom Bernoit had followed into the citadels of the nations. He had faded and Bernoit was shocked by the sight. This wretch was far removed from the bold general whom he had last seen at Borodino. On that morning he had galloped past, in his old artillery coat, waving his famous cocked hat to the cheering troops, just as Bernoit had seen him so long ago on the field of Austerlitz. But now there was no cheering, no acknowledgement. The Emperor passed silent through his sullen people.

At his side rode the Prince of Neuchâtel, Berthier, the Chief of Staff, an ugly man, thoughtful under his blue cap. Behind came Murat, King of Naples, chastened and sad for all his fine ostrich plumage, and beside him General Rapp, dark and grim. All the others were there, household and staff, Jomini and Narbonne and the rest whose names were known in every home. The flower of the Empire, these, whose proud faces were familiar to Bernoit from different, happier days. Gone were their splendid white feathers, the beautiful array of full dress uniforms, blues and greens and reds, with dolmans and busbies and gold lace aplenty. Now they were clad for warmth alone and they were dismal to the eye. Even their horses, the best cared for in all the army, were thin, mangy beasts, and the saddle furniture was filthy and soiled. Yet worse than this was the sad, worried expression of all these men as they rode unspeaking through the rabble which once had been the army at their command.

As the Emperor moved away a woman near Bernoit raised a shrill voice.

'Are you leaving us behind? How are we to get to Vilna?'

Others took up the cry and it grew to a roar as the Emperor, secure among his loyal guard, led his staff across the Berezina into White Russia. But Napoleon heard the echoed baying of resentment and hatred expressed by the disillusioned throng he left behind. They had come a long, long way from the cheering army that greeted him on that glorious morning at Austerlitz.

The mob pressed in behind the Emperor, heedless of the oncoming units of the Guard which had to struggle hard to make their advance. Bernoit and MacDonald were swept forward in the press. They were aware of the regiments behind forcing their way through. A number of other soldiers saw the problem and they locked arms together and pushed back against the pressure while the guardsmen squeezed through the narrow corridor.

The row of soldiers held together for a long time, keeping the pressure at bay, while the Guard marched past. But the Guard were taking an eternity to cross and the crowd was growing at their back. They were all tiring and eventually a little gunner fell, exhausted. The broken line surged forward, driven before the tumultous thousands, closing the route of the Guard. The Second Lancers were close at hand and Bernoit heard their vile cursing at being cut off. MacDonald used his height to see what was happening. He reported to Bernoit, his voice in awe.

'They're the last. There are no more to come.'

Bernoit was appalled, but he knew that MacDonald was correct. He had been noting the various units as they passed and had seen how reduced they were. Three-quarters of their men were missing, and this was the reserve, the most protected, most cosseted corps in the army. So now there were no reserves. Bernoit wondered how they would ever reach the safety of Vilna.

The Lancers were among them, lashing out with the flats of their swords, using brute force to cut themselves a passage.

People who could not move from their path quickly enough were beaten aside or, if the pack was too solid, knocked down and ridden over. The Lancers had with them the last of the vehicles and horse teams remaining to cross. These came forward in stops and starts, their wheels churning dangerously close to the fringe of the crowd. Sometimes a man would be heaved forward and caught by the wheels, which threw him down to be crushed under the succeeding carts.

The tension eased suddenly and Bernoit was thrown forward in a surge to collide with one of the lancers' mounts and found himself pressed against the horse's chestnut flank. The horse backed at the blow and kicked out, missing him, but causing him to slip. As he fell he reached out desperately and managed to get his hand round the lance, set in its boss. The pressure behind him decreased and he levered himself back to his feet, but then he saw the lancer swinging down at him with his sabre and he was forced to let go. Like a bobbing cork in a stream he was swept back, bumping into the succeeding horses as they came past. Then he was trapped before one of the dreadful turning wheels, jammed against the side of the cart while the wheel bore down on him as if he was grain in a mill.

He heard the splintering of crushing bones and the agonising shrieks of a soldier who had fallen before him. Frantically he tried to break free and slip under the vehicle but could not. Then a hand was on his collar pulling at him, pushing the people aside in fury. The wheel scraped past him but his musket caught in the spokes and pulled him down. He wriggled it from his shoulder, so that freed from the restraint it spun down like a scythe fixed to the wheel. The hub of the axle caught his hips but the pulling hand held him up as he swung clear of it. As suddenly as it had come the waggon was gone and he spun into the vacuum left by it. The hand still held his collar. At last he could spare the time to look up to see his saviour and there was MacDonald, hatless, looking grim, the sweat running down his face. Bernoit tried to grin but he felt his face was frozen, and his legs shook under him.

'By God, that was too close,' he said.

'It was. I nearly let go a couple of times.'

Now they moved forward with the crowd, drawn obliquely by the unseen pressures across from the lancers' line of march and as they struggled to keep their balance they saw this, the last unit of the guard, achieve the bridge and dismount to lead their horses across from the corpse-littered bank of Central Russia.

The mob pressed on towards the river, each individual determined to get across regardless of anyone else. Some of the people clung to their horses, trying to lead them, and here and there the sensitive beasts would panic and crash out in a thrashing fury of lashing limbs. Others were trying to take their carts and carriages across, careless of the peril these occasioned in the crowd. Just ahead of Bernoit a phaeton was in trouble, its horses rearing and the driver screaming curses as the wave of humanity swept it aside like flotsam. Its wheels could not take the strain of the sidewards movement and the carriage wobbled. The driver saw his danger and threw himself clear, on to the heads of people below, creating a momentary eddy which filled quickly as the crowd closed in and swept over those who had fallen. The phaeton was toppling and the people near saw their danger and panicked to get clear, but the mass was unyielding. The carriage crashed down, crushing and maiming.

The crowd swirled round the ruin and Bernoit was swept round the roof of the wrecked carriage, trampling over the screaming bodies trapped below. A soldier was clinging to the side of the phaeton crying like a man demented.

'My wife, my wife is under there. Will no one help me?'

No one stopped and Bernoit passed on unhearing. The horses were thrashing furiously, trapped in their harness and screaming in almost human terror. Occasionally they struck a deadly blow with their flying hooves, knocking people down under the endlessly moving feet of the crowd. The mob pressed forward, tighter and tighter as it approached the river.

The pressure was unbearable and Bernoit felt himself constricted by the solid bodies pushing at him from every side. His arms were pinioned against his ribs and could not move and he felt his lungs compressed by the unyielding back of the man in front. MacDonald had kept his arms free and had thrown them round the shoulders of his neighbours. Bernoit felt his friend's strong hand clinging to the collar of his fur. The squash was tighter than ever and Bernoit gasped for air, trying desperately to breathe with his shallow, flattened lungs. His feet were lifted from the secure feel of the ground and he was carried along, rigid, suspended, floating in the sheer massive press.

As they approached the river they began to stumble over the bodies of fallen men and horses. The precarious stability of the

157

crowd began to dissolve. A man would fall and be swallowed up as if he had drowned. Bernoit's feet made contact with something and felt the soft flesh sag as he shuffled along the corpse. His foot caught under the man's pack and he almost tripped but managed to bring his other foot up in time. He swayed perilously over to his left. MacDonald's grip tightened, but the sudden irregular movement had sent ripples out among his neighbours. Bernoit saw the man beside him slip and slide down. He grabbed at Bernoit's coat in a desperate effort for support.

Bernoit felt himself being pulled down and he almost panicked. He was constricted, helpless. But the man had left a gap and Bernoit could free his arm. He smashed his fist down hard. The other let go and fell back, and in the ensuing swirl Bernoit managed to free his arm and throw it round MacDonald's shoulder.

There was a dead horse ahead and the press of humanity was gathering like a tide to sweep over it. Again Bernoit felt the dreadful crush on his chest. He nearly suffocated as he was lifted from his feet and pushed forward on to the obstacle. The pressure grew and grew as those in front struggled to climb over. The press behind was too heavy and they were lifted and thrown forward. It was as if they had been keystones in a dam. The released pressure forced everyone in its stream up over the dead beast in a torrent where balance was impossible.

Bernoit felt his feet touch the ground, once, twice, as he was thrown forward helter-skelter, spinning in the human maelstrom, clinging to others, seeking his balance. The people in front began to go down. Those behind, unable to get their footing, finding their forward support gone, were cast down on top. Bernoit, thrashing, pushing at people to retain his balance, felt his sleeve gripped and wrestled to free himself but was swept on regardless. The sleeve ripped from his arm; the force of the release threw him to his knees. He felt men fall behind him and scrambled on his hands and knees up the growing heap of human beings.

He was quick enough in his panic to reach the top and hurl himself over and tumble down to the other side. He slithered somehow to his feet by grabbing at the coat tails of others and pulling himself up. Behind him more were being cast on the dying heap, but now the tide was sweeping over the mound, staggering down, tramping all to death. Bernoit once more found himself in the pack and was carried along as helpless as before. MacDonald was nowhere in sight.

Now they were beside the river and a new hazard was emerging. The people on the fringes of the bank had no protection and those pushing past were driving them into the black, freezing water. Bernoit was being forced perceptibly towards the bank and tried to alter direction, but to no avail. He found himself on the very fringes of the crowd, being pressed closer and closer to the river with its drifting ice floes and floating corpses. The bridge was only ten paces away. He saw a young woman clinging to a baby and as he looked she was knocked aside and teetered for a moment before beginning to fall. Urgently he reached out and grabbed her, swinging her up beside him. She was nearly safe and smiled her thanks, her face pretty and tender. But Bernoit was pushed from behind and to save himself he had to let go. She fell back silently, still holding her child, to sink in the hungry water. Bernoit fought to retain his balance. By clutching at others he was again carried along in the flow which brought him at last to the bridge.

Here the trestles came up to his waist for the bridge began some distance back up the bank, where detachments of grenadiers and pontonniers were struggling hopelessly to direct the mobs. Bernoit wrapped his arms round the trestle and began to climb up as others were doing before him, but he felt very tired. He called to the people on the bridge to help him but no one turned to his aid. Each trudged past, intent only on his own survival. But the people behind were pushing and at last he managed to wriggle on to a beam and pull himself up on to the deck of the bridge.

Movement was much easier now for there were no obstacles to block the way and the procession had become orderly and regular. Bernoit imagined that, like himself, everyone else felt quieter in their minds now that they were actually on the bridge. The control parties at the bridgehead were clearly achieving something. However, there was still danger, for the surface was thick with manure and the whole structure was shaky and sagging. There was no guard rail and Bernoit was dreadfully aware how easy it would be to slip, and fall into the river. He wondered how long the bridge would be able to stand up to this heavy traffic.

There were groups of Dutch engineers standing up to their necks in the icy water carrying out repairs. Bernoit remembered General Eblé and his men last night. And here they were again, still at their wretched work. One of them dropped from exhaustion and cold, and quietly disappeared. Their fortitude was amazing. Their faces were drawn and haggard, and blue with cold. Bernoit hoped that there was dry clothing, and shelter and food waiting when their work was done, but he doubted it.

As he crossed he realised that he had been hearing gunfire all day and he noted from its direction that Victor must now have fallen right back on Studyanka and be surrounded by Wittgenstein's army. On the other bank there was firing from the south and he concluded that Chichagov had come up and was being held back by the troops which had already crossed. He supposed that Ney's corps would be there somewhere, but he did not really care. He was cold and tired and the sweat which had run so freely was now chilling on his body. He wanted only to find somewhere sheltered to sleep and pushed forward, anxious to reach the other bank.

At last he came to the end of the bridge and found himself walking over the frozen marshland. Even in summer this would be a depressing quagmire but now it was a frozen white waste, badly churned up in places by the mass of men and horses and vehicles which had crossed. The ice was broken and twice Bernoit stepped into the clinging mud, and had the utmost difficulty in pulling himself free. When he reached firmer ground he sat down to rest.

The main body of the crowd was curving in great, merging columns away from the two straining bridges out on to the road through Fremin to Vilna. Bernoit watched them wearily. He would not follow yet, but would find a place where he could sleep. Behind him he could see the Young Guard standing in line protecting that flank against any further Russian advance and he noticed the Lancers, who had crossed before him, drawn up in support. There was a fearful amount of shooting going on and cannon-balls and shells came whistling overhead. He wondered how long the bridgehead could last.

Looking back at the crowd he tried to see MacDonald, but he realised that in this enormous mass it would be impossible to identify any individual. He gave up the exercise with a deep regret and wondered if he would ever see the tall, silent man again.

Nearby, some soldiers had a fire going and he rose and staggered over to share its warmth. The men around it sat huddled and cold and many who had chosen to swim across the river sat naked, with their clothes spread out, in the pious hope that they would dry. Bernoit nestled himself into this group to benefit from its shelter and started to inspect his equipment to see how it had fared in the mêlée.

His beautiful fur coat was ruined, both sleeves gone, the rest shredded into separate pelts. His heavy greatcoat was no better, buttonless and tattered. He would require to find some new protection for his body. Still, he could salvage the fur to bind his feet and wrap his head. That prospect appealed to him but he was too listless to actually do anything. He would rest in the glow of the fire. Tomorrow, he could seek a corpse with all that he needed. It might be as well to take a new cartridge case, for the old strap had almost gone. Certainly there would be no difficulty in replacing the musket, although he regretted the one he had lost for it had belonged to Necker.

He lay back to sleep, knowing that he should really be attending to these matters. It would be dark soon and he realised, with an awful appreciation of its meaning, that in this great, lost mass of humanity, he was alone.

13

The cold daylight was beginning to fade and the straggling lines were drawing closer for protection as the night set in. Already fires were being lit as the weary men and women prepared to settle down for the night. It was some time since the Cossacks had last ventured a raid, killing a few stragglers before being chased away by the remnants of the cuirassier regiment nearby. It had been snowing all day but Bernoit had made a good march and the horrible memories of last night were distant from his mind as he looked around for a place to shelter. For days he had been following the same routine because he had been all alone since he had crossed the Berezina a week before.

Last night he had been lucky to be near a window when the townspeople smashed their way into the room and began their slaughter. He had been able to leap into the street outside and escape the carnage. The ferocity of the attack had appalled him and in vengeance he had returned to the house with the men from the street. The brutality of their retaliation had so reminded him of his time in Spain. He recalled the blood running from the door and the mutilated bodies in the room where he had slept. He had been fortunate to avoid the cruel hands of the villagers of Moledechno.

His good fortune did not appear to have left him for he had been on hand when the commissary waggon had broken down. The rapacity with which they had plundered it, all those who were near, had left nothing for others who came later. All day he had been anticipating the meal he would enjoy tonight, and as he marched the bottle of cognac in his pack gurgled merrily. Nonetheless, he knew that he was helpless on his own. If he sat by one of the fires and tried to cook his potatoes the others there would steal from him and he would be unable to defend his meal. He watched all the time for

162

some place where he could shelter alone and eat undisturbed.

Not far away he saw a strange mound of snow and his practised eye told him that there would be refuge there. It was distant enough from the mainstream of the march to be ignored by most people as too exposed to attack, but Bernoit was prepared to take that risk. He trudged up the slope, knee deep in the snow, to approach it. As he came near he saw that it was an abandoned waggon lying at a crazy angle and the snow had drifted over its canvas cover. He would be snug in there.

He drew open the cover and crawled into the gloom inside. Snow had formed a soft floor lying level between the bottom of the waggon and the side. He grunted with satisfaction. He could spread his blanket there and lie down with comparative comfort, and he would light a small cooking fire at the entrance. It would be beautifully heated, although he realised there would be problems with condensation. Perhaps there was a tarpaulin in the driver's box. He would have a look later. In the meantime he must cut some firewood.

He pulled off his pack and placed it on the snow floor and carefully propped his musket against the slanting floor of the waggon. He heard an intake of breath, a slight gasp startling him, and he peered anxiously into the other end of the vehicle. A huddled figure was there, only just visible as his eyes became accustomed to the dark. A face was watching him intently and he saw in the dim light that it was a woman.

'We'll be cosy enough in here,' he said, but the woman said nothing, staring at him nervously with dark, round eyes.

'We'll be all right, don't you worry. I'm just going out for wood—we'll have a fire going in no time.' But the woman still said nothing, and Bernoit was saddened because he was lonely. He turned to leave when he had a thought and rummaged in his pack to produce the cognac which he offered to her, crawling over to hand it to her.

'Here, take some of this. You'll feel better,' And the woman took the bottle from him, without saying anything, but she nodded listlessly. Bernoit saw that she was young, fifteen or sixteen, and she looked very pretty to him. He felt his loins stir and said abruptly, 'Don't move. I'll be back in a couple of minutes and we'll get a fire going.'

He clambered out of the shelter and moved further up the slope to a thicket he had seen earlier. It would be dark very soon and he toiled quickly, hacking with his sword at the stubborn undergrowth. He cut only branches which would burn well, and trimmed them into manageable size. The work was hard and he felt himself beginning to sweat despite the cold. He piled his little logs into bundles and when he thought he had ample he began to carry them back to the waggon. All around him were the glowing points of light where the ruined army had made its bivouacs for the night, and the glare from the fires was rendering the sky orange as the daylight ebbed away.

Bernoit stacked his firewood carefully in the waggon but it looked a pitifully small amount. He hoped there would be enough to keep the fire burning most of the night, but he doubted it. Well, that was a problem which could wait. He was too tired to go seeking more wood now. If the worst came to the worst he could start burning the timber vehicle, although that would diminish the value of the shelter. He set his fire on the snow floor, took out his tinderbox and struck a spark. He blew the tinder into a flame which he applied to the dry twigs he had assembled and blew again until the flame grew and the fire started to sparkle and crackle.

Content, he turned to the girl, 'There,' he said, 'we'll be lovely and warm in a minute.'

She sat, clutching the bottle of cognac, and nodded mutely. He remembered the tarpaulin and scrambled past her to search in the driver's box. The woman did not move as he passed. As he expected, the box had been broken open and he had to dig under the snow to search with his hands. It was too dark to see what he was doing, but he could feel the usual tackle, frozen ropes, blocks and then he felt the oilcloth. He swore with pleasure and dug furiously until he had freed the clumsy thing. He pulled it back into the waggon and spread it out, struggling with its stiff folds.

'This'll keep us dry!' he exclaimed with a grin to the woman. To his surprise he saw her smile in the firelight and for the first time she spoke:

'You must be cold. Here.' And she handed him back the bottle. With his numb fingers he pulled out the cork and took one short drink.

'It's good stuff this, eh?'

She nodded back and smiled again and Bernoit thought she looked very lovely and felt pleasure at her closeness.

He turned back to his fire and placed another two logs on it.

He would soon be able to cook. He removed his pannikin from his pack, half filled it with snow and balanced it on the fire. Then he picked out his stolen potatoes and piled them on the tarpaulin, adding after a moment's thought the one sausage which he had been able to retain. He drew his sword and winked at the woman.

'Even the Emperor would be glad of a meal like this,' he joked and began to cut the meat with his sword. But his fingers were clumsy and he carelessly nicked his thumb. He swore in irritation and hacked at the sausage impatiently.

The girl laughed at his bad temper and said teasingly, 'But the Emperor would have someone to do that for him.' Her voice was sweet and musical to him.

The snow in his pannikin had melted now so Bernoit dropped in the potatoes and sausage.

The fire was slowly heating the interior of their shelter, spluttering and sizzling in its pool of molten snow, but the wood smoke was becoming a nuisance. Bernoit drew back the canvas cover slightly to let the smoke escape and was impressed to note that the flap was already stiff with frost. He looked out and dimly saw the outline of the valley with the speckled jewels of the campfires. He blessed his good fortune and wisdom in selecting this shelter. Men must be dying in their hundreds out there on a night like this.

The food was almost ready and the girl was kneeling by the fire watching. Her hood had fallen back and he saw that she had long, brown hair. He felt an end to loneliness with her presence for it had been days since he had spoken to anyone as a companion. He wondered if MacDonald or Larguien were out there somewhere, huddled by a campfire, trying to eke warmth from the bitter night.

He lifted the hot pannikin from the fire, gasped at the searing pain, and gingerly placed it on the snow.

'I nearly dropped it then,' he said.

The girl dipped her fingers into the pot and lifted out a potato, juggling it from hand to hand, and nibbled at it hungrily. He watched her gratefully, reflecting that it was good to share his meal with her. It was strange that they had both assumed that she would eat, and that nothing had been said about it. These supplies had been meant to last him for several days and he would have killed rather than share them.

He took a morsel himself and it was hot in his hands but he

stuffed it into his mouth and let it scorch his tongue. It tasted incredibly good and he reached out for more. He had not realised how hungry he was. They both gobbled the stew with the fury of the starving. Their whole being centred on that little pot of food and they ate without stopping, without speaking, but noisily, and even in their haste they took pains to lose not the slightest morsel. Too soon it was finished and the pot was empty, save for the watery juices lying on the bottom. Bernoit seized the pannikin and began to drink, but he became aware of the grey round eyes watching him. He only took one share and passed the pannikin over. She took it without thanks and drained it and then placed it on the snow where they looked at it sadly.

'Ah well,' murmured Bernoit and reached for the bottle.

She moved close to him and leaned on his shoulder and gently placed her hand on his chest. Her eyes looked into him, deep still pools.

'You are very kind,' she whispered, and she smiled at him, but her face was serious and calm. He felt her breath on his cheek and held her gaze and he was at ease.

Gentle it was with the girl beside him and the snow outside cocooning them from its chill. The fire-cast shadows danced merry around them and nothing stirred without. His arm around her, they nursed away their loneliness and she, soft against him, her grey eyes wide in wonder. Then in the tender silence her lips were cool upon him and her neck smooth to his. Her breath rustled hot beside his ear. Their aching bodies wrapped together and he came into her and they were one. And the misery all around them knew nothing of their love.

Cold found them thus and parted them. A drowsy Bernoit rose and stoked the fire and gathered up their furs and clothing and brought them to make a bed. Together they lay in the softness and her head was on his shoulder. Her caressing fingers rippled on his chest and paused to search his scar, puckered and hard. Concern flickered in her eyes. Gruffly he spoke to her.

'Jena that was. A long time ago.'

She smiled her love at him and closed her heavy lids. Lulled, they slipped deep into sound and dreamless sleep.

Quiet they lay and the glowing logs crackled to keep them safe. Yet the night was long and the flames, unfed, starved and, like the suffering souls without, began to fade. And stricken to the heart, the fire slowly died. In time the embers chilled and frost crept in beside the sleeping pair. Bernoit, roused by the icy cold, opened his rested eyes and saw the glimmer of dawn in the eastern sky. It was time to move again.

He woke the girl and she smiled a bright welcome to the day.

'We'll get going as soon as we're ready,' he suggested.

Reluctantly they exposed their nakedness to the bitter air and hastened to clothe themselves. He broke the last of his bread and gave her half.

'Have you anything to carry?'

'No,' she replied, 'I have nothing now but my clothes.'

Bernoit gathered his bits and pieces together. He wiped out the pannikin with snow and packed it carefully away, together with his cognac. His knapsack was nearly empty and there was now no food in it. He thought ruefully back to the days when it had been crammed with meat, and wondered what he would be able to scavenge in the course of the day. He put on his crossbelts, feeling his sword and bayonet settle against his hip and the rigid shape of his cartridge box under his ribs. For a moment he contemplated taking the tarpaulin, but decided it was too clumsy and heavy, and he left it lying. He swung on his pack, pulled his blanket over his head and shoulders and picked up his musket.

'Come on,' he said, 'let's see what today brings,' and gently he lifted her from the waggon. She put her arms round him and drew his head down to meet her hungry mouth.

'There, my gallant *voltigeur*,' she said; 'today will bring tonight.'

Thus encouraged, Bernoit led her away. It was strange to be marching with a woman after his days of loneliness. He felt that he had lost some of his independence and freedom and now there were two mouths to feed. He strode on at his regular pace, but she could not keep up and he had to slow down to stay with her. He watched her bravely stepping out, her face grim and determined, and he smiled to himself. Her companionship was well worth the extra effort that would be required of him.

The march, barring the girl's presence and the slower pace, was monotonously identical to all the wretched days before. The same blackening corpses sat round their last fires, the dead and dying men sprawled out along the road. Everywhere were broken vehicles and abandoned guns, the horses frozen in their traces. Endless stretched the long undulating steppeland, one great, white, frozen plain bespecked with ruined villages, woods and stiffening corpses as the ice gleamed with sullen hatred at the ragged, pitiful columns of the dying that struggled across its freezing surface.

The drifting snow of the previous day had frozen hard in the night giving them a clean surface to walk on and their fur-wrapped feet clung to the ice, preventing their slipping. Sometimes the frozen crust would not support them and they fell through into the softer snow below. Once the girl sank to her waist and Bernoit had to stop and help her free.

They felt a need to communicate that was more than physical and so they talked and their conversation eased the march. Bernoit found himself confiding the small things about himself in a way he had not known since his wife, Thérèse, had died in Spain. There was joy in companionship and freedom in speech that he had not felt from the day that Étienne Vernier had been slain.

She, too, had been alone. Her man had fallen at Borodino and then she had followed the retinue of General van der Gelder. Posing as a stable boy she had been discovered but had been well enough treated by the General's staff. At the crossing of the Berezina she had become separated and had been friendless since.

In time as the morning wore on their conversation became sporadic with only intermittent remarks, and Bernoit found his mind drifting into its old marching shell, devoid of thought other than the regular crunch of his tramping feet as his legs found their rhythm and his pack and musket settled their weight on his shoulders. League after league they marched over the interminable steppe and his eyes saw nothing but the crystalline formations of the snow as it sparkled under his plodding feet in infinite beauty and tedious variety.

They stopped to watch a remarkable sight, an entire brigade of light cavalry gliding past in sleighs. These men were chasseurs but had lost most of their horses and some intelligent officer had thought of using sleighs. There must have been two hundred sledges, each drawn by one horse and holding two or three well armed men. They gazed with envy as the soldiers slipped quickly past, unwearied and safe from attack.

Then the brigade was gone and they saw that they were isolated, and the nearest formed unit was some infantry about a half a mile away. Instinctively they began to edge closer to it, for

168

they knew only too well how quickly Cossacks could appear. Moreover, there was a village not far ahead and they had both learned to fear Russian peasants.

They had made their move just in time for they heard the shots and screams behind them as Cossacks darted over the ridge to cut a bloody swathe of death through the straggling bands. They fled straight towards the formed infantry and Bernoit saw that the regiment was hastily forming square. He looked over his shoulder and saw that the Cossacks were in greater number than usual, a veritable horde sweeping towards them. There was only just time to reach the square before the Cossack lances caught them.

The girl fell. Bernoit ran on for a pace or two before he realised. He turned back to help her up and threw his arm round her. He doubted if there was time to reach safety, yet he held to her and dragged her along with him in the desperate race. Again she fell and he stopped by her.

'I'm sorry,' she cried pitifully but he shook his head. It was too late now and nothing mattered. He quickly unslung his musket.

The enemy were almost upon him now but the square was just behind him and they reined up, afraid to approach. One, bolder than the others, spurred forward and stabbed at them with his lance. Bernoit fired and the Cossack toppled back from his pony. Seizing the girl by the arm, Bernoit dragged her into the protecting ranks, unaware that the enemy had ridden off in search of easier targets.

She was in his arms and he felt her tears against his neck.

'I'm sorry, so sorry,' she wept.

He held her to him and comforted her, oblivious of the men around forming back into column and preparing to march. A friendly officer touched his arm and said gently, 'I think you'd better stay with us. That was damned perilous.'

Bernoit nodded and moved with the girl in his arms, supporting her as they fell in behind the marching regiment. He made a note to reload his musket at the first opportunity but now he had to give his efforts to cheering the girl along as she strode out, gallantly doing her best to keep up with the hurrying column.

The day passed without further incident and, although they needed frequent rests, they managed to stay within reach of the regiment, but it was not till well after nightfall that they finally reached Smorgon. Every house in the town was packed with soldiers and there were the usual dreadful scenes in the streets. It was now very cold and the unruly were ripping apart coaches and houses and burning them in huge fires in the open streets.

Bernoit considered that in this cold they should have shelter. He felt the girl snuggle to him when he put his arm round her. 'Let's see if we can find room in the inn,' he said, and she looked up at him and smiled.

It took them a while to find a place where there was room and warmth, but eventually they found a house which did not seem too crowded. They could not find an empty room so they entered one which had only half a dozen men in it and Bernoit sat the girl down and started to remove his equipment. As he eased off his pack he saw that the men were wearing tattered brown rags which he could only just identify as Portuguese uniforms. It ruffled him slightly for he could recall the Caçadores, the Portuguese riflemen in Wellington's army, and he had bitter memories of their brown andy yellow uniforms. However, he spoke jocularly in Spanish.

'Good evening, muchachos. It's colder here than Oporto.'

One man was breaking up furniture and heaping it on the fire.

'Yes,' he said, 'it is very cold, but we'll be warm enough tonight,' and he spoke in rapid Portuguese to his comrades. They laughed loudly and leered at the girl. The spokesman added something and there was a tenseness. Bernoit knew immediately that something was wrong.

'Come on,' he said, 'let's get out of here,' and he reached for his musket as she stood up, not understanding. An arm restrained him and two men were at the door.

'No, senhor, I think not.'

He kicked out at once and tried to draw his sword but they threw themselves upon him. Down he went in a welter of flying fists and feet. Someone tried inexpertly to knee him in the groin. He took the blow on his upper thigh, and rolled back and broke free. His sword was out instantly and he held all six of them at bay.

'Get out!' he yelled to the girl. 'Get out of here!'

She moved too slowly and two of them darted to catch here. Bernoit lunged forward at her attackers but was seized by the others and disarmed. They threw him back in a corner and one of them presented his own sword to his throat.

The man who had spoken before and who seemed to be the ringleader walked over to Bernoit and said quietly, 'Frenchman, you are a fortunate man. My beloved is a country. But now you will know, as I know, what it is to witness your beloved's rape.'

Bernoit roared and tired to struggle to his feet but the arms pinioning him were too strong. The sword pricked his throat and he felt the blood trickle down his neck.

The girl kicked and struggled as they tore at her clothes·and she screamed aloud for help. They silenced her by threatening to castrate Bernoit. A blade jabbed at Bernoit to emphasise the threat. He squirmed in horror. The sharp steel was perilously close, piercing his trousers. A gleeful voice said:

'I don't think you'll make any noise, will you?'

Bernoit scowled and fought the dangerous desire to spit in the man's grinning face.

She was naked now and they were pinioning her legs and arms. She thrashed and wriggled but they held her on the floor before Bernoit's appalled eyes. One of them threw himself upon her and forced into her. She screamed, a racking shriek of agony and offence, and she spat in her rapist's face.

The assailant was mauling at her breasts and biting them and Bernoit could see that his teeth were drawing blood. He roared in fury and tried to break loose. But those blades were at his throat and his genitals. He spat, powerless. His guards sneered at his rage.

'Always the same,' one of them winked. 'Relax and enjoy it.'

Bernoit sagged back. He hoped she could stand up to it. As she lay there naked, subjected to the obscenities of these vile people, he made a point of remembering every face, concentrating on every minor detail of expression. MacDonald would be the man for a job like this. Bernoit swore that given the chance he would have vengeance from every man of them.

He had lost count of how many there had been but now the jesting bayonet-wielder was handing over his charge. Bernoit watched them like a cat. In their sexual anticipation they were being careless. He tensed, ready for a move.

Suddenly the door opened. Two Swiss officers walked in. Everyone turned to look, but Bernoit, taut as a spring, bounded to one side, clear of the sword at his throat. He found himself holding the bayonet. The sword flickered beside him and he twisted aside. He saw an exposed gap and thrust up under the man's chin. A scream, and then Bernoit dashed, yelling to the two officers.

171

They waved him back. They had drawn their pistols instantly and there were four lethal barrels pointing into the room. Bernoit backed against the wall so that there would be clear fields of fire. One of the Swiss beckoned to a servant who threw a blanket to the girl. As she drew it round her violated body Bernoit watched, close to tears. He realised that he did not know her name.

One of the officers was looking at him closely and Bernoit thought he recognised the face. 'Corporal Bertrand?'

'Bernoit, sir, Sergeant-Major. Captain de Begos.'

'Colonel.' And they looked at each other as old comrades.

'Well, Sergeant-Major?'

'You saw for yourself. This lady and I . . . '

'Quite! Well, Captain Galveias, what have you to say?'

Bernoit was amazed for the ringleader wore no insignia of rank, though he replied arrogantly:

'You'd take the word of a common soldier?'

'I saw what I saw. But above all I've served with him and I've served with you. Get out of here and take this riff-raff with you — including that,' and the Colonel pointed to the tortured man whom Bernoit had stabbed. He added to his companion, 'Captain Langst, see these gentlemen out of doors, if you please.'

When the Portuguese had gone, de Begos tucked his pistols away and moved to leave the room. He paused at the door. 'I had thought to take this room myself but in the circumstances . . . If it's any consolation to Mademoiselle the Captain belongs to one of the finest families in Portugal. A splendid ally. Be very gentle, Bernoit. I'll have a sentry in the corridor.' And he left, closing the door behind him.

She was sitting still, staring at the door, when he went to her, tears dripping from his face. 'Oh my darling, my darling,' and he wrapped his arms round her body. For a moment she sat stiff and wretched and then collapsed sobbing against him. Harshly, she wept at the foulness and the pain and Bernoit was compassionate with love. He tucked the blanket close to keep her warm and in time her misery gave way to sleep. With her dark hair spread on his chest Bernoit lay listening to her heaving breath and bitterly watched the flickering firelight on the ceiling. He seethed to avenge her and, scowling, remembered the faces of the men. Eventually sleep came to him.

It was late when they woke and daylight filled the room. Bernoit could see that she was severely worn by the night and his anger soared again. But hunger gnawed and he knew she needed food.

'I'll try to find something to eat,' he said, but she clung to him in terror.

'Don't leave me!'

He found himself restrained against her torn, bruised breasts. And sleep, anew, cleansed them.

Later, much later, he wakened in a sudden panic to be away, to be rid of the vileness of Smorgon. They rose and hastened to dress. He paused to look at her beauty and said:

'You're very lovely.'

Flustered, she took fright and covered herself. Bernoit turned his back to protect her modesty while she dressed. She came up behind him and wound her arms round him, kissing his ear.

'You're very good to me,' she murmured.

'Come on. Let's find ourselves a meal.'

But in Smorgon that day there was nothing to eat and they left the city a little before noon, with only a drop of cognac in their bellies to keep out the bitter cold. For it was cold, icily cold, and the cold sought them out as they marched, finding weaknesses in the warmest of clothing, chilling them with the cutting wind and offering them no relief.

'Never mind,' said Bernoit, 'once we're in Vilna everything will be all right. Plenty of food, clean uniforms, warm beds, you'll see.'

But Vilna was three, maybe four day's march ahead and in the cold that was an eternity. Above all they were hungry and they felt themselves perceptibly weaker for lack of nourishment. At every fire they came to they stopped to rest and seek food, but there was never any. They stopped at farms as they passed and in hamlets but found nothing, and so they starved while the sun, hidden behind the deep banks of snow cloud, moved remorselessly over them, hidden all the while until it sank below the steppe as if it had never been there.

They found a fire that night in the shelter of a burned out barn and they sat round it deriving warmth from each other and the others who sat huddled round. They broke timbers from the building and cast them to the flames in the pious hope that this would bring heat, but it was so cold that the snow around the fire did not melt, but turned to ice. And no one at the fire had food for himself, let alone to share.

173

Bernoit sat there with the girl enduring the long vigil of that night and they leaned against the wall of the old barn with their blankets wrapped around them. His arm lay round her neck and his hand settled on her breast and she huddled close to him, her hair tucked under her hood, her hand lying in the warmth of his thighs. Time and again they felt the chill reaching their backs and had to jerk forward to break the icy contact which had frozen them to the wall. She had wanted to move close to the fire but Bernoit remembered the fate of Yvel so they stayed back, nestled against the wall, and from time to time one of them managed to doze in the soft, comforting arms of the others.

When dawn came they were both asleep and only the movement of others stirred Bernoit or they might have lain entwined for ever, like the fringe of frozen corpses round the fire.

Bernoit looked at the girl and nearly wept. The night had wrought terrible vengeance on her and she was gaunt and hollow-eyed. She looked up innocently and asked, 'Is there anything to eat?' and Bernoit saw hard-bitten veterans like himself turn away and shuffle off, afraid to answer. He shook his head sadly and said as cheerily as he could, 'No, but let's have a hot drink.'

He took out his little pannikin and filled it with snow. Patiently he waited while it melted and then tried hard to boil. Around the fire a few lethargic faces watched curiously as he added cognac to the bubbling water and handed it to her. She drank thirstily and he could see the hot spirit take effect. Then she stopped guiltily and offered the pot to him.

'I'm sorry, I've taken more than my share.'

'No darling, take it all.'

But she insisted and he swallowed the fiery liquid and felt the day improve. It did not improve very much. The temperature must be very low, he thought, as they prepared to move away. The whole landscape was frozen, one eternal sea of ice, glittering evilly and treacherous under foot.

It was a dreadful morning. As they marched they saw men collapse beside them, chilled and unable to go on, and they stepped over them, leaving them to die. On every hand there were corpses and as they passed woods they saw that the crows were sitting in the trees, dead, frozen to the branches. Sometimes they passed fires where men sat staring into the flames, waiting for death, and occasionally they stopped at such a fire to rest. All the time Bernoit was aware of the girl beside him and he kept his arm round her for he could see that she was failing.

About midday they came to a fire where men sat listless and they stopped to rest, hoping perhaps to catch some morsel of food. But no one there had anything to eat. They had news, however, and it was terrible in its implication.

'Antoine's right enough. He left last night. We heard it from a bloke in the Second Lancers ' And the speaker emphasised his comments by gesticulating with the stump of a recently amputated arm.

'He wouldn't leave us, not like this.'

'He bloody has,' chipped in Antoine, the grenadier.

'I don't believe it! Why would he leave us?'

'Oh, he told me, didn't he? Take one bloody look around, son—there's not much to leave. Anyway he left Murat in command.'

With a feeling of awful certainty Bernoit knew that they were speaking of Napoleon and was appalled that he could abandon yet another army.

'Just like Egypt,' he said. 'And only last week I saw a friend shot for desertion.'

'Dead right there, pal,' said the grenadier. 'I was in Egypt. Ought to have learned—at least it was hot there.'

'There must have been some reason. He'll have gone to bring an army to relieve us,' said a gunner sergeant.

'Yeh? What army? This is the only one he's got. Look at it.'

'But he left the King of Naples in command.'

A thick German accent spoke: 'Oh, that is good, no? The King of Naples. I tell you about the King of Naples, your precious Murat. I am a lancer, no?'

'You're a Prussian,' exclaimed the Bonapartist gunner. 'A German traitor! Get away from this fire. No wonder the Emperor doesn't trust you lot.'

'Tell me, do you trust your Emperor now?'

'Ha ha! Very good Hans,' laughed the one-armed man. 'I like that. Just you stay where you are. What were you saying about Murat?'

'Just that he destroyed the cavalry.'

'He is the greatest cavalryman in history,' protested the Bonapartist.

'I think, my little gunner, that to be a great cavalryman you have to know about horses. Murat knows how to kill horses. That

175

is all. To take care of them, of this he knows nothing. He is a colourful popinjay—a useless princeling and impostor. And your Emperor has placed us in his trust. God help us all.'

'I'll tell you what,' said the one-armed man, 'if our little man has cleared out it's because even his blessed star can't get us out of this one.'

Bernoit turned to the girl. 'Do you feel up to moving on?' he asked. She eyed him wearily but nodded assent and rose to her feet. The one-armed man looked up.

'You don't hang about, do you? Fancy some company?' and without waiting for an answer he rose with his grenadier friend and joined them. Uninvited, the Prussian lancer also joined them, with a contemptuous look at the sad circle round the fire.

'These men will all soon die,' he pronounced in epitaph and they marched on in silence.

They were a strange little band. Bernoit and the girl, the one-armed man and his grenadier friend and the Prussian trudging along in his clumsy riding boots. They were isolated from anyone else, from the corpses, from the dying men at the fires, from other groups like themselves, and from the disintegrating columns of ordered troops. They moved along quietly with only the constant tramping of their feet on the hard ice disturbing the lethal silence of that awful frost. Their outer garments froze and their breath, crystallising immediately, formed icicles on their whiskers and beards and in a delicate, beautiful tracery on the girl's hair.

At first they took comfort from their common plight, each caring about the other, but soon they were only aware of the shadowy spectres around them as foot followed foot in the timeless treadmill of the retreat. Bernoit's arm slipped from the girl's waist and gradually she became another shadow to him as his mind closed in, wrapped in its chill tomb of death and frost. They drifted into the main flow of the march and, uncaring, trampled thoughtless over the unhappy souls who had fallen. Once they came to a general, trapped beneath his horse, crying to be set free. Bernoit, recognising the man's plight for one selfless instant, stepped around him, but others unseeing walked over him. Thus they carried on, a thinning column of dying men, so close to death that it was of indifference to them, something which instinct told them to avoid, but of which they had no fear, no understanding. Deep in their minds, at the very kernel of their consciousness, was the desire for food and, as the day began to die like all who had perished during it, this desire became an urgent, crying need.

It was the one-armed man who saw the barn, just as night was casting its shadow over this misery. 'There's the very place,' he cried. 'There's a fire. There's bound to be something to eat. There'll be shelter and warmth.' The little group moved towards the beckoning fire, amidst the flock of others attracted like moths by the flame.

It was at that moment that Bernoit saw that she had gone. He could not remember taking his arm away. He could not even think when he had last seen her. She was not there, among them, and he had no knowledge of when he had lost her. He was stricken, thinking of her, alone out there, lying perhaps under the ever trampling feet. He cried out in anguish, knowing the hopelessness of search for her, and the one-armed man took him gently by the shoulder and led him into the shelter of the barn.

14

It was cold, wickedly cold, colder than Bernoit had ever known, ever imagined. It was so cold that the large fires in the barn were giving out no heat and the men sitting round them hunched frozen and dead, while others climbed over their stiff, icy corpses in the vain hope of warmth. In the little open hut beside the barn men had drawn in an enormous fir tree and placed it on the dying fire but the flames licked around it without success.

Bernoit's feet and arms were agonisingly cold and it was very tempting to sit motionless and let them go numb, but he had seen this happen to many other men, so he stamped his feet and flapped his arms to prevent them from freezing. He could feel the ice clawing into his body, stirring in the marrow of his bones, penetrating into his heart, his lungs, his stomach. He sat there on the mound of frozen corpses, unaware that his coat was stiffening in the frost; unaware of the ice that formed between him and his seat; unaware of anything except the appalling cold . . . and hunger.

Others, too, sat there freezing to death, blank faces, bearded and filthy, watching the useless fires with black, empty eyes. Sometimes one of them would move forward and throw more wood on the fire and it would blaze hurriedly, sending sparks among them, in the murky smoke-filled place, and the soaring flames would throw out a light which might just have been heat.

Into this hall of dying others crawled for shelter, because, impossibly, it was even colder out in the open where the bitter wind cut cold to a man's innards. A general crawled in, an elderly man, an engineer, and he settled himself before the flames. From his pocket he drew a morsel of bread and held it so that all could see. Every living eye watched as, bite by bite, he devoured it, eating with such care that not a single crumb was lost. When he had done he hunched forward to gaze into the fire as if will, alone, could extend his meal. And all who had seen turned away to dream of food in what little was left of their conscious minds.

Bernoit sat unmoving in the cold, for he felt very weak. His mind returned again and again to the general slipping that last crumb into his mouth. He felt that if he could only eat that one crumb he would be content. It was impossible to go on without food. He had no energy, no desire to do anything or to move. He could just sit there and let the numbness creep over him. He was too weak to do anything else. If only he could find something to eat, to restore his strength. His body cried out for nourishment. If he had food he could endure the cold, but he knew there was none so he sat there, stamping and flapping his arms, unconsciously, becoming weaker and weaker and thinking all the time about that last crumb.

Later, much later, when the pile of corpses had climbed icily to the roof and the dying sat brooding, mindless, Bernoit thought that he could smell burning meat and knew that he had finally lost his mind, so he sat stamping and flapping, waiting to die. But something was tugging at his sleeve and he looked round, puzzled, trying to understand. The one-armed man was there, grinning at him, pulling and gesturing, but Bernoit could not comprehend what he was saying and shrugged, incurious. The grenadier was there too and reached out his hands to Bernoit.

'Here, eat this—it's good,' and he put a large piece of hot meat into Bernoit's hands. Bernoit looked up, perplexed. Where had this come from? It was charred and smoked and he saw that it had been placed right in the centre of the fire. It was too good to be true and he suspected there must be some trick. He looked around with cunning but no one was watching him, except the one-armed man and the grenadier, grinning at him. He grinned back and then ravenously bit into the meat.

It was delicious, sweet tasting and fresh, fine tender meat, cooked so that the juices ran down his chin and clogged greasily on his beard. There was plenty of it, hot, beautiful food. Even as he ate he felt his condition improve. He had not eaten meat like this before. It tasted vaguely like fresh pork. He wondered what it was and where it had come from. He smiled up at the two men and paused briefly in his meal to say, 'It's very good.'

'There's plenty more,' said the one-armed man and Bernoit followed the half-concealed flicker of his eye to the nearby corner of the barn. Crouched on the mound of corpses was the Prussian

179

lancer, his sabre out, cutting ample slices from the thighs of the dead.

Bernoit nearly vomited and threw the meat from his hands. 'For Christ's sake,' he swore, 'you filthy bastards.'

'You were enjoying it until you knew,' the one-armed man said plaintively, his feelings hurt.

'We probably saved your life with it,' said the grenadier.

'You should finish eating it,' the one-armed man said. 'You'll die if you don't.'

Bernoit turned away in disgust, but he knew that they were perfectly right. His personal revulsion was a mere vanity, a dangerous luxury. Eating man in these circumstances made more sense than his normal trade of killing man. The two men facing him were genuinely aggrieved, hurt by his rejection of their aid. He tried to make amends.

'I'm sorry,' he said, 'I shouldn't have done that. It's just . . . '

The grenadier smiled again, 'It's all right pal, we understand. I was the same myself the first time. We've been eating it for days. It's kept us alive.'

The one-armed man added, 'A lot of the lads don't like the idea. You've got to keep it quiet. We wouldn't have bothered you only we felt bad about the girl.'

The girl. Bernoit had forgotten all about her. Where was she now? Lying dead, frozen stiff on the great white wastes? If she had been here he would have made her eat. There was nothing he could do to protect her now, to put his shielding arm round her soft, fragile body and brush the frost from her long brown hair. He felt the tears start in his eyes and they ran down his cheeks in his wretchedness. He recalled in ultimate misery that he had never learned her name.

The two soldiers looked at him in pity and quietly moved away, leaving him sitting motionless on his bed of corpses as the cold sought new ways of entering his wasted body and froze the tears on his face.

He had not moved for a long time and now he felt his body still and numb. He began to stir himself, rubbing feeling into his chilled limbs. He brushed the icicles from his face. If he stayed like this he would die. He wriggled restlessly at the thought of the Prussian lancer cutting slices from his flesh. His eyes drifted down to the charred meat he had thrown away. It lay where it had fallen and none of the dying men around him had taken it. His mind rebelled from the idea but he was very hungry and he knew that he was stronger from the morsel he had already eaten. It had tasted so delicious.

In the end his hunger won and he crawled forward and gingerly retrieved it. He looked around guiltily to see if he was being watched and he felt the eyes of all living men watching him. He hesitated, but then necessity overcame his sensitivity and he bit into it. It did not taste so good as before and it was cold now and greasy. He felt his stomach heave at what he was doing, but his hunger asserted itself and he ate ravenously, hurrying to gobble it all down, only half chewing each mouthful.

When it was all finished and he had licked the last greasy traces from his fingers he sat back, satisfied, to return to the same old business of stamping his feet and flapping his arms to keep the chill, chill night from killing him. For it was even colder in the dark hour before dawn and many of the people in the barn perished.

At last the night began to fade and a dull, grey light grew in the sky. Bernoit saw that he could leave now and he began to crawl away from the fires, up over the stiff-limbed dead and dying. They formed a high barricade, reaching to the roof, where men had come in during the night to die on the corpses of those who had come before. Up and up he climbed, until at length he was able to crawl out through the door and slip down to the frozen snow. Later, when he remembered that night, he estimated that some four or five hundred men had perished in the barn during the bitter hours of darkness.

The march that day was terrible. Cold, exhausted and alone, Bernoit dragged his weakened body across the glistening ice and only the knowledge that this was to be the last day of the march kept him going. It was almost impossible to believe that at last the appalling retreat was going to end, and that fresh supplies and warmth waited in Vilna. The main Russian pursuit had ended long ago and only Cossacks and light cavalry harried the marching men; they and the vengeful peasants. There would be rest and reorganisation and he would find himself once again with his comrades, secure among the reserve divisions. It was difficult to believe, but during that long, cold march the belief kept him alive. And so he came at last to Vilna.

The town seemed well organised and there was a Dutch

battalion, in arms, acting as marshals to direct arrivals to the billets prepared for them. Bernoit was too exhausted to be bothered listening to them and when he had entered the gates he made for the first house he could see and pushed his way in. He was fortunate, for as yet the main rush of fugitives had not arrived and he could take his leisure and seek out the warmest room. There were some Croatian pioneers there, taking up most of the room, but with assistance from others, mostly Bavarians, he evicted them and pushed his way into the fire where he lay down to sleep. Someone in the room shouted for food and the people in the house brought this to them. Bernoit ate with relish. The thoughtful garrison commander had provided soup and meat and bread and the tired, hungry men gorged themselves on this feast. It was a very different meal from the last grisly affair.

Bernoit's sleep was disturbed, for there were always people trying to fight their way into the room. But violence resisted them and the occupants stayed where they were. In these spells of wakefulness he heard the roar of the surging crowds trying to force the narrow gates of the town and could imagine the panic and the pressure there. He congratulated himself on having arrived before the main part of the column. His long, rigorous marches had not been in vain.

At some stage during the afternoon a man wearing a civilian coat and a turban forced his way into the room, announced that he was a general, and tried to commandeer it as his own. They swore at him and refused to go, and eventually he gave up trying, but evicted a Polish infantryman from one of the beds and threw himself down on it. Bernoit watched the incident and then turned over on his floorboards beside the fire and lay listening to the riotous tumult in the streets outside. It was a strange background to his drowsy cosiness and was faint on his mind as he slipped back to sleep.

Night had fallen when he was awakened by someone shouting and he sat up. A boy was kneeling beside him throwing logs on to the fire. Again the voice shouted from the door, 'General Wrede! Is General Wrede here?'

'Aye, I'm over here,' said the man on the bed, and Bernoit was vaguely shocked to learn that this weak man was the redoubtable commander of the 20th Bavarian Division.

'Colonel Rossetti, sir, King Murat's staff,' said the speaker at the door, walking to the bed. 'His Majesty requires your immediate presence to assist in clearing the streets. I have here orders from the Prince of Neuchâtel.'

'I trust Berthier and your King are well. No doubt they can cope.'

'Sir, with respect, the orders are for immediate attention.'

'I heard you, Colonel, you may leave the Chief of Staff's orders with me,' and the General rolled over, turning his back on the aide, terminating the conversation. Rossetti stormed from the room leaving the men lying there in impressed silence. The boy stoking the fire rose to go and Bernoit caught him.

'Food,' he said in Russian, 'more food.'

The boy nodded and left, returning later with more soup and bread.

They slept undisturbed through the night and it was daylight when they were wakened by the people of the house bringing them breakfast of biscuit and hot black coffee. An officer entered and showed a notice to the general. Bernoit knew enough German to understand from what was said that it had been posted on the door of the house. The document summoned all generals to attend a conference at headquarters that morning. Wrede shrugged and threw himself back on his bed.

It was later that the same officer came running into the room shouting excitedly. This time Wrede swore, leapt to his feet and rattled out orders to the men in the room. The speech was too rapid for Bernoit's ear, but the others were reaching for their weapons and preparing to leave in considerable agitation. Bernoit, unable to understand, pleaded in French, 'Please, sir, what is happening?'

Wrede looked at him, surprised to find a Frenchman in the room. 'Cossacks, man, Cossacks! They've broken in and are arresting everyone! No one at headquarters is doing anything! Get your weapons and come along.'

Bernoit knew galloping panic as he reached for his musket. If the Russians had taken the town there would be wholesale slaughter. Wrede's intention seemed to be to make for headquarters and Bernoit decided that staying with the general was probably the surest way to survive. They were all pulling their warm clothing together and Wrede wrapped his head in handkerchiefs, with the ridiculous turban perched on top. The Bavarian soldiers were looking askance at Bernoit and he realised that they only now identified him as French, concealed as he was in his motley clothing. One of them made an ugly comment. Bernoit scowled defiantly; Germans did not worry him. But Wrede had heard and snapped, 'Enough of that! We're going to need every man for this.' He drew his sword and led them into the street.

There was confusion everywhere and the streets were littered with the customary corpses, fires and wrecked vehicles. There was no sign of the enemy as they pushed through the crowding rabble, but every time they paused for directions the men they asked fled in panic at the dread word 'Cossack'. Soon they began to hear reports of whole districts which the Russians had captured. Apart from the mobs in the streets there was no sign of French soldiery and Wrede sent detachments down the side streets to clear them. As they approached the centre of the town they came to a street broader than most and Wrede led them down it, running with his naked sword. The others, including Bernoit, some fifteen or so strong, followed, their bayonets fixed, their fingers on the triggers, nervous lest the dreaded cavalrymen appeared at the other end of the thoroughfare and charged.

A Polish officer stepped from a side street walking brisky. He was wearing the smart uniform of the First Lancers of the Guard and his czapka was set on his head at a jaunty angle, its tall plume nodding as he walked. Wrede called to him, 'Take me to headquarters! The Russians have entered the city. They are killing everyone and yet the Guard remains in its billets!'

The officer paused and looked at the General as he came up. He recognised him and saluted smartly before replying quietly:

'I shall be pleased to guide you, General. I am required at headquarters myself. But there is no need for alarm. The town is well protected, pickets are everywhere and the gates are held by infantry. There cannot be any Cossacks within our lines.'

Bernoit was reassured, but felt a strange sense of anticlimax. He was embarrassed standing there with his musket at the ready, his bayonet fixed. Self-consciously he relaxed his position, unfixed and sheathed his bayonet and tried to recover the appearance of a French veteran of twenty years. He felt like a raw recruit at having been panicked so easily. God knew how Wrede felt. The Polish officer spoke again, contempt sounding in his voice, 'General, you have no need of your sword. Please sheath it or you will affront His Majesty, King Murat.'

The Bavarians who had not understood the conversation in

French saw the general sheath his sword and realised what had happened. Sheepishly they abandoned their warlike positions and trailed after him to headquarters. Bernoit, having nothing else to do, tagged along behind, but when they reached the courtyard under the castle where Murat had sited his headquarters, one of them remembered that he was French and chased him away.

He wandered aimlessly in the square and warmed himself at the fires which were being lit, burning carriages, camp beds, tents and other equipment. He supposed that he ought to try to find his corps, but that could wait till later; it was cold and he felt weak. He decided to seek a place to rest where he would be out of the cold.

It was not easy to make an entry into any of the houses round the square for they were full of soldiers and at every door he was turned away. He thought of returning to the house he had slept in during the night, but he knew that it would have filled up already and that he would be unable to force his way in. He spat in disgust at the stupid panic that had made him leave and cursed the German general for his lack of self-control. He would otherwise be lying snug in front of the fire eating the endless supplies of soup which seemed to be available there. He was despairing of ever finding shelter.

He wondered if he could panic the occupants of the next house he came to and when he pushed the door open he shouted, 'Cossacks, the Cossacks are in town!'

An old grenadier sergeant was sitting on the floor and looked up at him coldly. 'Good for them,' he said. 'Let the Guard deal with them. I don't hear any disturbance outside so I'll stay put thank you, while you go out and attend to the matter.'

Bernoit shrugged and tried to grin. 'I thought it might work,' he said, trying to edge himself into the building, but he was taken by the shoulders and firmly pushed back.

'Close the door as you're leaving,' called the grenadier. 'You'll let the cold in.'

In the street again Bernoit reflected that his alarm-raising might work better if he were further away from headquarters. In this district he had not heard the rumours of the disaster that had been prevalent in the outskirts of the city. He determined to try the last few houses in the square before heading into one of the more remote suburbs.

In the remaining houses it was the same story. There was the usual rabble of troops from a variety of nations, selfishly defending their own snug niche against any intruder. One house seemed to contain only French soldiers, infantrymen mostly, and in desperation he tried in vain to argue with them and bully them into admitting him, but it did no good. He made one last appeal to them as fellow citizens, but they began to become annoyed by his persistence and for a moment an ugly scene appeared inevitable. Then, from the back of the mob in the doorway, a man was pulling people aside and pushing his way through.

'Hey, don't throw him out lads, he's my mate—hey, Bernoit! Come on lads, let me through. God, it's good to see you.'

It was MacDonald. Bernoit's heart leapt with pleasure as he saw the big man fighting his way through the crowd to get to him. Then they were holding each other by the shoulders, grinning and laughing together.

'Come on inside, it's really cosy in here,' and MacDonald escorted him back through the packed hall into a little room at the side. The formerly hostile soldiers settled down again, uninterested in anything other than themselves.

The room into which MacDonald led him was just large enough to hold the half-dozen men stretched out there. In one wall was a small fireplace, and the fire was glowing red from its embers. A pile of wood lay in one corner, probably broken up furniture, for Bernoit noticed that the room was devoid of furnishing other than blankets and curtains strewn on the floor. The window was heavily frosted, but there was one broken pane through which Bernoit could see the looming walls of the castle. He noted that the men in the room were all giants like MacDonald and he could imagine the ruthless way in which they would have taken over the room and imposed their rule on the house.

'By God, I was pleased to see you then,' said Bernoit. 'I'd been hoping you were all right.'

'I'd thought you were a goner in that shambles at the Berezina. One moment you were there and then you were away.'

'Christ, that seems years ago.'

'Yes, it's been a long march. You've been on your own?'

'More or less,' Bernoit replied, sadly remembering the girl.

'I teamed up with these lads in Smorgon. They're a good crowd, you'll be all right now. God, man, you look done in. Sit down by the fire and I'll get you some food.'

Later Bernoit was awakened by an excited clamour by the window and rose to see what was going on. It was dark now but the square outside was brightly lit by the glowing fires.

'The bastards,' growled one man; 'they're pulling out.'

Bernoit pushed his way to the broken window-pane.

'They can't be,' he asserted, 'we're snug in here for the winter.'

Yet deep down he knew that the man was right. In the street below he saw the Imperial Guard marching in long columns from their quarters and assembled among them were the carriages and waggons of the army's headquarters. He distinctly saw a large group of horsemen gather, indicating the presence of Murat's staff.

'What the hell's he pulling out for?' someone asked. 'We could hold out here once we're reorganised.'

'Maybe he's moving out to fight,' another man suggested.

'Balls—take a look—the whole bloody headquarters transport is there. He wouldn't be moving that if he wasn't retreating.'

'Good of him to pass the word.'

'Yeh, Cossacks'll be in here tomorrow. A lot of the lads'll be caught out.'

'We're bloody lucky to have a ringside seat like this.'

'Yeh. We'd've been bloody left behind if we hadn't.'

'Oh well,' said MacDonald. 'Let's get organised.'

'It's going to be a long, cold march.'

Bernoit had said nothing since his original assertion but now he began to swear in a string of expert and unrepeated obscenities. There would be no more warm billets, no more hot food. His dreams of rejoining his corps were destroyed yet again. There would be no orderly life, reassembling the regiment, organising the new drafts as they came in, preparing quietly through the winter for the following season's campaign. Instead there would be the continuing chaos and misery of this endless march across the hostile, frozen landscape. He still did not know that on the night when the peasants had attacked him in Moledechno the Emperor, in that same village, had issued his despairing bulletin announcing that the Grande Armée had ceased to exist. But Bernoit did know that the army was doomed by this final withdrawal.

MacDonald turned to him protectively and asked, 'How are you off for clothing, food?'

Bernoit gestured to indicate his plight and together they

187

collected blankets to wrap round him and MacDonald managed to scrounge some bread to stuff into his empty pack. The other soldiers in the room were preparing themselves in similar fashion and eventually they all seemed satisfied that they were fitted adequately for the journey.

They would have looked comical in different circumstances. Some, including MacDonald, had fur coats which they had drawn tight round them, but the remainder wore a strange assortment of garments: blankets tucked over the shoulders and hooded round the head, drawn in at the waist with a belt holding the whole together; women's shawls wrapped round their shoulders; fur trimmings tucked in at the neck; civilian cloaks drawn close. One man was wearing several layers of ladies' satin dresses with a hussar's pelisse over the top. Their headgear varied as much: forage caps tied round with handkerchiefs; turbans; shakos; bearskins, and Bernoit's strange arrangement of furs, fashioned that evening after crossing the Berezina.

They collected their weapons and pushed through the anxious bustling crowd into the street. The Guard had left the square but the street was busy. From every house poured men who, like themselves, had realised what was happening. Yet there were many, very many who ignored the signs and stayed behind, piling wood on their fires, lying sleeping in the deep recesses of houses throughout the city. These people were of no concern to Bernoit, and he and his comrades departed on their way. As they approached the west gate they saw that other corps were on the march and knew that their assessment had been correct. Without attempt at resistance, the city of Vilna and all who remained within its walls were being abandoned to the hatred of the Cossack hordes.

Through the dark, freezing hours they marched and such was the extent of the white, wasted landscape that it was light under the starlight. But the light brought no respite from the cold and men dropped frozen to the ground. In the long columns of the stragglers and in the formed lines of the fighting units men perished, and with them died horses and many, many of the few surviving women and children. The stiffening corpses and the broken vehicles were left behind, a tragic wake that marked the route. Back to the gates of Vilna it could be traced, and across the steppe to the Berezina, through the forests to the Dnieper and Smolensk, over the rolling hills to Borodino it lay, and beyond, to the charred ruins of Moscow itself. And all the time the line of ruin and death grew longer and the sombre light of day brought no relief but exposed their anguish to the watching sky.

For days the doomed procession marched and death did not abandon it. Cossacks slew and tortured but the survivors did not stop, but trailed on over the interminable ice of the steppe, and when night came they sheltered in villages, within the mean hovels or huddled against the outer walls. Starvation ate at them so that Bernoit remembered the grisly lesson he had learned from the one-armed man, and saw that MacDonald, too, had learned. At every dawn they left their fires with the litter of dead and dying, and buildings burning with men trapped, helpless, within. And all the time the Cossacks harried them and the Russian people wreaked the vengeance of their nation on their wasted bodies.

15

In the late afternoon of 13 December Bernoit and his companions arrived in Kovno and saw, on the opposite bank of the Niemen, the friendly soil of Poland. Here, in June, they had crossed into Russia and marched, confident of victory, in flowing streams of men and horses with their bands and eagles, kettledrums and standards, guns and caissons and all the glitter and fluttering plumes of their emblazoned glory. Now all had been extinguished by the terrible winter and men wept to see how few were left, to remember all that was lost.

One bridge, alone, remained over the frozen river and the thousands of souls flocked to cross. There was no attempt at order and no trace of formed troops. Generals and marshals mingled in the rabble, deprived of command, lacking even their aides, and on the other bank the crowd dispersed, each man seeking his own refuge in the woods. Behind them they left their weapons, discarded like leaves on the ground.

Yet Murat, abandoning all in his flight, had thought to leave spirits in the town, though he left nothing else for those who came. One of Bernoit's gang found such a store, kicking open the door to peer into the noisome place.

'Come on, lads! We'll have a drop and then be on our way.'

The magazine into which he led them was filled with drunken men, and spilt liquor lay reeking on the floor. Casks had been split open and men stood there catching the brandy as it flowed from the broken staves, lapping from frostbitten hands, swilling from cups and tin canteens. Purpled faces diffused in joviality, escape from everything in the giddy drink. Then, besotted, they reeled in embracing goodwill, or fell vomiting to the sodden, filthy floor. Half a dozen men in mutual support swung arm in arm and roared out the bawdy verses of their regimental songs. In splendid good humour one man stood on a cask and called cavalry insults to the infantry below until some Italians bundled him from his perch.

'Long live the King of Naples!' one cried, deliberately provoking the jeers of the bemused crowd.

'Courage, friends! Like the Emperor he is safe.'

'Our little Corporal has gone to raise another army,' someone protested, and a drunken chasseur slurred out:

'Long live Emper — eror.'

'Murat's dashed off to screw your wives,' a grenadier shouted at the Italians.

'He's a good chap,' said another. 'He's left us all this lovely brandy.' And he began to croak out the timeless words of a marching song, before collapsing to the ground.

Bernoit's companions had not intended to stay for long in this disgusting scene, but they were sick and tired and drinking brought its own relief. They jostled with the others at the casks to take their share and found themselves drawn willy-nilly into the deceptive merriness. Already one or two of them had the flushed faces and stupid grins of the other revellers. A soldier slumped over one of the kegs and vomited copiously into it, while others, unseeing, continued to drink its contents.

It would have been easy to stay and enjoy the drowning of their faculties until they staggered into the open and fell in the snow to perish in the cold, or be taken when the enemy entered the city. Yet Bernoit felt the alcohol sour in his empty belly and pain stabbed his bowels as it did when he knew fear. In sudden clarity he saw the sprawling drunks and foresaw their fate. He became urgent to be gone and sought out MacDonald who was swilling deep.

'We've got to go. Soon it will be too late.'

The dark man scowled and refilled his cup. Bernoit seized his arm and drew him close and the stinking spirits were on his breath.

'Look, man. We'll soon be drunk. Can you imagine that? The enemy will be here soon.'

MacDonald's eyes began to clear and he knew the force of Bernoit's argument. They tried to round up their comrades and only MacDonald's forceful tongue brought them success, against the stubborn will to drink. In the end most of the gang rallied round, but there were several who would not be encouraged away and who remained, heedless of their friends' entreaties.

191

From the heady stench of the place, the night air was fresh despite the cold, and they paused at the door to gasp at the contrast. A burning building lit the narrow alleyway and the flames roared and cracked over them, illuminating everything. A drunken soldier pushed among them to force his way through and lurched out before them, and then fell so that they had to step over him to make their way between the buildings. From the opposite end a man was striding purposefully towards them and they moved aside to let him pass, for there was challenge in his eyes.

He stopped and boldly faced them, compelling them to halt. Bernoit saw the firm eyes and knowing them felt fear, for he could not deny this man what he sought. The others stirred, nervous, also recognising him. It was Ney who stood before them.

'Will you also flee with the rest, he demanded, 'or will you stand with me?'

They tried to shuffle past, as if they had not heard. Everyone knew what it meant to be with Ney on this campaign for four rearguards had already been destroyed as they fought at his side. No one desired to join him in this last, solitary vigil. Bernoit sidled past in shame, his eyes averted.

'Hey! Bernoit! You'd not leave me here, in this place, alone? We've done too much together, old fellow. I need true French-men round me now.'

Bernoit stopped, miserable with guilt. It was appalling that Ney should have to come seeking in the streets for men to command. He remembered Krasnoe and the Dnieper, and knew that the Marshal had defeated him. He owed too great a duty, too deep a loyalty to go free from this appeal. No other man could have made him stop, but the decision was made and Bernoit turned and came to attention. It was strange to behave like a soldier again, and reassuring. He jutted out his chin.

'Sergeant-Major Bernoit, Marshal. Rejoining the corps.'

Ney nodded in brief acknowledgement, his eyes twinkling. He inclined his head to the rest of them, but they had melted away, all save MacDonald who stood firm at Bernoit's shoulder and slapped his hand against his rifle in salute.

'MacDonald, sir, Voltigeur. 46th Line.'

'MacDonald, eh? Any relation to the Marshal?'

'My father claims kinship, sir.'

'You Scots are all related to each other. I remember you—

you're the fellow with the rifle. I see you've still got it. Good. We will have need of it.' He turned back to Bernoit. 'You pair have stuck together well.'

'We are all that are left.'

'Aye, and now you've rejoined Third Corps. Well, that makes about a dozen of us.' But he grinned at their dismay. 'Come, comrades, we will show the King of Naples how real soldiers fight.'

He led them through the town, collecting as they went a few others who were prepared to follow him, and brought them at last to the ramparts. A battalion of German conscripts was there, a thin line stretched too far by the long perimeter, guarding the withdrawal of the ruined army. Bernoit discovered that they were from the garrison of the town and had never been tried in battle. It was more encouraging to learn that guns had been assembled at the gate on the Vilna road, ready for the morning's action. Another battalion of the Germans lay in the town, and in addition there were perhaps a score of generals and aides and others like himself forming the Marshal's retinue. His reserve, Ney jested.

From the bleak wall where he stood beside the shivering German sentinel, Bernoit could see the bivouac fires of the Russian army and knew that a mighty force was opposed against this pitiful resistance. He observed the gaps where the horse lines were, and saw what he took to be the positions of the sledge-borne artillery. Platov was there with his Cossacks and Bernoit wondered how long it would take him to overwhelm the tiny allied reaguard. An hour or so, perhaps, but no much longer, and then the Cossacks would be in among the helpless souls in the town.

He felt the black, old fears returning. He had so few hours left to live. Perhaps he would be wounded and left to die a lingering death in a crowded Russian hospital. They had not even tried to evacuate the wounded from Kovno. How many times had they left their injured men behind? The whole retreat was landmarked with their desertion. Viasma, Smolensk, the Dnieper, Studyanka —the list was endless. He remembered Necker. Well, he'd be going the same way now. God, it was cold.

The bitter hours of night dragged on and only the changing of the pickets broke the silence of the waiting men. From the north in one last spiteful fury the wind came howling down and brought flurried snow to torture the soldiers huddling in the slight shelter of the battlements. Throughout those dark hours they heard the cries of the drunken mobs roaming disordered through the streets or fighting to push their way across that single bridge. And before them lay the Russian army where men also perished in the cold and starved from famine, but where they knew that day would bring the purging of their land.

In time the darkness eased and the dismal halo of dawn loomed over the enemy camp. Buildings and embrasures began to take form and the cold, still soldiers stirred and checked their weapons. Orders were called out sharply and a single trumpet blared brassily. Drums rat-tatted the approach of day and bade the listeners stand to arms. And in the east, not far from them, the Russians were summoned to take victory from the dawn.

The cannonade began just after light, engulfing the Vilna gate where the French guns lay silent. Ney came stumping along, gathering his retinue together as he headed, cursing, in that direction.

'Why don't our guns reply?' he complained. 'Can it be that our artillery need orders before they open fire?'

They ran behind him along the wall and into the terrible fire of those accurate sledge guns. Down the steps they followed him and through the gate, pushing past the gunners milling there and forward to where the battery had been posted.

'Now we'll drive off these Russian fellows!' Ney roared.

But they could not. The artillerymen had fled and only an officer and some sergeants remained. In their fear they were spiking their guns, disarming the last gun even as Ney arrived. So now the French had no artillery.

The Marshal was beside himself in wrath. The battery commander plaintively squealed his explanation and his abject terror further infuriated Ney. Enraged, he drew his sword and swung it in a vicious cut. The gunner actually screamed. Another blade gleamed and halted the blow in violent clash. A quick-thinking aide had intervened.

'Prince, do not sully your sword with this coward's blood.'

Speechless in fury, Ney bellowed his venom, but wrenched his blade aside and turned away. Craven, the artilleryman slunk from his presence, spurned by them all. Bernoit stood with the others, the generals and the common soldiers, while they waited for the Marshal to bring his anger under control.

'General Marchand! We'll need your German fellows here now. We'll form them up in line. Those Cossacks aren't going to wait for long.'

But only one of the German battalions came forward to take their place in the line; the other had fled without once coming into battle. By the time the nervous conscripts appeared the steady gunfire had taken its toll of the Marshal's little band and, even as the Germans dressed off on their sergeants, the Russians commenced their attack.

Steadily the enemy marched forward, unopposed by gun or horse while the guns pounded the allied position. Even the tested veterans of the retinue were disturbed by the lethal hail, dismayed by the solid phalanx of the Russian advance. Bernoit wondered how the conscripts were feeling. It was impossible to resist those thousands and their guns with a paltry three hundred men.

Ney alone seemed unconcerned. He was cheery and confident and spoke gently to the frightened boys. The senior soldiers saw and remembered themselves. Bernoit stiffened his shoulders and checked his lock. The Russians were almost in range.

'Steady, lads,' cried Ney. 'We know these fellows don't like our volleys. We'll drive them off in a minute.' He paused for a moment, timing the Russian advance and then called:

'Major . . .'

The battalion commander raised his sword in salute.

'Present!'

Three hundred muskets came up in regimental precision. The leading Cossacks flinched to see those ugly muzzles aiming directly upon them. Any second . . .

A cannon-ball smashed into the parapet before Bernoit showering him with splintered stone. The shock numbed his cheek-bone and his probing fingers found lacerated flesh and felt the blood running hot. A man was screaming nearby and he looked over and saw that the ricocheting ball had hit the German major in the chest. No man could survive such a wound, but the officer, in his agony, did a thing that Bernoit had rarely seen. He drew his pistol, calmly placed it in his mouth and blew out his brains.

It was too much for his men. Their muskets wavered, they heeded not Ney's desperate order to fire. Another roundshot crashed among them and they cast away their weapons and they fled. One musket did go off, firing when it hit the ground. A sergeant of tirailleurs with fourteen years' service on his sleeves spun in poignant bewilderment and crumpled to the ground.

Unarmed, the conscripts were falling over themselves to escape, clamouring to get through the gate. Ney turned furiously to the officers around him.

'Marchand! Ledru! After them—bring them back! Gérard! Find guns and bring them here! Heymès! Round up any men you can.'

The officers dashed off on their urgent tasks and Ney now looked to the men left to him. There were only four. MacDonald, Bernoit and two others.

'Well, boys, now we'll have some fun.' He bent to pick up one of the discarded muskets.

The Cossacks had behaved with their customary curiosity. Rather than press their advantage when the threatened volley had dissolved, they had remained where they were, watching to see what would happen next. Now as the five remaining Frenchmen opened fire their hetman rode out in front, urging them forward. The Russians heard his pleas and started to move.

'MacDonald!' Ney commanded. 'Shoot me that officer.'

Meticulously, MacDonald primed his rifle and then nursed it against his shoulder. He squinted along the barrel and corrected his aim. An intake of breath, a spurt of smoke, and then the single shot crashed out.

The hetman sagged lazily over the brow of his saddle and slipped quietly to the snow. His horse whinnied and walked several paces away. Leaderless, three thousand Cossacks swarmed, perplexed, and came again to a halt.

It was uncanny to be there in the cold morning, Bernoit himself with Ney, and MacDonald and the two fusiliers, defying an entire army while all their comrades sought refuge. Even the Marshal's proximity was unreal. They were accustomed to see him among them, bravely leading, encouraging, ever in the position of danger, but always the great general, the powerful prince. Now he was truly one of them, as close in comradeship as though he shared their mess.

'Let's pepper them a bit,' he called with glee. It was as though he was actually enjoying himself, deprived of decision, bereft of responsibility.

It was fortunate that the Germans had not fired that volley for

196

now their muskets lay in charged abundance. Fired by Ney's enthusiasm it was almost sport to seize the loaded weapons and discharge them into the motionless, close-packed Cossacks. How many rounds he fired Bernoit did not know, but his shoulder ached from the recoils and his ears rang with the concussion. Eventually the Cossacks wearied of their casualties and withdrew from range.

'By God, there's a tale to tell your grandchildren,' the Marshal laughed out. 'Another five like us and they'd have run back to Moscow!'

But there were not five others, and the Russians, though they did not know how few opposed them, saw that the French were weak and began once more to advance. Yet they did not charge, but rode forward slowly, expectantly.

Ney leapt, musket in hand, on to the parapet. A sigh rose from the enemy and they stopped. No gun fired; no man spoke. Long minutes passed and still the Cossacks sat, watching in wonder. Their proud bearded faces gazed on the Marshal, their lances upright as though in salute. Nothing stirred, save perhaps a restless horse pawing impatiently and the wind-blown spindrift, hissing over the steppe.

The Russian command could not tolerate this situation and an officer bustled up to bring the men to order. MacDonald fingered his rifle hopefully, but the range was too great. In the tense silence Bernoit bade him hold his fire.

The Cossacks reluctantly started forward again.

'Stop! I am Michel Ney! Prince of the Moskowa. Do you dare to approach me?'

The words rang clear across the whispering air. Though they could not understand what was said the Cossacks stopped again. They knew who he was and were fascinated. Like Murat, whom they revered as some splendid cavalry god, Ney was a legend to them. They had been watching him for weeks past as he fought, fearless and unharmed, at the very rear of the dwindling army. And now he seemed to be alone, here before them, challenging them to approach. They sat quiet in their saddles, staring with respect and awe.

Of course it could not last. One of their hetmen, frustrated by his stubborn troops, nudged his horse forward and began a long charge down upon the solitary Marshal.

Spellbound they watched, the two forces; the thousands of

197

Russians and the four Frenchmen; as between them this medieval display took place. The hooves thundered across the driving snow: the lance came down and settled for the kill. Closer and faster the flying rider came. The French soldiers raised their weapons to slay the man.

'Leave this to me,' the Marshal snarled and they stopped, abashed. It was like interfering in a duel. Yet MacDonald kept his rifle trained for fear of mishap.

On and on the horseman hurtled and his robes and pennant trailed in the rushing wind. He loomed close, swirling the snow around in clouds. The deadly lance was pointed straight at the Marshal's heart and all men held their breath. MacDonald, tense, tightened the finger on the trigger. The lance-point was five yards short when the Marshal moved. He whipped up his musket and shot the hetman dead.

It was as though he had a mystic power. The watching Cossacks stirred uneasily and drew back. Ney roared at them in challenge and they backed, disturbed. Their officers could do nothing with them, could not make them advance against him, and they broke away in dread.

'Thank Christ for that,' Bernoit gasped.

New turned to grin at them.

'That's one my grandchildren will never believe,' called one of the fusiliers.

'Nor will my own, Bécoulet, my boy,' the Marshal replied.

Frustrated, the Russian command saw that their troops had failed them. They turned back to their guns and resumed the cannonade and the balls smashed heavily into the crumbling parapet. It was incredible that five men could cause the enemy so much trouble. Yet as the pounding gunfire crashed around them Bernoit wondered how much longer they could hold out. The hours were slipping past and the enemy were losing their opportunity of taking the town this day. Surely they would realise how few men resisted them.

Now the Russians were sending skirmishers forward and the Frenchmen found themselves compelled to revert to the German muskets. Each man had his own pile of the loaded weapons gathered around him and the five men were able to maintain an extraordinarily rapid fire. But the stock of firearms was running low. Soon they would have to withdraw, if they were ever to do so.

A welcome shout hailed them from the gate. It was General

Gérard at the head of thirty men. But Gérard had more than mere men: he had guns, three beautiful guns. They were only light field pieces, it was true, but the men were so encouraged that they felt that now they could face all the armies of Russia.

Bécoulet, the fusilier, called, 'Hey, Marshal—now we'll see the devils run.'

Ney smiled, his glance embracing all four of them.

'I'll not forget what you four men have done. All France shall hear of it. But now take your rest. It is well earned.'

'We'll rest when you do, Marshal,' said Benoit stubbornly. 'The job is not done yet.'

It was glorious to see the guns belch forth and watch the enemy shrink from their increased volleys. The little band held on, well into the afternoon, and endured the constant bombardment. Their casualties were few only because, spread out, they were such a tiny target.

In the middle of the afternoon Marchand and Ledru returned, bringing with them a battalion of infantry which they had somehow contrived to rally and arm. The exhausted defenders cheered as, company by company, the infantry marched out to take its place in the line. The Russians seemed to be completely bemused and to have formed no plan to force the town.

Yet even as the reinforcements fired their first shots, and took their first casualties, they all heard the uproar of a new attack.

'The bridge, by God—they'll cut us off,' a soldier cried in near despair.

Ney had seen the danger and hastily conferred with his generals. There was a lull in the fighting in this sector and Benoit took the time to observe the discussion. It did not last for long before the generals nodded and broke away. Marchand and Ledru walked quickly over to their freshly engaged battalion and Ney raised his voice to address the others.

'My boys, we have done well and now must manage on our own once more. These other fellows are needed at the bridge. They'll keep our road home clear.'

Benoit could have wept. The precious infantry was marching away leaving them to continue their defiance of the enemy's thousands. There were so few of them, just thirty men and the three guns. How much longer would they have to stand? Till nightfall probably, another two hours at most. But suppose the enemy did attack again, what hope would there be for this

199

handful of men forced back on the disputed bridge? He was very tired and the icy wind had chilled him to the bone.

Yet the Marshal seemed tireless, striding down behind the line, speaking encouragement to every weary man. He seemed to have no fear, to be undismayed by their plight. He disregarded the dangerous situation at the bridge in his rear, although they could already hear the opening salvoes as Marchand's men became engaged, and concerned himself only with the position in front. The enemy fire was increasing to an iron rain of death and the little line was taking heavy casualties at last, yet the Marshal never ceased to move among them, pausing for a heartening word.

'Well, Bernoit, you old rascal, you're still with us. At Valmy—'

He never finished. A roundshot crashing past struck one of the guns. A scream of tortured metal rent the air. The gun carriage dissolved into dashing splinters, ripping open the men who stood near. Lazily the gun tilted over and then toppled on its side.

'It's time we got back to the wall,' said the Marshal.

Indeed they would only just have time. The Russians were perilously close to their left flank. One of the guns spat out a flail of grapeshot, delaying the enemy for some precious moments. The smoke-blackened defenders now had time to withdraw in order, skirmishing as they fell back, taking the last two little guns with them. Behind them they left the useless battery, the litter of discarded firearms and their comrades who had fallen.

The ramparts of the wall seemed scarcely more secure to Bernoit. There were far too few of them to hold the new position. The cannon were placed in the very mouth of the gate and were firing so rapidly that even though ice formed on their cartridges the barrels were hot to touch. Bernoit's own musket was hot. He had been firing it constantly since the supply of loaded muskets had ended. Now the flint was wearing out and there was no time to change it. He looked around him for another, less abused. MacDonald was still beside him sniping with his rifle, and Bécoulet and the other fusilier.

Again and again the Russians made their tentative advances and were repulsed. Bernoit in all his years had never known an action so furious, and yet in the biting cold it all seemed slow and dreamlike. Occasional knots of friendly soldiers appeared from time to time, shamed by the resistance into joining them. So it went on as the day lengthened and began to wane, and all the

200

time Ney was with them, firing his musket with the others, cajoling them to even greater efforts like (but infinitely greater than) some sergeant of grenadiers.

Till nightfall they fought without retreat, until the grey, cold day surrendered to the black, comfortless night, and only the flare of the guns gave sight of their enemies. It was impossible to tell where the Russian soldiers were, or what they were doing. They knew that they could last no longer. Their vigil was done.

Ney ordered the cannon to be overloaded and burst. Then, and only then, did they commence their withdrawal. As they left their posts the Russians, seeing an end to the stubborn defence, swarmed joyously into the town. Now the little band of defenders had to fight ferociously to save themselves. From house to house they dropped back, in bitter combat through the narrow streets. Sometimes they fired the buildings behind them to seal the enemy from their withdrawal.

It was a nightmare to the weakening, war-sick Bernoit. His ears whined in deafness from the endless banging shots. Men were falling everywhere and his eyes ached from straining along his sights at the half seen, blurring targets. Around him buildings crackled in consuming blaze, the flames scorching as if to cauterise his bloodshot eyes. He felt the heat on his torn cheek and remembered the pain. His fingers found that the flesh had fallen over in a flap, and was frozen. And still there were more men to shoot and kill.

A troop of mounted Cossacks appeared from nowhere. In the confined space it was hopeless to resist. They bustled in panic. The Cossacks screamed their battle-cry and charged. Someone, Heymès perhaps, the aide-de-camp, yelled:

'Into the houses! Get indoors!'

With others, General Gérard had flung himself against a flimsy portal and it burst before them. Bernoit threw himself behind them. MacDonald was there beside him as ever. But there was no time for relief. Gérard was calling them to order; the Cossacks were hurtling down the street.

Ney had been at the very rear. Defiantly, when others fled he had stopped to fire his musket. His defiance cost him dear, for despite their cries he would not run. Slowly he paced backwards, unflinching, his void musket held in challenge. But in the squalid streets his magic was of no avail against the blood-crazed Russians. Alone he stood as the leading rider

201

hammered down upon him. The lance dipped to take the prize.

Helpless, they watched for he stood between his assassin and their friendly muskets. There was nothing they could do. The angle was too acute to avoid hitting him. Bitterly they tensed to reap their vengeance. Then one single shot cracked in their ears.

MacDonald had fired. Only a rifle could have done the job. The Cossack was swept from his steed. The lance curved in an arc and landed, quivering, at the Marshal's feet. The horse whipped past.

Heymès dashed from among them and threw himself forward to save his beloved chief. He seized him and bundled him aside. Now their muskets could tell. Bernoit could see nothing—a blurred mass, no more, yet he fired. They all fired, and the leading horses went down. Heymès came sprinting back, dragging his precious charge behind. There was none of the dignity due to a Marshal-Prince of the Empire.

'By God, that was a close call. Now we're in a pretty fix.'

The Marshal may have been shaken by his harsh treatment, but already his eyes were darting around, examining their position. It was not good. The Russians were quick to realise whom they had trapped in the building. Their men were moving up rapidly to surround them.

'Well, the buggers know I'm here so we must expect some trouble. We'll hold out for a bit and let the others get clear and then we'll make a dash for it.'

He wasted little time in assigning them to their various positions. Bernoit he placed in command of a party of three men in one tiny room at the rear. He took MacDonald away with him, jesting.

'I want you close to me to see what you're up to. You parted my hair just then with that damned rifle of yours.'

They did not have long to wait. One of Bernoit's men, a cuirassier, called to him from the window. Bernoit peered anxiously and in the glow of the enveloping fires he saw Cossacks, dismounted, clumsily stalking down the lane.

'Marshal! They're advancing on the back wall! About thirty of them.'

He looked at the cuirassier. He was nervous, a youngster of perhaps eighteen. His beard was a straggly down, his eyes clear blue. He was out of his natural element, should have been boot to boot in some fine cavalry charge. In his anxiety he was fingering his firelock. Bernoit said sympathetically:

'Not yet, sonny. We'll have them cold in a minute—when we can't miss. And for God's sake keep back from the window.'

Ney was bellowing orders. They would fire a couple of rapid volleys into the men at the rear and then break out. Eagerly Bernoit's soldiers raised their weapons.

'Wait for it!' he yelled, judging the timing to a nicety.

Someone below fired, far too early, and a ragged volley shattered the tense silence.

'Reload! And for Christ's sake wait for the order.'

But the young cuirassier was too zealous. He thrust his reloaded carbine through the window before Bernoit could stop him. There was a burst of enemy fire. The youth wheeled round and looked at Bernoit, the black, round hole neat in his forehead. Blood trickled down his face staining the immature beard. Already the boy's eyes were masked in death and he fell back, full length, upon the floor.

'Fire!'

There were dead Russians lying in the snow.

'Fix bayonets!'

They leapt from the windows, from the doors. A clash of steel against the surprised Cossacks. An exposed chest. Thrust, twist and up with the foot to kick him clear. Then a long dash down the alley as the bullets snapped angrily about them. Someone was down. Jump over the prostrate body. Round the corner and stop to reload.

'Come on!'

But Bécoulet was hit and could not go on. Ney paused for a moment with Bernoit and MacDonald, and the fusilier whose name Bernoit did not know. It was hopeless, Bécoulet was beyond aid. Their little company of five was broken.

'Adieu, Marshal.'

'Adieu.'

They were deserting Bécoulet and felt unclean. But it was forward again to the next corner. And the next, and halt to fire into the pursuing throng. Then sprint down the twisting street. Here was Gérard, grim-faced with news.

'Marchand hasn't been able to clear the bridge. We can't get through.'

'Then we'll cross on the ice!'

On again, driving some of the drunks before them, showing them the way. It was snowing again. More horsemen and a hurried volley to deter them. A wavering Russian line ahead and charging them with cold steel. So cold, the steel was, in the falling snow. A simple peasant face in agonised surprise. Another long street with the wind whistling chill against them. Russian wind blowing as if to hinder their retreat. A final volley at the men behind and then they were on the river bank.

'Go on — get across.'

The Marshal stood still, watching them as they slithered down the snow and found their footing on the ice. One by one they filed past him and gratefully trudged over the frozen surface and up to the safety of the Polish bank. The Russians would not pursue them here. Only when the last man had passed him did Michel Ney move.

Slowly he clambered down the bank and stepped out on the frozen river. He was the last man of all the Grande Armée to leave the soil of Russia. As they watched him walk calmly over the ice they saw the enemy assemble on the bank that they had left. The Russians made no move but gazed at the lonely figure striding across the Niemen. He became aware of them behind him and when he reached the midpoint he stopped to face them. In a final gesture of defiance he raised his musket and fired one last, parting shot. Then he swung the weapon down and broke the stock against the ice. The campaign was over. He turned and continued on his way. He, alone, was undefeated.

Bernoit and MacDonald stood side by side looking back into Russia. Their eyes could see the burning town and the milling Cossacks on the opposite bank. Their minds saw more than this, carrying them back over the bitter snow-cast leagues. So much misery; so many dead. Bernoit felt the tears flood his eyes. Back there lay half a million of his comrades. He would mourn them all his days.

MacDonald took the rifle in both hands and cast it far from him. He would need it no more. Sadly the two men turned their backs on Russia and walked in silence into the forest.

Epilogue

The Seine was sluggish in the morning fog, slipping almost reluctantly below Bernoit as he leaned on the parapet of the Pont-Neuf. Two wharfingers were pulling their ugly boat upstream, the oars rising and falling to leave trailing eddies in the slow water.

Above the Louvre the white flag of the Bourbons hung limp in the December mists and somewhere from an inner courtyard a drum rattled harshly, summoning the mock soldiers of the Royal Guard. Bernoit drew his civilian cloak around him and enviously eyed the strolling British soldiers on the Quai, shabby in their tattered scarlet. The King was back in Paris, but only by the grace of foreign arms. No real French soldier would serve him.

A horse clattered on to the bridge and Bernoit turned to see a Russian general ride past. He watched sullenly as the medal-bedecked officer passed him by and headed off to the south, to the Luxembourg, no doubt, where Ney's court martial dragged its spiteful course.

Bernoit sighed heavily. The early air was fresh, still free from the mixture of smoke and the smell of horses that would fill the later day. It was strange that there were so few people about. He breathed in deep, glad of the sharp weather. His vigil had been long and dismal, sitting by the bedside in the darkened room while his sister, Émilie Vernier, faced her lingering death. Here on the bridge he felt at peace, away from the gloomy house in Rue des Prouvains where the wasted body lay.

Poor Émilie! She had never really recovered from Étienne's death, had constantly toyed with the little mementoes which Bernoit had collected on that dreadful night at Viasma. Only young Paul, approaching manhood, had given his mother some purpose in life. But Paul had been killed at Waterloo.

Bernoit spat into the water. He was all alone in the world, deprived even of his regiment. He began to walk towards the south bank. There would be affairs to put in order, a funeral to arrange. Yet he needed company and decided these matters could wait. He would go to his favourite café and drink some cognac. It was too early to expect the usual crowd to be in, but there might be one or two of the old soldiers like himself, contriving to survive without a pension. It would be pleasant to hear their grumbling, and catch up with news and gossip.

He strolled along the quayside, enjoying the macabre greyness of the day which so perfectly matched his mood, and as he approached the Invalides he made to turn south. A voice hailed him.

'Bernoit!'

It was Larguien! The officer came striding towards him, beaming from ear to ear. He too wore civilian clothes, his right sleeve flapping emptily, lacking the arm which he had lost in that last advance at Waterloo.

'Bernoit, I'm so glad. I didn't know . . . Since the Berezina . . . '

'Oh, I heard all about you, Colonel.'

'Don't call me that—you'll get me shot,' Larguien said in mock terror. 'Don't you know I've been proscribed?'

Bernoit was appalled. Were the Royalists never to end their persecution of Bonaparte's old soldiers? He looked his astonishment. Larguien grinned ruefully.

'Yes. They're after me all right. Fortunately I have friends. I'm getting out tonight—going to America. Just in time, I am told. After last night they are in full cry.'

Bernoit looked puzzled. He had had no news for days.

'What, man, haven't you heard? Ney is sentenced to death.'

Bernoit was stunned.

'That's impossible,' he protested.

'No. He's to be shot. It's his pledge to King Louis that did it. They say he's a traitor.'

'Traitor, is it? Ney? Was it this nonsense of the cage?'

'Well, you can't promise a king to lock an emperor in an iron cage and then change sides. The Bourbons were relying on him to destroy our little man. Instead he led their army over to the Emperor's camp and returned France to Napoleon.'

'It could have saved France.'

'Perhaps. But it did for Ney. He was the King's general, you see, that's the law of it, and it's held to be treason.'

'Treason, my arse! Revenge.' Bernoit was quivering in wrath. 'What about the amnesty? There were to be no reprisals.'

'Only the Allies signed: the Bourbons never did. The Amnesty of Cambrai is to be disregarded—a fraud to disarm the army. They are determined on hunting down every senior officer involved in the Hundred Days.'

'Wellington will never allow it. He won't let them shoot Ney.'

'I hope you're right. They shot La Bédoyère.'

A man was watching them closely from the opposite corner. Bernoit felt suddenly conspicuous. Despite their clothing there could be no mistaking their military bearing. Their wounds also marked them out: Larguien's missing limb, that nose, his own torn cheek.

'Let's get away from that fellow. I know a café full of old grumblers who'll keep you safe.'

Larguien consented and they moved away. The man followed at a discreet distance. Had the streets not been so empty they would never have noticed him. Bernoit commented on the fact.

'That's because the populace have all gone out to Grenelle to watch the execution. I trust it amuses them.'

'Perhaps they'll rescue him.'

'Perhaps.'

The café was busy for the time of day, filled with old soldiers, mostly sergeants like Bernoit, but there was also the odd lieutenant and captain. One or two of them rebelliously wore the vestiges of their former uniform. A word from Bernoit sent three of the hard-bitten veterans outside to deal with the Royalist spy. Larguien would be safe in this company until the hour came to meet his friends.

The men had assembled in outrage at Ney's death sentence. Their talk was angry against the petulant King. They spoke of dissension, of rebellion if that was possible. Napoleon was gone, but they remembered his son, the four-year-old King of Rome, languishing in the imperial care of his Austrian grandparents.

'Let us restore the little one to his rightful place. We'll march to Schönbrunn and bring him home. We need no guide—we've been that way before.'

The grizzled old fellow who spoke bore scars in testimony of his two previous visits to Vienna. They all growled in agreement. They knew the way and the Austrians had learned better than to gainsay them. Of course it was nonsense, for disarmed and leaderless they could do nothing, but it was some satisfaction to mutter such things, to hear the warlike marches in their speech.

Yet always their thoughts returned to Ney. Rumour and speculation abounded. There was a British plot to free him, someone said. It was known that Wellington himself was involved.

'He'll not let this fat old king shoot the Marshal. The Bourbon is powerless without him. Wellington signed the Amnesty—his honour demands his intervention.'

There were murmurs of assent to this speech and more wine at the table to drink the Marshal's health. Bernoit turned to Larguien.

'You see how it is. Even now we will not live with defeat. These royalists could never survive without their foreign friends.'

'Yes, but they will always have their foreign friends. They will never again trust us with swords and guns. France will be long under their yoke. For me it is beyond bearing—I have served too loyally to tolerate proscription as a traitor. Only in America will I now find the peace to live as I will.'

Bernoit sucked his pipe thoughtfully before replying.

'Many of the old fellows are going out there.'

'Why do you not come with me? There is nothing left in France for you.'

A disturbance at the door prevented Bernoit's reply. More old soldiers came crowding in, their faces joyful and in excitement they told their tale. They had been out at Grenelle to witness the execution but nothing had happened. There had been no firing squad; no escort, no prisoner. Wellington must have interceded. It was said that the Marshal had escaped.

'Hey! Groignard—another bottle! We'll drink to Milord Wellington.'

In noisy jubilation they filled their glasses and rose to celebrate the tidings. They seized upon Larguien as the senior man present and called on him to declare the toast. A lame old gunner cleared a table and urged him on to it, and Larguien stood there, glass in hand, stooping under the roof-beams and looked round at their happy seasoned faces.

'Soldiers of the Empire!' he began and they cheered loudly to be thus addressed.

But Larguien got no further. The door crashed open and the interruption brought silence to the busy room. Old Vézanet stood there, who had served in Ney's squadron in the long distant days of the 6th Hussars. Misery was reflected on every contour of his craggy face and tears bedraggled his splendid grey whiskers. In the expectant hush that fell as they watched the old hussar lean against the door-post they felt a chill dread of the news he bore.

'They have shot him.'

'No! That's impossible, I was at Grenelle . . .'

'At the Luxembourg Gardens. Secretly—in fear of the crowds. I have seen the body. Ney is dead.'

Bernoit placed his pipe on the table and stared at the ring-like patterns of spilt wine until they became blurred by the tears welling in his tired, old eyes. His last hero had fallen. All his love and loyalty were as nothing, too late, too small to save him who had saved so many. He felt anger grow within him at the memory of that last defiant shot on the Niemen, of the reassuring figure looming by the roadside when the first snows were falling. Larguien had been there also, then.

The younger man was gazing dry-eyed at the wall.

'Marshal Victor was one of those who condemned him,' he whispered bitterly. 'Has not enough French blood been shed? Has not there been a surfeit of teachery?'

'There is no honour in our enemies,' Bernoit growled. 'Even Wellington betrays his word.'

Groignard came hobbling round, one-legged, to fill their glasses.

'Come, comrades, now we can only drink.' He tilted the bottle back to his mouth and gulped deeply. 'Farewell to memory. Our little man's in St Helena and the Marshal is gone ahead of us. He's never left us behind before.'

Groignard slumped, sobbing over his own wine casks. There was only oblivion to be sought. Anger and misery, hatred and sorrow were poor emotions for men such as they who had known so many glories. They began to drink in heavy, palpable silence.

But Bernoit was in no mood for such escape. He wanted to be out, wandering aimless in the vanquished city. Larguien, too, was anxious to be gone. Together they left the gloom-filled tavern and outside they stopped, unsure which way to turn. Larguien hesitated, and then spoke quietly.

'Will you come with me?'

Bernoit looked up at the deep clouds marching across the sky and saw a solitary bird circle over the city. The plane trees were bare in the dank, empty streets and the shutters were closed against the cold. A discarded broadsheet stirred in the breeze and rustled past them and the smells of the city came to him. Winter would be long. He faced Larguien and saw the sorrow in his eyes.

'No, I cannot now leave France. I will go home to my village. I was a shepherd once. In the south the spring will not be late.'

Sadly, the two men said farewell and parted to seek their lonely ways.